Season of Hope

Laurel Ridge Series, Book #1

Tara Baisden

Sterling Ridge Press LLC

Cover designed by Sterling Ridge Press LLC

Published by: Sterling Ridge Press, LLC www.sterlingridgepress.com

ISBN: 978-1-966093-01-5
Printed in the United States of America

First Edition: October 2024

For permissions, contact: tara@tarabaisden.com or visit www.tarabaisden.com

About The Author

Tara Baisden is a Contemporary Inspirational Romance author who proudly calls the beautiful state of West Virginia her home. Nestled on a sprawling mountainous property, she is surrounded by the peace and serenity of nature. Her days are happily spent in the quiet of country life, writing heartwarming stories of love, faith, and second chances. Tara also enjoys quilting, working in her garden, tending to her beloved pets, and soaking in the beauty of her surroundings.

With deep roots in West Virginia, family is everything to Tara. One of her favorite pastimes is gathering on the front porch with loved ones, sharing stories, laughter, and enjoying the simple, meaningful moments that life offers. When she's not crafting her novels, Tara can often be found exploring the rich history of her home state, visiting local historical sites, and, of course, stopping by every bookstore she passes! Her passion for reading and discovery always fuels her next adventure.

Tara is the author of the Laurel Ridges Series of novels, which includes: Season of Hope, Finding Grace, His Perfect Plan, and Love Redeemed, all of which have been beloved by fans of inspirational romance. Her novels reflect her love for faith, family, and the timeless beauty of West Virginia.

Known for her sweet and clean romances, she creates characters that feel like family and settings that make readers want to visit again and again.

You can find out more about Tara and her latest releases at www.tarabaisden.com or follow her on social media for updates and behind-the-scenes glimpses of her writing process. Stay connected—you won't want to miss the heartfelt stories of love and family she has in store!

Also By Tara Baisden

<u>Laurel Ridge Series</u>

#1. Season of Hope

#2. Finding Grace

#3. His Perfect Plan

#4. Love Redeemed

Dedication

To all the remarkable people behind the scenes who kept me caffeinated, sane, and (mostly) on deadline—you know who you are, and I couldn't have done this without your cheerleading and well-timed distractions. Seriously, you deserve a trophy.

To my incredible parents, for always believing in me.

To my children, who are my greatest accomplishments, and remind me every day what love and hope truly mean.

And to everyone embarking on a new season of life, may it be filled with hope, laughter, and the courage to embrace whatever comes next. Here's to your very own Season of Hope!

About Laurel Ridge

Welcome to the fictional town of Laurel Ridge, West Virginia!

Nestled deep in the heart of the Appalachian Mountains, Laurel Ridge is a place where time slows down, allowing visitors and residents alike to enjoy life's simple pleasures. With its quaint, brick-paved streets, historic storefronts, and the ever-present backdrop of rolling hills and dense forests, Laurel Ridge is a hidden gem that attracts tourists looking for both serenity and adventure.

A Rich History

The town was founded in the early 1800s by pioneering settlers who were drawn to the fertile land and abundant natural resources of the region. Laurel Ridge began as a small logging community, relying on the towering forests that covered the surrounding mountains. The New River, one of the oldest rivers in the world, provided an essential transportation route for lumber, as well as a lifeline for the early settlers.

As the years passed, the town evolved from a logging outpost into a thriving hub for craftspeople and artisans. By the late 19th century, it had developed a reputation for its hand-crafted furniture, textiles, and pottery, all made by skilled locals. The town's proximity to the New River also made it a destination for adventurous souls seeking to kayak, fish, or hike along the riverbanks.

A Place of Renewal

Though the logging industry faded by the early 20th century, Laurel Ridge adapted to the changing times. Its natural beauty and deep connection to West Virginia's mountain heritage drew travelers from near and far, transforming it into a beloved tourist destination. Local shops, run by generations of the same families, line the town square, offering handmade goods, locally sourced foods, and, most of all, warm hospitality.

The town's signature event, the Harvest Festival, began in the 1930s, celebrating the craftsmanship, music, and traditions passed down through the generations. Each year, visitors flock to enjoy live Appalachian music, taste locally grown produce, and witness demonstrations of old-world techniques like blacksmithing and weaving.

A Town of Faith and Community

At the heart of the town stands Laurel Ridge Community Church, a small, white clapboard building with a steeple that reaches toward the sky. Built in 1876, the church has been a pillar of faith and strength for the community for over a century. Its bell, crafted by the town's original blacksmith, has been ringing on Sunday mornings ever since, calling townsfolk to worship and reminding everyone of the enduring values of faith, hope, and love.

The church's history is intertwined with the town's, serving as a refuge in difficult times and a gathering place in moments of joy. Over the years, the church has grown to include an outreach center that supports local families and tourists in need, providing everything from free meals to spiritual counseling. The church's welcoming atmosphere reflects the town's deep sense of unity and service.

A Growing Tourist Haven

Today, Laurel Ridge has grown to a population of around five thousand people, yet it has managed to retain its small-town charm. Its thriving tourist industry draws visitors year-round. Tourists can stroll through mom-and-pop shops, and dine at the beloved Martha's Diner, famous for its homemade pies and retro charm. The town square, with its white gazebo surrounded by flowering bushes, is often the site of outdoor concerts and farmers' markets, creating a sense of nostalgia and small-town pride.

For nature lovers, the New River offers breathtaking views and the thrill of adventure, whether it's fishing in its crystal blue waters or hiking along the rugged trails that weave through the wilderness. Tourists and locals alike cherish the scenic beauty, often finding peace in the simple pleasures of watching the river flow or taking in the panoramic vistas of the Appalachian Mountains.

Laurel Ridge, with its rich history, strong community spirit, and natural beauty, is more than just a tourist destination—it's a place where past and present blend seamlessly, offering everyone who visits a chance to experience the best of West Virginia's mountain heritage. You'll find that Laurel Ridge is a town that captures the heart.

Welcome to Laurel Ridge. I hope you fall in love with this charming small town and its residents.

Contents

Chapter 1

Wendy Lane wiped her hands on her apron. She stepped back to admire her display at the entrance of The Farmstead Store. Her eyes traced over the cascading arrangement of baskets, each one brimming with the bounty of the farm's harvest. The deep crimson and delicate green apples, freshly picked from the orchard, glistened in the afternoon sun that streamed through the windows and open barn-style doorway. Vibrant orange and muted cream miniature pumpkins mounded in wooden crates and scattered among the rustic shelves of the display. Jars of preserves, neatly arranged, displayed endless shades of red, orange, and hints of violet. These jams and jellies were made from the last fruits of summer and the first harvest of fall. The honey on display shimmered in amber and gold. Its thick liquid caught the light like droplets of liquid sunshine. A sweet promise of warmth on colder days ahead. Jars of rich apple butter, the thick contents a deep caramel color. Wreaths of dried corn husks and wheat stalks, and garlands of golden leaves, draped just so, completed the scene. The display transformed the entrance to the store into a welcoming autumn haven for visitors.

From the kitchen, the comforting aroma of freshly baked apple pie filled the store. It wrapped around everything like a cozy blanket. It invited customers to linger and savor the warmth of this harvest haven.

Wendy folded her arms loosely over her chest, taking it all in—the apples, the pumpkins, the glow of the preserves. The comforting scent of pie threaded through the air, imbuing everything with a sense of home. It wasn't just a display of the season's harvest; it was the very soul of the farm.

Wendy felt the crisp early autumn breeze on her skin coming in from the doorway. A smile tugged at her lips as she let herself savor the moment. But Wendy knew the afternoon rush was imminent. Her eyes flicked to her sister, Amy, who was chatting with a young couple at the counter. Amy balanced a tray of apple cinnamon rolls with casual grace, her eyes sparkling with a hint of mischief.

"I'm telling you, add a dollop of our apple butter on these," Amy said, her voice animated. "You won't regret it. Best decision you'll make all day...well, except for coming here."

The couple laughed, their faces glowing with the joy of vacationers who had escaped the hustle of their everyday lives. Wendy's smile grew. Amy could light up a room with just her presence, drawing people in with her warmth and humor. There wasn't a business strategy in the world that could match the way Amy made others feel welcomed and cared for.

Wendy shook her head, amused, as Amy handed the couple their change with yet another dazzling smile. Though Amy preferred the orchard and the pumpkin patches over being stuck behind the counter, today she seemed to have embraced her role with enthusiasm.

"If we keep selling apple cinnamon rolls like this, you'll have to open another store!" Amy called over her shoulder, a teasing grin on her face.

Wendy let out a dramatic sigh, pushing a few stray strands of hair away from her forehead. "And you'll be the one running it, right in the middle of the orchard. You'd like that, wouldn't you?"

Amy laughed, shaking her head, her blonde hair swaying in its loose knot. "Hey, the pumpkins don't judge me for putting too much butter in the pastries, like Grandma does. That's why they taste so..."

"Ahem," came a voice, soft but sharp. Wendy turned to see their grandmother, Ruth, emerge from the kitchen, a tray of scones balanced in her hands. At seventy-three, Ruth moved with an ease that spoke of years spent mastering the art of baking and working the land. She slid the tray onto the counter.

"Let me guess," Ruth said, her brow lifting. "Amy's debating butter again? Honestly, Wendy, why'd you let her anywhere near the store today?"

Wendy exchanged a conspiratorial smile with her grandmother. "Desperation, I imagine," she quipped.

Ruth rolled her eyes and turned her sharp gaze to Amy, a flicker of humor dancing there. "Your sweet-talking better bring in the sales today, or it's back to the kitchen for you...flour up to your elbows."

Amy clutched her chest in mock horror. "Me? Mess with scones? Heaven forbid! You should know better, Grandma."

Wendy chuckled as her eyes drifted to the kitchen, where more trays of baked goods cooled on racks. Ruth had been at the helm of their family recipes for as long as Wendy could remember, her steady presence like an anchor on their busiest days.

The familiar rhythm of the day began to pull Wendy forward, the tasks ahead nudging at her mind. The Apple Festival was only two weeks away, and she still had a dozen loose ends to tie up. Booth assignments, vendor confirmations—Wendy half-joked that this year's festival might be the thing that finally did her in.

"While I've got your attention," Ruth said, her tone as light as the breeze filtering in through the door, "I saw someone driving up toward the cabin just now. Our well-known author, maybe?"

Wendy blinked, her lips curling into a small smile. "Are you keeping tabs on him already?"

Ruth shrugged, an amused twinkle in her eye. "Small towns run on good gossip. A gal's gotta keep up on all the current events, dear."

Amy's eyes lit up as she chimed in, her voice taking on a dramatic tone. "Oh yes, Luke Carter, our mysterious guest. Tall, brooding writer seeking refuge for his tormented soul." She raised her hands, as if painting an invisible portrait. "The tortured writer, in love with words."

Wendy groaned, rolling her eyes. "You sound like a bad romance novel, Amy."

Amy flashed her a grin. "Bad romance novels are still selling pretty well, if I'm not mistaken. Writers are always a little tortured. He's probably one cup of apple cider away from spilling his entire tragic backstory."

Ruth crossed her arms, her gaze full of humor. "Maybe he just wants some peace and quiet, Amy. Not everyone's a walking drama."

Wendy shook her head, unable to keep from laughing. "He's asked for privacy. And as far as I know, yes, he is here for peace and quiet. I assume he's here to write, not to share his personal life with us."

Amy waggled her eyebrows. "For three whole months, Wendy. Just imagine! Ninety days of hosting a world-famous author. Who knows, maybe you'll help him find the perfect ending to his story. Hint. Hint. He's a widower, and you're still single."

Wendy shot her sister a look. "I'm too busy," she replied, her tone sharper than intended. She shifted her weight, feeling the familiar pang of wariness settle in her chest. It wasn't that she had anything against the man or any man for that matter—but the mere thought of dating stirred old memories she'd rather leave buried, especially those tied to David. Wendy's heart had been through enough twists and turns. She didn't have the energy, or the trust, to give anyone a chance ever again.

David's betrayal still lingered, like the fading smell of smoke after a fire. Long gone, but impossible to forget. She had let herself believe, once, that rekindling a relationship with her high school sweetheart would lead her toward a life of shared dreams on the farm. He had played his role perfectly, diving into the daily rhythms of her world, until Wendy found out the truth.

So no, she didn't need a man in her life. For all she cared, Luke Carter was just another average Joe passing through, one more man whose promises might fall apart like autumn leaves in the wind.

Her gaze drifted to the display of apples sparkling in the afternoon light. "I just don't see the point anymore," she muttered to herself.

Still, she thought about him. A bestselling author escaping to the backwoods of Laurel Ridge for three months. Solitude was one thing, but choosing a place as remote as their cabin seemed... interesting, to say the least. Wendy remembered his email: short, professional, no hint of warmth. He wanted peace and quiet, and to be left alone.

Wendy wandered over to one of the nearby windows, her eyes falling on the hills beyond the store. The green and gold of the landscape was slowly shifting, the trees giving way to the burnished reds and oranges of autumn. It was beautiful, breathtaking, even. Wendy rested her hand against the cool glass, her eyes tracing the gravel road that led up to the cabin on the hill beyond the orchard.

Luke Carter. The name lingered in her mind. She knew a little about his work. Bestselling author, famous for his emotional and evocative storytelling, but something about his request for solitude intrigued her more than she wanted to admit.

Wendy walked over to the counter and picked up her phone, hesitating for a second before typing his name into the search bar. The results filled her screen almost instantly. Images, articles, and interviews. Wendy clicked on a few, her eyes scanning through reviews and headlines that seemed to paint a picture of the man who'd be staying in the cabin for the next few weeks.

She paused at a black-and-white author portrait. Luke Carter looked to be in his late thirties, his expression contemplative. His dark hair was tousled, his eyes focused somewhere just past the camera lens. There was no smile, no warmth. Just an intensity that hinted at a mind at work. Wendy couldn't help but feel he looked like a man who carried his thoughts heavily, as though they weighed down his shoulders.

She clicked on another interview link, her eyes skimming over the words. His tone was professional, almost detached. There was a mention of his writing process, his inspiration, but nothing that hinted at who he was beyond the words he put on paper.

Readers seemed to adore his books — 'heart-wrenching tales of human resilience that leave readers breathless and aching for more,' as one review described them—but Wendy wondered about the man behind those stories.

What kind of life created that kind of writing? The intensity in his eyes seemed to suggest that he held a lot inside, perhaps even more than he allowed onto the pages of his books.

She thought of his email again, brief and impersonal. He'd asked for privacy, for peace and quiet, and not to be bothered, and Wendy would respect that request. But the more she read about Luke, the more her curiosity grew. Why would a bestselling author want to disappear into the backwoods of a small town like Laurel Ridge for three months? She understood needing solitude to write, but there was something in his clipped words that suggested more.

Another more recent article she found online was a short piece about a book signing he'd canceled. There was no explanation given—just a note that Luke Carter had taken time off from public appearances. Wendy felt a pang of something she couldn't quite name, a mix of sympathy and curiosity. Was it burnout, or something else? His books spoke of resilience, of love and loss, and Wendy wondered if the writer was trying to find some of that resilience for himself.

She sighed, closing the tab, and placed her phone back on the counter. It wasn't any of her business. Luke Carter was entitled to his privacy, and she had no reason to pry into his life. But she couldn't shake the feeling that there was more to him than what the articles let on.

"Well, Mr. Carter," she murmured, "I hope you find what you're looking for. And maybe, just maybe, these mountains can help you in some way."

Chapter 2

Wendy adjusted the last of the glass jars along the display shelf, making sure they were perfectly aligned. Her hands, roughened from years of farm work, seemed out of place amidst the jars of preserves—almost too sturdy, too familiar with the weight of crops and the grip of a tractor wheel, to handle something so delicate.

With the faintest sigh, Wendy stepped back, rubbing her hands down the front of her apron. Her gaze swept over the store—over the wooden crates spilling with freshly picked apples, the dried corn stalk wreaths, and the brightly colored miniature pumpkins displayed near the entrance. This was the heartbeat of the farm. Her parents' dream turned into reality through her hands.

Her grandmother stood nearby, quietly rearranging a collection of carved wooden signs. Wendy watched her move, admiring her steady hands, which had been creating magic in the kitchen and on this farm for nearly her entire life. Ruth's body might have been slowing, but her mind and spirit remained sharp and unwavering. She was the unbroken center of their family—the one who had held everything together after the sudden loss of Wendy's parents—and she kept them all grounded in ways no one else could.

"You've been pretty busy today Amy, you look exhausted," Ruth said, glancing over her shoulder at Wendy, her voice carrying that familiar note of concern that Wendy had heard a hundred times before.

Wendy forced a smile. "Oh, you know how it is with the apple festival coming up," she replied, trying to infuse her tone with lightness. "There's never enough time this close to the festival—the vendors, the booth assignments, plus I've got to make sure we have enough stock. We're expecting a lot more visitors this year."

Ruth paused, her fingers trailing thoughtfully over a wooden sign that read "Faith, Family, Farm." She lifted it from its place, as if examining the words themselves. Her expression was soft but thoughtful, lined with years of wisdom laced with love.

"You know," she began, placing the sign back down and turning to face Wendy, "slowing down and taking a little time for yourself isn't the worst thing in the world."

Something in Ruth's tone made Wendy's heart tighten, a reaction as immediate as breathing. She had this way, Ruth did—this quiet, observant way of reaching the truths Wendy tried hardest to ignore.

She forced a chuckle, running a hand through the strands of hair escaping from her loose ponytail. "Slow down? Grandma, I'll slow down when the festival's over and everything's wrapped up. Besides, it's not just the festival. If we don't keep up with production, we'll lose the momentum we've built this past year."

The corners of Ruth's lips tugged into a knowing smile, her eyes rich with understanding. "The festival, the farm, this harvest season... they're all important, I know that. But I wonder if..." She trailed off for a moment, searching Wendy's face. Then, more quietly, she added, "Has there been too much filling up the empty spaces in your life? And not enough... letting life just happen? I worry about you, Wendy. You never take time for yourself. You never go out with friends anymore and just have a little fun. Not only that, but you work non-stop."

Wendy's practiced response turned sharp on her tongue and died before it reached her lips. She wasn't sure how to answer her grandmother's question; wasn't sure she even wanted to. A tight breath lodged in her chest, and all she could do was fidget with the edge of a small basket of gourds beside her.

If Ruth saw her discomfort, she didn't press. Instead, she watched Wendy in that familiar grandmotherly way—the way that spoke of patience and love wrapped in a gentle concern—that kind of unspoken tenderness that said I've been there too, and I know exactly how you feel.

After a moment, Ruth reached out, resting a hand on Wendy's shoulder. Her touch was warm, a slight tremble in her fingers, a hidden strength that Wendy had leaned on since she was a little girl.

Ruth squeezed Wendy's shoulder, grounding her before the memories of the past could pull her too far under. "It's alright to trust again, Wendy," Ruth said, her voice deeper now, her eyes searching as she swayed to conversation. "Not every man's out to break your heart. Just because one thought so little of you and this farm..." her voice faltered, but only for a split second before she continued, "doesn't mean others won't see it the way you do. You don't have to carry those old wounds from David forever, child."

Wendy's skin flushed, and she could feel the tightening beneath her ribs. The mention of David still came like the sudden sting of stepping on a thorn.

David. His name, his betrayal, still cast a shadow, even if she would rather not admit it.

It had been such a whirlwind when he came back into town two years ago. He'd swept in like the autumn breeze, all charm and nostalgia, and she'd let herself believe they could build something together like the dreams they'd once shared in high school.

But then... the discovery. That heart-sinking evening when she found the emails—a cold, calculated plan between him and his development company to sell off the farm once they were married, to plow her family's roots under concrete. He'd said it was for her—a fresh break, a smart move. David had called her life a dead-end.

Since then, she'd buried herself in work. It had been easier to fill every inch of her life with busyness, to throw herself into the farm, the store, and the endless "to-dos" of running it all. Safer to focus on keeping Nature's Gifts alive than to look beyond it... to herself.

Wendy's voice crept above a whisper as she mumbled, "My life's full enough."

But Ruth's gaze didn't waver. She stood there, steady as she had when Wendy was a scared sixteen-year-old, just trying to understand the hole her parents had left behind after they had died in an auto accident.

"Is it?" Ruth asked, and her tone was so gentle—so simple—that Wendy wished she hadn't asked at all. Her breath hitched despite herself, anger mixing with a sudden helplessness she didn't want to feel, not here, not now.

Ruth's hand remained in place on her shoulder, her grip firm and undeniable in its tenderness. She didn't push further, didn't scold. Ruth never did that. Instead, she waited, letting her words soak through the fragile walls Wendy had built piece by piece around her heart.

"This little routine of psychoanalyzing me," Wendy said, desperate for humor to ease the tightness in her chest, "it's not going to last, Grandma."

Ruth smiled. "We'll see about that," she said, unconvinced by Wendy's attempt to end the conversation.

Wendy glanced around the store, feeling as though she were that girl again—sixteen years old, standing in the same store, feeling equally overwhelmed by a life too heavy to carry on her own yet terrified of letting others help bear the burden.

But she wasn't that girl anymore. She had responsibilities now, and the farm didn't run on hurt feelings and insecurities—it ran on hard work, grit, and intention. She couldn't afford moments of weakness or slowing down—not when everything about this farm meant stability, tradition, and survival.

Ruth's voice softened, pulling her back from her scattered thoughts, bringing with it a familiar gentleness—one that pushed at the growing knot in Wendy's stomach. "The Lord's got big plans for you, Wendy," Ruth said, her palm warm and reassuring as it patted Wendy's arm. "He's not finished with you yet, even if you would rather not stop and take a moment to realize that."

Wendy knew what Ruth was getting at—she always did. She knew her grandmother held on to faith like someone holding on to a handrail while crossing a rickety bridge. Steady. Unshakable. More than anyone, Ruth had shown her that life wasn't just a collection of random moments tied by circumstance. There was more to this life's path than anyone could ever see upfront, and no matter how painful the load, there was always purpose behind it.

But it wasn't easy for Wendy to see that—not when everything seemed so precariously balanced. Not when the ghosts of her past still lingered so close.

"What if... I'm not ready for what's coming? What if—" Wendy caught herself before she could continue, swallowing hard as she struggled to keep the emotions from bubbling over.

The longer she stood there in front of Ruth, the more her defenses began to crumble, piece by piece. It wasn't just David that hurt the most; it was everything she had lost before him too—it was the fear she carried that at any moment, something precious could be ripped away again.

Ruth's eyes, still filled with that knowing softness, engulfed her like a shelter. "God's never asked us to be ready," she whispered, her words as smooth and steady as the autumn breeze outside. "He asks us to be willing."

Wendy blinked, her throat tight, words too tangled to muster a proper response. For a moment, the surrounding store seemed far too small—too quiet—and her heart, all at once, weighed too much in her chest. She wasn't sure what to say.

Wendy considered Ruth's words.

Maybe she was right—maybe.

"Sometimes, Grandma," Wendy said, lowering her gaze as she reflected on their conversation. "Life's easier when you keep all the empty spaces filled. It's easier not to think about the past and just stay busy. I'd rather not think of what has happened or ponder on what's to come into my life."

Ruth gave her another quiet pat, her presence standing like a sturdy oak in a world teetering on the edge of change.

"Maybe, child," Ruth whispered, her voice carrying warmth and time-worn patience, "But that doesn't mean it makes those spaces whole."

The words lingered in Wendy's thoughts. She let them sink in, even as old fears clawed at her, even though she wasn't sure if she could put them into practice just yet, or if she even wanted to.

Chapter 3

The truck's engine rumbled to a stop, the deep hum fading into the quiet of the surrounding woods. Luke Carter's hands remained on the steering wheel longer than necessary, his gaze fixed on the rustic cabin ahead. Nestled among the towering maples and oaks of Laurel Ridge, West Virginia, it looked exactly as advertised—secluded, weathered, and gloriously quiet.

"This is it," he muttered. He forced himself to say it aloud, as if to make it real. "Time to write."

His eyes dropped to the small leather keychain hanging from the ignition, the bold letters of "S. Carter" staring back at him. A familiar tightness clenched his chest. Sarah. He swallowed, the sudden tug of grief taking him by surprise, like an ambush. Even after two years, moments of grief crept in. He dragged in a breath, fighting it back, his fingers pressing against the wheel.

Luke pulled his gaze from the keychain, his eyes narrowing as they drifted back to the cabin. He'd promised his editor a full draft by Christmas.

With a frustrated grunt, he shoved the truck door open, stepping out. The early fall air wrapping around him, sharp but gentle. The slight breeze stirred the tree branches, coaxing a few dry leaves into a gentle dance before they settled on the ground. Everything felt quiet and still here, as though this piece of the world existed in its own space separate from the outside noisy world, far from the urgent crunch of deadlines and rising tides of pressure. It was a stillness that pressed around him, foreign, yet welcome—the kind that heralded change.

Maybe this place could offer him what nothing else had—a quiet so deep it might finally drown out the ache. He didn't need inspiration... he needed to forget how much he'd lost. To be left alone with the empty pages and the hollow parts of himself.

Maybe.

Luke grabbed his duffel bag from the passenger seat, slinging it over his shoulder. The steps leading up to the cabin groaned as he climbed them, the worn wood shifting beneath his weight. He paused for a moment, letting the air surround him. The scent of damp leaves mingled with the resin of pine, a crisp sweetness rising from the apple trees beyond. The cabin was simple—no frills, no pretenses—just functional, the way he needed it to be. He took the heavy iron key hanging from the nail beside the doorframe, feeling its cool weight in his palm. There was something almost ceremonial in the way he turned it in the lock, as though it might unlock something within him, too.

The front door swung open, revealing a simple, cozy interior—wood-plank walls, a stone fireplace, and an overstuffed plaid couch looking out over a modest kitchen. It was the kind of place that didn't need anything fancy. It just felt... right.

He dropped his bag on the floor and made his way over to the oversized front window that looked out over a sparse patch of woodland. Beyond the trees, a sprawling pumpkin patch stretched across the land to the right, with rows of orange dots scattered like a sunset on the earth. To the left, an apple orchard, trees heavy with fruit. A farmhouse and a couple of barns nestled comfortably in the distance. Perfect. No nosey neighbor's next door like he was used to in his suburban life. Peace and isolation for a man desperate for both so he could focus.

Running a hand through his hair, he let out a breath through his nose. This was his life now for the next ninety days. A cabin rental in the hollows of some mountain town, hoping—no, grasping—

With a sigh, he kicked off his boots by the door, leaving them in a haphazard pile, and half-heartedly nudged his bag toward the couch. He opened the top and rifled through just enough to pull out a notebook, a couple of folders, and his laptop, setting them on the small wooden table that would double as a desk near the front window.

The thought of jumping straight into writing weighed on him. His stomach growled, cutting his anxiety short. The rental agreement had mentioned a modestly stocked refrigerator. He wandered over to the kitchen to see what exactly "modest" meant.

Opening the narrow door of the small refrigerator felt like prying open a time capsule. A hum came from the appliance as he pulled open the old-fashioned latch and peered inside.

It was surprisingly well-stocked—fresh farm eggs in a bowl, a tub of butter, and a small assortment of cheese sat on the top shelf. Below them, cold glass bottles of milk and apple cider crowded beside a wrapped package of smoked bacon, a loaf of bread on the side. A mason jar labeled 'Grandma's Homemade Apple Jelly' caught his eye. In the crisper, gleaming apples, and farm-fresh vegetables—carrots, leeks, potatoes—rested beside a carton of mushrooms.

Luke surveyed the scene, feeling a pang of unexpected gratitude. Whoever arranged this had gone out of their way to provide more than just the bare necessities.

He closed the refrigerator door and looked around the small kitchen, its modest setup charming. Basic but functional—pinewood cabinets hung over a polished countertop and a vintage stove. A small microwave, coffee maker, a trusty old kettle, along with a cast-iron skillet resting across one burner on the stove. A trio of mason jars held dried herbs on the window shelf, carefully labeled. Sage, basil, and thyme.

Luke ran his hand over the worn edges of the countertops, noticing a crock of wood cooking utensils near the stove. They appeared hand-carved and were smooth to the touch. Whoever ran this place had put care into it. These weren't the usual cheap plastic cooking utensils from the dollar store.

He rummaged through the cabinets, canned soups, beans, and various dried goods. Jars of oats, grains, and pasta arranged neatly next to more jars filled with spices. Simple food, but enough to survive on. The arrangement spoke of self-sufficiency in a way that was both comforting and eerily isolating.

Luke closed the cabinet door with a quiet thud, his movements deliberate, as if the very act of doing something—anything—would somehow stave off the lingering thoughts he'd rather not face. He grabbed the jug of cider from the fridge.

He uncorked it and poured himself a generous glass. The moment the rich amber liquid hit his cup, a sweet, familiar fragrance filled the kitchen. He sat down at the rustic wooden table. The legs creaking softly as he eased into the chair. The chill of the glass pressed against his fingers before he took a long sip.

The flavors hit him instantly. A combination of fresh apple and autumn's essence flooding his senses. As the refreshing coolness slid down his throat, it stirred something buried deep within him—an old, unexpected memory of simpler times. Of hot cider on cold October evenings, of childhood bonfires and laughter with people who had once been so close. He could almost feel that familiar warmth, pulling him back to a time of childhood simplicity.

Luke leaned back in the chair, his eyes wandering to the living room, where his duffel bag slumped on the floor, waiting to be unpacked. Clothes, toiletries—a few attempts to ground himself in the practical. His laptop and notebooks waiting for him to get to work on the table.

Writing used to fill my days, he thought, his shoulders sinking under the weight of his expectation. The blank pages in the notebook or the blank screen on his laptop felt like a cruel joke, mocking him with their potential. What once came easily, like breathing, now felt like digging through stone with his bare hands.

What did he expect would happen by coming here? That, somehow, the stillness of the mountains and the isolation of this cabin would bring the words rushing back like an unstoppable flood? That the beauty of the place would snap him into working order again and allow him to weave stories with the passion he once had?

He placed the glass back on the table, slowly sliding it to the center with two fingers. The faint scrape of glass against the wood was the only sound in the room.

He exhaled deeply, leaning forward, and resting his hands on his knees.

He clenched his jaw, the familiar gnaw of failure eating at him.

The crunch of tires over gravel jerked Luke out of his thoughts. His brow furrowed as he made his way to the front window and glanced out, irritation bubbling at the intrusion. He walked to the front screen door, pushed it open and stepped onto the porch, letting it creak shut behind him.

A boxy white delivery van had stopped beside his truck. 'Nature's Gifts Farm & Orchard' was painted in neat letters on the side, a colorful logo of apples, pumpkins, and sunflowers splashed beneath. The driver's door swung open, and a woman climbed out, her brown hair pulled into a loose ponytail that swayed as she moved. A plaid flannel shirt, well-worn jeans, dirt-smudged boots, and sun-kissed skin made her the very picture of country living.

Luke's gaze moved to the basket she carried. It was brimming with baked goods—pumpkin bread, muffins, scones, and a mason jar of apple butter. The scent of pumpkin reached him before she did, sweet and inviting, and his stomach growled, betraying him.

"Fresh delivery," she called, her voice carrying the simple rhythm of someone who belonged in these mountains. Her steps were sure, her energy brisk, as if work was second nature to her. "You must be Luke Carter."

Luke blinked, realizing she was waiting for a response. "Yeah, that's me," he said, his voice coming out rougher than intended.

She smiled, her hazel eyes lighting up. "Wendy Lane. I run Nature's Gifts Farm and Orchard." She nodded toward the van behind her. "Your rental package includes a complimentary basket—our way of saying welcome to the farm and Laurel Ridge."

Luke's mouth tugged into a reluctant half-smile. *Complimentary, huh?* A gesture that was probably more of a local tourist gimmick than anything else. He forced himself to respond, even if the words felt stiff. "That's... thoughtful."

Wendy's smile didn't falter. "Thought you might enjoy a taste of what we grow around here." She extended the basket, her gaze steady, warm. It contrasted starkly with the cold wall Luke felt himself holding up. He hesitated before accepting it. "Thanks. I, uh—this smells great." He tried to keep the sarcasm at bay because, truthfully, it did smell incredible, but his discomfort lingered, gnawing at the edges of his manners.

Wendy seemed unfazed by his lackluster response. "You picked a beautiful time to visit," she said, her eyes shifting to take in the landscape. "Early fall here is something special. Wait until you see the leaves change."

Luke gave a curt nod. "I imagine it's...spectacular."

Wendy chuckled uncomfortably. "Well, if nothing else, it's quieter than most places. I suspect you'll enjoy the solitude," she said. "No high-speed internet or fashion shows out here. We're more of the 'apple-pie-on-the-porch' type."

Luke blinked, not sure what to say. He settled for, "I doubt that'll be an issue."

Wendy tilted her head, her long ponytail swaying behind her. She opened her mouth as if to say something more, then seemed to think better of it and nodded instead. "Well, I won't keep you," she said, her hands finding their way to the pockets of her jeans. "But if you need anything, you can usually find me at the Farmstead Store just down the drive. We've got plenty of produce, jams, and..." she glanced at the cabin behind him with a look of consideration, "...well... if the quiet becomes too much, you can come visit us there."

Luke stiffened at the words, his stomach twisting. People. Questions. Conversation. The very things he had come here to avoid. He forced himself to meet her gaze, managing, "I'll keep that in mind."

Wendy's smile lingered, her eyes warm in a way that made Luke feel like she saw more of him than he wanted. "Well, welcome to Laurel

Ridge, Mr. Carter." She took a step back toward the van. "I hope you enjoy your stay with us, and I'm sure we'll see you around."

Luke watched as she climbed into her vehicle, her movements relaxed. The van's engine growled to life, and Wendy gave him a knowing smile before she turned the wheel, guiding the vehicle back down the gravel road. Luke stayed there, watching until she disappeared around the bend, leaving only the stillness of the mountains.

A sigh escaped him, the weight of solitude settling back over his shoulders. This was what he wanted—peace, quiet, no distractions.

Except, the way Wendy had said "welcome" rattled something loose inside of him. A door he'd thought he'd closed long ago, somewhere back when Sarah lost her fight with cancer. Wendy had made him feel as if she actually cared about him.

Luke shook his head, turning back to the cabin. He stepped inside, noticing the air was cooling as the sun dipped lower behind the mountains. The raw chill made him shiver, a reminder of how quickly warmth slipped away, like sand slipping through his fingers. You didn't know how much you'd lost until it was gone.

Focus, Luke. Stick to the plan. Write.

He set the basket on the kitchen table.

A rustling sound followed by a small thud came from the front porch.

Another visitor?

Irritation sparked. He shot a glance toward the front windows, dread pooling in his stomach at the thought of more unsolicited cheerfulness.

He stopped short at the screen door, his breath catching as he saw a small bundle of firewood sitting by the doorway. Next to it, a woven basket filled with fresh-cut flowers—goldenrod and late-season asters, their colors vivid in the cool autumn air. Another gift?

He frowned. Someone had gone out of their way to do this. Wendy, probably. She'd seemed the type. He hadn't heard another vehicle. As he glanced down the gravel road, he noticed a golf cart retreating.

His eyes shifted back to the flowers, a knot of unease tightening in his stomach. It wasn't just a gesture; it was a kindness, and kindness had a way of digging under his skin, making him feel vulnerable. He picked up the firewood, carrying it inside, setting it by the stone hearth.

He glanced back through the screen door at the basket of flowers. The last time someone had given him flowers had been...

The hospital. Sarah. Bouquets that meant well, but did nothing to stop the inevitable.

His chest tightened, the memory rising.

The flowers could stay outside.

Taking a deep breath, he kneeled to set the kindling for a fire. The cabin wasn't freezing, but the act of building a fire gave him something to focus on. Something besides feeling the emptiness. Something besides the writing that waited for him. As he worked, the image of the flowers stayed in the back of his mind, nagging at him. Guilt, maybe, or something softer, something he wasn't ready to name.

He stood abruptly, crossing the room in a few long strides. He opened the screen door and grabbed the basket of flowers, his sigh gruff as he brought it inside, setting it next to Wendy's basket of food on the table.

Luke stood there for a moment, staring at the two gifts. The ticking of the clock on the fireplace mantel filled the silence, each tick a reminder of time slipping away—of the looming book deadline, of the isolation he thought he needed.

He sank into the kitchen chair, the weight of it all pressing down.

He reached for the pumpkin bread, peeling back the plastic wrap, the aroma of cinnamon and nutmeg filling the air. Luke tore off a corner and took a bite. The pumpkin spice was perfectly balanced—sweet, warm, comforting. A taste of autumn. The bread practically melted in his mouth, a surprising sense of comfort washing over him.

Simple. Human. Something he hadn't felt in a long time.

Chapter 4

The rooster's call sliced through the quiet of the early morning, breaking the delicate hold of sleep with a familiar insistence. Dawn was staining the horizon with its first pale colors when the rooster crowed again, as if staking his claim on the day. Wendy lay in the warmth of her bed, not startled by the sound but rather comforted by it. The early cries of the rooster, the soft rustle of hens flapping their wings, and the fading echoes of night owls retreating into their hidden corners. This was the morning symphony of farm life.

And Wendy wouldn't trade it for anything.

She sat up, rubbing the sleep from her eyes. The cool morning air greeted her, brushing across her skin like a whispered reminder that autumn was arriving. Soon, the mornings would carry a sharper chill that cut through even the thickest quilt. Wendy glanced down at the one she'd kicked aside during the night, resisting the urge to pull it back over her shoulders. Instead, she swung her legs over the side of the bed, her bare feet pressing onto the floorboards, which felt cooler than they had the morning before. Summer was losing its grip, slipping away day by day.

Wendy rose, stretching her arms over her head, her joints loosening in that satisfying way that marked the start of another day. She tugged on her worn jeans and slipped into a long-sleeved t-shirt, twisting her brown hair into a messy ponytail atop her head. She moved out of her room, her feet carrying her down the narrow hallway, her hand brushing against the familiar walls. Wendy knew every inch of this place, every creak in the stairs, each groaning floorboard in the hallway.

The house was old, but it held together well—a testament to her parents' dedication, God rest their souls. Wendy had kept that same devotion, putting in her own love and labor to maintain the sturdy home. She reached the kitchen and flipped the light switch on. The kitchen was her pride and joy. She smiled at the sight of the wooden table worn smooth by years of meals, prayers, and memories. The faint lingering scent of yesterday's bread and the ghost of cinnamon and spices from the tea she'd brewed the previous night welcomed her like an old friend.

She moved to the counter, her fingers brushing against the cool metal of the coffeepot as she lifted it. The rich scent of brewing coffee began to unfurl through the air, a comforting aroma that wrapped itself around the room. She poured herself a cup, steam rising in delicate wisps, and her gaze drifted out the window, her mind already running through her endless list of tasks.

Wendy turned the crank of the old bread slicer, feeling the rhythmic resistance as she worked through a loaf of bread. The year had been both generous and demanding, and October was approaching fast. The Apple Festival—an event that loomed large in her mind before it actually arrived—was closer than she liked to admit. The last of the apples for the year needed to be harvested, pumpkins needed to be picked, orders needed filled, and so much left to prepare.

But there was something else tugging at the edge of her thoughts. Or rather, someone. Luke Carter. She didn't enjoy dwelling on him, but maybe it was because of the unexpected resemblance. Not in looks, but in the way he had held back, that tension in his shoulders like it cost him too much to share his thoughts or even hold a conversation. It was a restraint she had seen before, from someone else she'd rather not dwell on.

Wendy sliced the bread a little faster. Less than a day had passed since she'd delivered the welcome basket to Luke. His lack of words and warmth felt familiar—too familiar. David had been the same way when he returned to Laurel Ridge. Withdrawn at first, like he had the weight of the world on his shoulders, until... Wendy shook her head, banishing the thought. Luke's guardedness was none of her concern. She wasn't about to fall for the same act twice.

Still, there was something about Luke that left her feeling... unsettled, or perhaps, on edge. Like someone who comes waltzing into your life, stirring up feelings or thoughts you hadn't expected to address. It was like he came blowing into her life with the turning cool winds—bringing change she didn't have time for. Or wanted, for that matter.

She brushed the thought aside and slipped the bread slices into the toaster. The machine hummed softly, warming up. But Wendy's thoughts drifted again, replaying her brief encounter with Luke. His seriousness, the way he spoke, his reserved demeanor—it had stuck with her.

Hopefully, Luke's stay with them would do him some good. Help ease whatever weight he was carrying. These mountains had a way of changing people. She'd witnessed many visitors' demeanor change throughout their stays in her cabin in the past. She had seen plenty of weary people come needing a break from life, only to leave happy and renewed.

Wendy shook her head, dismissing her thoughts. Luke Carter wasn't her responsibility, and she had plenty of other things to focus on today.

The sound of footsteps thudding down the stairs broke through her thoughts. Wendy turned just in time to see her sister, Amy, stumbling into the kitchen, her eyes still half-closed.

"Morning," Wendy called, her voice bright with the natural energy she always carried at dawn.

Amy groaned in response, her disheveled hair pulled into a loose ponytail that looked like it had battled against her pillow and lost. She made her way straight to the coffee pot, her expression one of determined survival.

"You have to stop saying that so cheerfully," Amy muttered, her voice thick with sleep. She filled a mug to the brim and brought it to her lips like it was a lifeline. "It's too enthusiastic for this time of day."

Wendy laughed. "I'm a morning person. I can't help it. You should try it sometime."

Amy gave her a bleary, unamused look, her nose wrinkling as she sipped her coffee. "I don't understand why God invented six a.m."

"So we could get an early start on farm life," Wendy replied, her tone serious but her eyes sparkling with mischief.

Amy rolled her eyes, slumping into the nearest chair, her coffee still in hand. "Farm life should start at eight. Or maybe nine, if we're being reasonable. I need time for my body to accept the concept of sunlight."

Wendy handed Amy a plate of toast. "Eat something. Perhaps then you'll start to resemble a human being."

Amy mock-pouted, taking the plate from her sister's hands. Wendy knew better than to expect much conversation from her sister before she'd had her first cup of coffee.

As they ate, the sunlight crept into the kitchen, warming the room and chasing away the last traces of dawn's chill. Amy leaned back in her chair, her lips curving into a sly grin.

"Soooo…" she began, her voice laced with mischief, "how'd the delivery go yesterday with Mr. Famous Author?"

Wendy pushed herself up from her chair, taking her plate to the sink, her head shaking in amusement. "Not much to tell. He was… polite."

Amy raised an eyebrow, the teasing still dancing in her eyes. "Polite? That's it?"

"Polite. Quiet. Thoughtful," Wendy said, drying her hands and turning to face her sister. "And not in any hurry to make small talk."

Amy laughed, spreading butter on another slice of toast. "Mmm-hmm, classic tortured artist. Was he wearing all black and carrying a fountain pen? Because that's what I'm imagining."

Wendy rolled her eyes, her laughter bubbling up. "No, but he definitely had that 'leave me alone' vibe. The kind that makes you think he's here to escape life and doesn't want to be bothered by us mere mortals."

Amy nodded, her eyes twinkling with humor. "Brooding artist, check. Probably hiding some epic dark story."

"Or just wrestling with his demons," Wendy replied, her tone softening. "But it's not our job to figure him out. He's our guest, and he's asked to be left alone, so don't get any ideas."

Amy's grin widened. "Still, having someone like him around is pretty interesting, don't you think? A famous novelist in our cabin?

That's a big deal for Laurel Ridge. I can hear the gossip trains chugging away already."

Wendy took a breath, crossing her arms and leaning against the counter. "He's a person, Amy. Just... like any other person who rents the cabin. He probably has his reasons for wanting to be left alone."

Amy shrugged, popping a piece of toast into her mouth. "Maybe so. But come on, the man's a pretty big deal—and you can't tell me your curiosity hasn't been piqued just a little."

Wendy didn't respond right away. Because, if she was being honest, she was a little curious. Curiosity had burned her before, though. Once upon a time, she had thought unraveling David's secrets would bring them closer. She'd been wrong about that. Sometimes the secrets people carried weren't meant for mending or unearthing—they wound those involved.

There had been something about Luke, though—something in the way he carried himself—that hinted at a story worth knowing. But stories didn't always end well, and it wasn't her place to pry.

Amy wasn't about to let it go. "Come on, sis," she pressed, standing up and taking her dishes to the sink. "You're telling me he didn't stir up anything in that practical heart of yours?"

"No," Wendy said, moving to the back door and checking on the supplies stacked there for today's deliveries.

But Amy was relentless. "You should have offered him a tour of the orchard and the store," she said, following Wendy with a grin. "What kind of person could resist a stroll through the orchard or fresh-baked apple pie and a bit of southern hospitality?"

Wendy turned, planting her hands on her hips, her expression stern but with a hint of humor in her eyes. "We're not here to entertain our guests, Amy."

Amy cackled. "At least humor me! It's exciting to have someone like him staying here. Stop being so practical."

Wendy stepped out onto the porch, Amy close behind her. Wooden bins were stacked there, waiting to be filled with apples for today's orders. She glanced at Amy, her voice thoughtful. "Sure, it's exciting. But that's all the more reason to give him space. He's carrying something heavy—I could tell that much. It's not our job to fix whatever is bothering him. He'll open up to us if it suits him. If he needs help or even just a friendly conversation, he knows where to find us."

Amy sighed. She hooked her arm around Wendy's shoulders, giving her a playful squeeze. "Fine. But you are a little curious about him, aren't you?"

Wendy met her sister's eyes, raising an eyebrow. "Curiosity isn't the same as prying."

Amy smirked, grabbing her work boots. "Alright, alright. You think Grandma will try to rope him into coming over for Sunday dinner?"

Wendy couldn't help but laugh. "Two days, tops, before she 'accidentally' has too much food and needs someone to help finish it."

Amy grinned as she hopped off the porch, her voice trailing off. "I'll keep an eye out for that."

Wendy watched her sister disappear into the yard, a small smile lingering on her face.

Before Wendy could get lost in her thoughts of Luke Carter too deeply, the soft shuffle of footsteps brought her back. She looked over to see her grandmother approaching, her eyes twinkling, her shawl draped over her shoulders.

"Started early again, I see," Ruth said, her voice carrying the warmth of someone who had lived a full life and learned to take things as they came.

Wendy nodded. "There's a lot to do today."

Ruth adjusted her shawl, settling into the rocking chair on the porch. "Oh, child, you need to learn to relax. Come, sit with me for a while"

Wendy smiled, shaking her head. "Relaxing isn't on the schedule today."

Ruth leaned forward and patted Wendy's arm, her silver curls catching the early light. "It never is, but the work always gets done, doesn't it?"

Wendy leaned against the porch railing, looking out over the orchard. "I suppose so. Today's all about getting orders ready, deliveries, and checking on the younger apple trees. We're also low on jars for apple butter, so I need to head into town this morning."

Ruth nodded, her eyes following Wendy's gaze. "All in good time, child. Just remember not to run yourself ragged trying to make everything perfect."

Wendy chuckled. "I'll be fine, Grandma."

Ruth's eyes narrowed. "I thought I saw someone go up the drive yesterday to the cabin, taking a rather large basket of whatnot up to that fancy author. How'd that go?"

"Oh... you saw that?" Wendy asked, half amused, though she wasn't surprised. Nothing escaped Ruth's notice.

Ruth nodded, a knowing smile playing on her lips. "Hard not to. What's the man like?"

Wendy hesitated, surprised, yet again, by how easily her grandmother could get right to the point. She shifted, feeling Ruth's gaze as if it could peel away her carefully built layers. "He was polite. Reserved. Didn't seem too interested in talking."

Ruth smiled. "Writers are an odd sort. They hold a lot inside. Plus, I read he lost his wife a few years back. He may still struggle with grief."

At that moment, Amy reappeared, still grinning from their earlier conversation. "Our renter is brooding and closed-off—definitely grunt-y, too, from what Wendy told me," she teased, her eyes dancing with humor.

Wendy shot her a playful glare. "Not everyone thrives on talking, Amy."

Ruth chuckled, a twinkle in her eyes. "Maybe he just needs some time. Some people don't know they need people until they've had too much solitude."

Wendy nodded, though she wasn't convinced. Luke Carter had looked like someone who built his walls high and sturdy. But maybe, just maybe, he would lower them enough for someone to see what was on the other side.

"Well, if anyone could make him loosen up a little, it's you, Wendy," Ruth said, as she glanced at Amy and winked.

"Me?" Wendy blushed, shaking her head. "Oh, I see where this is going. Don't even go there. Both of you don't even start trying to be matchmakers."

Ruth didn't miss a beat, her voice softening as she leaned back in her chair. "Not everyone's David, child. And not everyone's here to pull the wool over your eyes."

The mention of his name felt like a small sting of nettles. What she'd thought had been love with David had been something else entirely—an illusion. A carefully orchestrated ruse to benefit himself. Especially near the end, when his thoughtfulness had only been a screen for his plans to convince her to sell the farm.

Ruth's voice remained gentle as she continued, her eyes full of understanding. "Not everyone comes with a hidden agenda, Wendy. Sometimes folks are just looking for a quiet place to heal, just like you.

You're still healing, too. Sometimes, that means seeing things more clearly than you once did, and also letting yourself trust again."

That last line landed like a light nudge—not harsh, but undeniably true. Wendy couldn't muster the words to respond, so she simply gave her grandmother a small, grateful smile. Ruth's words echoed in her mind, lingering there like a softness she hadn't expected but somehow needed. She trusted her grandmother's wisdom, but trusting a man again with her heart—not as easy.

"Well," Ruth said with a contented sigh, easing the moment, "if we're done talking about mysterious authors, I'm going to get my day started. The apple butter sure isn't going to make itself."

Chapter 5

The bell above the door chimed softly as Luke stepped inside, the warm scents of bacon, maple syrup, and freshly brewed coffee wrapping around him. He paused by the entrance, his eyes scanning the restaurant. Martha's Diner looked like something from a different era—red vinyl booths, some of them filled with people murmuring over steaming mugs of coffee. The fluorescent lights overhead gave everything a faint, nostalgic glow, making the platters of eggs and toast in front of some diners seem almost radiant.

In one corner, an elderly couple sat, sipping their coffee, nodding now and then at familiar faces as they passed by. Across the aisle, a young mother wrestled with her child, her face scrunched in concentration as she tried to keep a dollop of jelly from landing on her clean blouse. Behind the counter, a round-faced woman in an apron moved from one customer to the next, pouring coffee into waiting mugs, her calm smile making each interaction feel like a moment shared.

"Good morning, young man," the woman called, her voice cutting through the chatter as she waved a laminated menu in his direction.

She spoke like she knew him already, like he was an old friend who had just walked in after being away for too long. "You look like you could use some coffee. Sit anywhere you like, sweetheart. I'll be right with you."

Luke hesitated, his eyes shifting from her bright expression to the nearest empty booth.

He wasn't sure if he was ready for the level of friendliness the woman had shown.

He pulled himself together and made his way over to the open booth, settling into the vinyl seat.

The woman appeared instantly. Her gentle blue eyes radiated warmth, framed by delicate wisps of salt-and-pepper hair neatly tied in a bun. The apron she wore looked like it had been part of the diner as long as the booths and the old bell above the door.

A cup of coffee landed in front of him, the steam curling upward. "Martha Kincaid," she announced, her drawl warm and welcoming. "Owner, and keeper, of what my regulars call the best darn diner in Laurel Ridge. Don't let anyone tell you otherwise—it's a fact."

Luke blinked, taken aback once again by her enthusiasm. There was a part of him that wanted to laugh at how quickly she'd laid everything out for him, but he wasn't quite sure if he should be amused or wary.

She tapped the menu she'd set down in front of him, her fingers drumming a light rhythm. "Take your time, honey. I've had all kinds of folks in here—city folk, travelers passing through, you name it. I'm sure you'll find something on this menu you'll like."

Luke nodded, still surprised by her energy. She gave him a smile that seemed almost too genuine, like they'd known each other far longer than a few seconds.

"Most folks go for the number five," she added, her smile broadening even more, her eyes crinkling at the corners. "Eggs, toast, bacon, hash browns. Simple, hearty, gets you through the morning 'till lunchtime rolls around. But if you're feeling a bit more adventurous, I'd recommend my special—perfect for those who like a sweet surprise with breakfast."

Luke chuckled, surprising even himself. "I think I may be feeling adventurous today," he said, the humor in his voice belying his usual caution.

Martha's eyes lit up as she jotted his order on her notepad. "Adventurous, huh?" She winked. "Well, you won't be disappointed. Apple-cinnamon French toast with my special homemade syrup. And I'll get you a little extra butter too...just in case."

Luke nodded, offering her a smile before she turned toward the kitchen. He inhaled, enjoying the scent of rich coffee and sizzling bacon that settled around him. It was comforting in a way that surprised him—like the kind of warmth that seeped into your bones and made you feel at home, even if you weren't.

Martha returned soon enough, her steps brisk as she set the plate down in front of him. Luke's eyes widened at the size of the breakfast—the French toast glistened under a generous helping of butter, the cinnamon, and apple filling the air with a fragrance that made his stomach growl.

Martha leaned against the booth opposite him, her arms crossed over her apron. "You're not from around here, are you?" she asked, a knowing glint in her eyes.

Luke chewed a piece of French toast, taking his time before answering. "No."

Simple. Direct. Enough to keep most people from prying further. But Martha wasn't most people.

"You don't really look like a tourist, not the hiking or kayaking type either. Just passing through on business?" she continued, her gaze steady, curious but not intrusive.

Luke swallowed, his eyes shifting to the window beside him. He hadn't even made it halfway through his breakfast, and already, it felt like he was being pulled into more conversation than he'd intended. "Just visiting for a while," he said, keeping it vague. "Rented a cabin out by Nature's Gift Farm and Orchard. Trying to get some writing done."

Martha's face brightened, as if everything suddenly clicked into place. "Ahh, the writer! Heard a bit about you. Luke Carter, right?" She grinned, giving him a friendly nod. "Well, now it all makes sense." She straightened, her smile softening. "Enjoy that French toast young man. And don't be shy, if you need anything...just holler. This diner's more than just food—it's full of good company, too." She winked, then turned and made her way back toward the counter.

Luke watched her go, a small smile tugging at the corner of his mouth. There was something about her easy, friendly manner that reminded him of the warmth he used to find at his childhood church—people who made you feel welcome, offering comfort without demanding too much of you.

He took another bite of the French toast; the flavors bursting across his tongue—sweet, with just enough spice to make it interesting. Absurdly good. Maybe too good.

He'd barely managed a few more bites before the bell over the door gave another cheerful jingle. He glanced up, not particularly interested, but the sight that met his eyes stopped him.

Wendy.

Her ponytail bobbed as she walked, her dirt-smudged jeans peeking out from under her plaid shirt. She carried a large wooden crate filled with apples. Her steps light, almost buoyant. Even from across the room, Luke could feel her energy—vivid and full of life, like she carried a piece of the orchard with her wherever she went.

Martha's face lit up as soon as she spotted Wendy. "Wendy, darling! You're saving us from another baking disaster!" she called, her voice carrying over the clatter of plates.

Wendy laughed, the sound clear and genuine as she set the crate on the counter. "Saving you from apple pie crisis number twenty," she quipped. "Did Sheriff Dooley place another big order again?"

Martha threw up her hands dramatically. "That man could eat a whole pasture full of cows and still have room for pie," she said, her laugh infectious as Wendy joined in. "He ordered a dozen pies for some meeting he has at city hall today."

Luke tried to refocus on his breakfast, but it was hard not to listen, not to be drawn in by Wendy's presence. As if sensing his attention, Wendy turned, her eyes meeting his. She smiled—a bright, friendly smile that seemed to make the diner a little warmer, a little lighter.

"Morning, Mr. Carter," she said, as she made her way over to his booth, leaning casually against it as if it were the most natural thing in the world. "Getting the full Martha experience already?"

Luke blinked, caught off guard by her proximity. "If the full experience includes life-changing French toast, then yeah, I'd say so."

Wendy's grin widened, her eyes crinkling at the corners. "Apple-cinnamon French toast? Oh, you've got good taste."

"Martha's persuasive," Luke replied, his voice a little softer, a hint of a chuckle escaping him. "It was hard to say no."

"She does have a way about her," Wendy agreed, casting a glance toward Martha, who was busy organizing plates at the counter. "I don't think anyone's ever left here without eating more than they intended."

Luke shifted in his seat. "I came in for a simple breakfast... but this?" he motioned to the plate in front of him. "This is something else. And the coffee's some of the best I've had."

Wendy raised her eyebrows, her tone playful, but something thoughtful flickered across her face. "Careful. Martha's coffee tends to get people hooked. We call it the gateway to Laurel Ridge."

Her voice was playful, yet Luke felt something weighty behind her words. She seemed at ease here, much more than he felt. And yet, there was a flash—something cautious mirrored in her green eyes. While she was perfectly at ease with small-town banter, he couldn't shake the feeling that she, like him, wasn't ready to fully open the floodgates with extensive conversation.

He took another sip of coffee, buying himself a few more seconds to gather his thoughts. "Just a heads-up," Wendy said, her voice dropping, a mischievous glint in her gaze. "I think Martha's already got you on the town's unofficial gossip radar."

Luke's smirk was polite but cautious. So people are talking already. "Guess there's no hiding out, even in a small town," he said, trying to keep it light, though a quiet unease prickled beneath the surface. Small towns could be suffocating if you weren't careful.

Wendy nodded. "Yep. But don't worry. The gossip will die down—eventually. Or maybe not, especially with the apple festival coming up soon."

"Apple festival?" he repeated, curiosity piqued.

The corners of her mouth tugged upward. "Oh yes," she said, leaning forward like she was letting him in on a bit of local wisdom. "It's a pretty big deal around here. You might not be able to avoid it—even if you try."

Wendy's eyes glimmered. "Coming up in two weeks. It's the biggest event in Laurel Ridge. Don't worry, I won't rope you into anything—unless you're craving some apple-picking or a pie-eating competition. But it's hard not to get pulled in by all the energy."

Luke grinned a little, though he wasn't entirely convincing. "Sounds... fun."

Wendy smiled, her tone softening. "You'll see. But I'll warn you. The festival takes over my entire farm. You'll experience a lot of noise and activity on the day of the event."

Just as Luke was about to say something—though what, he wasn't sure—the bell jingled again as a couple walked in. Wendy gave them a wave before turning back to Luke. "Anyway, I've got more deliveries to make. Don't be a stranger. If you need anything, just holler."

"I'll keep that in mind," he replied, watching as she waved goodbye to Martha before disappearing through the door. There was an ease about her, a brightness that hadn't been dulled by life's challenges. And yet, he wondered—was there something more under the surface, a flicker of something more cautious?

Chapter 6

Luke had been sitting on the porch for what felt like hours, his eyes fixed on his laptop screen. The soft, blue-tinted light no longer felt welcoming—it was harsh, accusatory, as if it were questioning his talent. The words stared back at him, hollow and rigid, lifeless and without meaning. They hung there like forgotten garments on a clothesline, swaying in the wind.

He closed his eyes and inhaled, but it didn't ease off the tension gathering between his shoulders. This morning, it had felt like his old self was back—the ideas had come faster than they had in months. Words spilling onto the page with a kind of clarity that made him almost hopeful. But now? Now they sat in front of him like a counterfeit version of what they should be. Lacking soul. Robotic. Forced.

Leaning back against the weathered wood of the chair, he let out an audible sigh as his mind wandered to memories of Sarah.

Sarah had loved porches. She believed they offered a space that couldn't be found indoors. In Ohio, she would often sit on their small porch, enjoying herbal tea and a good book.

But Luke was alone now, on a different porch, listening to the distant hum of cicadas, haunted by the empty chair beside him.

He missed her. He missed—everything about her. The life they had built together. The love they had shared.

He felt so utterly... alone and missed her companionship. He missed having a hand to hold, and someone to have a decent conversation with.

Sure, he had people in his life. He had a stunning career and loyal readers who engaged with him regularly on social media. He had fans that would send a friendly card in the mail. A few good friends would call now and then.

The world, in general, called him successful and assumed his life was full and rich. Indeed, the world spun around him as if he were as whole as ever, even as he felt like a shadow of the man he used to be. Success felt hollow now without someone to share it with. And Sarah... Sarah had known how to make life itself feel full, even in the smallest moments.

His gaze shifted back to the laptop screen, filled with the impersonal clumps of typed-out words. Three entire chapters. But each paragraph, each sentence, clung with a kind of desperation, like a hollowed-out shell trying to pass itself off as something more.

"A hollow victory," he muttered under his breath. With a soft click, he closed the laptop—an action that sounded almost apologetic, as though the machine too recognized he had nothing left to offer.

Luke sat there, staring out at the grove of trees edging the horizon. The light breeze moved between the leaves, rustling them. A gentle scent of apples tugged at him from Wendy's orchard. The mountain air was a blend of cool and crisp, invigorating in a way it shouldn't have been, considering how stuck and lonely he felt inside.

His attention drifted back to the surrounding farm. Even from the porch, he could see the orchard's perfectly aligned rows of apple trees, their branches heavy with fruit. Workers moved with purpose—each step deliberate, their hands steady as they loaded crates, filling the air with purposeful sounds that felt almost...rehearsed. There was something unhurried but focused about their movements, as though nature itself worked better than anything he was trying to do—a quiet reminder of life's continuity. It didn't stop to brood or pause to question.

Luke watched them enviously—the ease of their rhythm, the constancy of their work. Not a second was wasted. There was nothing hollow in their movements.

Some workers transferred crates of apples to the bed of a farm truck, while others maneuvered wheelbarrows brimming with pumpkins. Few words passed between them—only the occasional chuckle or murmured instruction—but their work was communal. They operated as a unit, flowing like water, where each person had their place. Luke couldn't help but feel more isolated by comparison, like an outsider peering in at something meaningful and whole.

Sighing once more, his eyes landed on the near-empty jug of cider next to him—a reminder of Wendy's kindness and generosity. There was also the last bit of the pumpkin bread she'd included with the cider jug. He picked it up and took a thoughtful bite, the warm flavors of pumpkin, cinnamon, and nutmeg bursting through in a rush that took him by surprise.

Again his thoughts moved to the past—transporting him back to other autumn seasons, standing around a backyard bonfire, the smell of burning leaves and laughter all around. He remembered a time when he and Sarah had carved pumpkins and laughed and joked together, without a care in the world. Sarah rolling out pie crust in their kitchen, her favorite apron tied snugly around her waist. He could still hear her voice, soft but melodic, telling him to grab the cinnamon.

She loved the fall. Loved everything about it.

Luke swallowed the bread, a pit settling in his stomach. The warm feelings and memories he once associated with this season, with those small normal comforts, had begun to blur recently, like photographs left out in the rain—edges smudged, faces fading. And those memories? They were slipping through his fingers like mist. He questioned if he was trying to hold on too tightly to the past, or if he should try harder to forget it entirely. His thoughts of her had slowed recently. He had to work a little harder now to remember details of moments spent with her.

Shaking his head and rolling his shoulders as though to shake off the feelings themselves, Luke stood up, stretching until he felt the tension pull out of his muscles. His gaze returned to the closed laptop on the table.

Not now.

He needed to move. To do something. Maybe that way, he could outrun that restlessness—the low thrum of unease that had settled inside.

The gravel crunched beneath his boots as he made his way down the driveway, each step feeling rhythmic, and intentional. Luke inhaled deeply, letting the crisp scent of the apple orchard and the fresh air fill his lungs. There was something grounding about it, like the air here was fuller, richer than anywhere else he'd ever been.

His eyes wandered to the workers again—their steady movements under the branches of fruit-laden trees. Without thinking twice, Luke stepped off the gravel path and moved toward one of the apple trees close to the roadside edge. He reached for an apple hanging low, cupping it in his palm. Its skin was smooth, cool, and firm.

Sarah would have liked this. He remembered the time they'd planned to go apple-picking. Five years ago? Maybe more. He'd canceled at the last minute on her because of a deadline. He could still see the way her lips had pressed into that brittle, too-easy smile when she promised him it was fine. But he knew better.

You always think there's more time—until there isn't.

Closing his eyes, Luke shook his head as if to clear the thought, and kept walking.

It didn't take long for the Farmstead Store to come into view. The barn-style doors opened wide, welcoming anyone curious enough to wander in. The area teemed with life—a handful of tourists were milling about outside, examining the pumpkins and baskets of apples set by the entrance, while children dragged their parents inside toward shelves filled with caramel-dipped treats. He could hear laughter intermingled with the sounds of customer chatter.

But his attention snagged to the side of the building—on the woman moving briskly as she unloaded crates from the back of a large pickup truck.

Wendy Lane.

There was a fluidity in the way she moved, as though this work was second nature to her. Each motion was full of precision and ease. The kind of ease you couldn't fake. Strands of loose hair fell from where she'd tied it back, sticking to her forehead. She paused, wiping her brow with the back of her hand.

Luke instinctively walked toward her, boots scuffing hard against the gravel. He stopped short, clearing his throat.

Wendy's head jerked up, and for a moment, surprise flickered across her face. But her smile came quick enough, warm and open, as if she welcomed the interruption.

"Afternoon, Mr. Carter," she said, leaning casually against the tail-gate. "Taking a break from writing?"

Luke glanced at the stacked crates beside her and then turned his gaze back to hers. A half-smile formed on his lips, as automatic as flipping a light switch. "More like my writing's taking a break from me," he joked. He paused for a beat, then added almost too quickly, "You can call me Luke."

"Alright," Wendy smiled, giving a small, approving nod. "Luke it is."

Before he could second-guess himself, he gestured at the crates in the back of her truck. "Need a hand?"

A flicker of something unreadable crossed her face, vanishing almost as soon as it had appeared. She hesitated for just a brief second—long enough for him to catch it—but there it was, a softness overshadowed by uncertainty, no matter how quickly she recovered. Perhaps it would have been subtle enough to miss if he weren't always so attuned to reading the slight shifts in people's expressions.

"Are you sure?" Wendy asked, her smile now hinting at playful skepticism.

Luke rolled up his sleeves, stepping closer. "I don't mind at all. I need to burn off some negative energy and take a break from writing."

She laughed, her bright sound breaking the tension for them both. "Alright then, Luke. Show me what you've got."

With a grunt, Luke hoisted the closest wooden crate onto his shoulder, noting that it was heavier than he'd expected. Wendy had already strolled ahead toward the side entrance of the store, so he followed.

Inside, Luke lowered the crate onto the floor near the fruit washing station, wiping the dust from his palms. Wendy was watching him with a teasing gleam in her eyes that bordered on admiration.

"Not bad, Mr. Famous Author," she remarked, leaning back against the barn wall. "Not bad at all."

Luke offered a crooked smile, brushing the dirt off his hands on his jeans. "I aim to please."

She tilted her head, her eyes gleaming as she studied him. Her earlier hesitation had passed, leaving only curiosity in its place. "Come on," she urged. "Better not quit on me now. We've still got a few crates left."

He nodded, and they made their way back to the truck. For the next several minutes, they worked, moving crates in tandem, slipping into a rhythm that flowed easily. Comfortable, even. They worked with the same kind of quiet focus he'd seen in the orchard workers—only this time, his mind wasn't wrapped around the novel, or Sarah, or the aching loneliness.

Once the last crate was moved, Wendy leaned against the tailgate of her truck, folding her arms across her chest. Her brows arched as she studied him for a moment, her gaze warm but with a touch of challenge.

"I'll admit it," she said, brushing back a loose strand of hair. "Pretty good job—for a writer."

He raised one brow, his smirk half-playful, half-proving a point. "I have my moments."

"I can see that," she replied, uncrossing her arms and standing upright. Her tone shifting to one of deeper consideration. "So...are you finished writing for the day already? The day's still young."

Luke blinked. "Writing?" He shifted awkwardly, glancing toward the ground before meeting her gaze again. "I got a few chapters down this morning, but... they're not my best work. I should probably try to get more work done at some point today."

Wendy offered him a soft, understanding smile—the genuine kind that made Luke wonder if she saw straight through the mess he tried to hide. "Well, even Hemingway had off days," she said with an encouraging note. "At least you wrote something."

Luke nodded, casting his eyes to the side. "Right. Something."

There was a pause—a brief but perceptible silence, as if both of them hung on what to say next. Wendy broke it by clapping her hands lightly together.

"Well," she chirped, "I appreciate the help. I'll have to let my employee, who called off today, know I've got someone lining up to take his job."

Luke chuckled. "Better not. I might have to quit my day job if that gets out."

Wendy's laughter rang out again—joyful, unburdened by the weight of awkward exchanges. "We'd be honored to have you."

"Does it pay well?" Luke asked with deadpan humor, hands back in his pockets.

"Oh, the best," Wendy shot back with a wink and a grin. "All the apples you can eat."

There was softness in her now—something unguarded.

"You going to stick around a little longer?" she asked, her voice casual. "We've got fresh cider inside, if you'd like."

Luke shook his head. The motion gentle, but not without some consideration. He gestured toward the gravel path he had come from earlier. "Think I'd better stretch my legs a little more. Then I have a laptop waiting on me back at the cabin."

There was something about the way Wendy smiled then—equal parts understanding and, somehow, hopeful.

"No worries. Don't be a stranger, Luke, and thanks for the help."

And for just a second, Luke paused. There was something so easy about the way she said it. Something warm and caring that made him uncomfortable. Like something in his chest stirred at the thought of being asked to stick around, not because he had something to offer, but because his presence meant something to another person.

"You're welcome," he murmured, his voice almost too quiet.

Chapter 7

Wendy slipped back into the cool air of the Farmstead Store, her heart a little lighter after saying goodbye to Luke, his smile lingering in her mind. She exhaled, feeling the gentle tickle of perspiration cooling at the back of her neck. Stray strands of hair clung to her face, and she tucked them behind her ears as she made her way to the deep sink in the stockroom.

The faucet creaked as she turned it on, the icy stream splashing against her palms. Closing her eyes, she drew in the coolness, almost wishing it could calm her inner stirrings as well. The brief interaction with Luke left her feeling... unsettled. Not in a bad way, and that was its own problem.

Grabbing a nearby towel, Wendy pressed it against her damp face, letting the coolness drain away the leftover warmth from her cheeks. She reached for the familiar forest-green apron hanging on its trusty hook and looped it over her head, securing it tightly around her waist. Time to refocus. Pies waited to be baked, jams and jellies needed stocking, and she needed to check in with her store manager, Leah, who was likely chatting away with customers in the store.

Still chewing on the thoughts circling in her mind about Luke, she passed by the crates of apples they had unloaded earlier. His offer to help had been simple, almost natural... but something about it felt too easy. Too familiar.

She smiled despite herself as she made her way to the swinging doors that led to the store, lost in her thoughts.

"Well, well, well..." Leah's voice caught her mid-step as she arrived at the counter. Her mischievous lilt was unmistakable.

Wendy froze for a beat, her pulse quickening. Here we go. She knew that tone all too well—Leah had the look of someone about to pounce. Wendy's stomach lurched as, sure enough, Leah crossed her arms over her apron, a slow, knowing grin spreading wide on her face.

"Don't think you can just stroll in here and pretend nothing happened outside, Miss Lane," Leah teased, eyes glinting like she'd just been handed the juiciest gossip ever.

Wendy's shoulders stiffened. A part of her was ready for the banter—to meet it head-on—but another part... Another part, buried beneath layers of caution, feared where Leah might drag this conversation if she wasn't careful.

Wendy tried to keep her tone light, but it felt just a little too breezy as she slipped behind the counter, rearranging jars of apple butter like precision stacking was her new mission in life. "What are you... talking about?"

Leah's smirk deepened, like she was savoring this. "Oh, honey, don't even try it. We both know you're terrible at playing coy. I saw him."

Wendy blinked, hand pausing over a jar. "Saw who?"

Leah raised an eyebrow and mimed fanning herself, her grin getting wider. "You know exactly who. The hunky stranger helping you unload those apple crates."

Wendy's face flushed as an all-too-familiar itch prickled at the back of her mind.

"He wasn't—Leah, it wasn't like that." Wendy's voice came out higher than she'd intended, the warmth in her cheeks intensifying. She spun around, hiding behind the stacked display of jellies, using the glass jars as her shield.

"Uh-huh," Leah drawled, eyes as full of amusement as ever. "And I'm about to start a dairy farm next week. Seriously, Wendy. Who was he? You've got to tell me. Because from where I was standing, he was definitely not your average farmhand."

Wendy fumbled for a response, fingers running restlessly over the jars again, twisting them as a distraction. "He's just someone staying at the cabin," she muttered. "His name's Luke. He was out taking a walk and offered to help me unload the apples."

A flicker of curiosity flashed in Leah's eyes. Her lips twisted into an exaggerated pout. "Just Luke? Just someone staying in the cabin?"

She glanced past Wendy, looking out the window toward the orchard as if Luke might come walking out of the trees any minute. "You know, Wendy, a guest in the cabin that looks like that is not exactly a casual thing. You can't expect me to ignore this."

Wendy couldn't help her exasperated groan.

"He's a famous author, okay? Luke Carter." Wendy crossed her arms across her chest, her tone sharper than she meant it to be.

Leah's jaw dropped, her eyebrows shooting so high that Wendy swore they might get lost somewhere above the display shelves. For a moment, blessed silence hung between them.

"What?!" Leah's voice shot up several octaves. "Luke Carter? The Luke Carter? Best-selling, makes-you-cry-over-a-teacup Luke Carter?!" She was bouncing on her toes, her excitement contagious—except Wendy wasn't catching it. Not today.

Wendy rubbed the bridge of her nose, feeling Leah's words starting to drain whatever calm she'd managed to hold on to. "Yes, the one and only." She tried to sound indifferent, but the heat rising to her cheeks gave her away.

Leah shook her head as if she'd heard the strangest, most unbelievable thing. "And you... what? Just didn't mention this to me before now? Like it's not a big deal that we have the world's most famous author staying with us?"

Wendy grimaced, half-amused, half-annoyed. "Because it's not a big deal. He's just renting for a few months. He wanted someplace quiet to stay while he's writing. That's all."

"Not a big deal?!" Leah scoffed, hands flying to her hips. "Girl, that man is responsible for an entire generation needing extra tissues! It's a massive deal!"

For a moment, Leah seemed too stunned to continue. Wendy grabbed a stack of order slips, pretending to be interested in what pies they might still need to whip up by afternoon. She almost allowed herself to believe the storm had blown over—when Leah piped up again.

"And how in the world did you manage to—"

"What's going on up here?" Amy's voice rang out as she strolled into the room, her grin already forming—like she could sense Leah's drama brewing and came to claim her place in the circle. "Did somebody spill a jar of gossip I haven't heard yet?"

Leah's eyes sparkled as if she'd been handed mythical treasure. "Ohhh yes—come, come. Wendy here was just telling me all about her little run-in with Mr. Novel Man, who, by the way, helped her unload the truck."

Amy's brows lifted as she moved closer, her fingers tapping on the counter. "Oh, really? And pray tell... what other escapades have ensued this fine apple-picking afternoon?"

"Oh, knock it off," Wendy muttered, exasperated now. She turned to grab a crate of jam jars waiting nearby, hoping the work would somehow save her from their relentless prying. "It was nothing. He helped unload a few apple crates. End of story."

Leah shook her head, her smile so knowing it bordered on telepathic. "I watched the whole thing from the window. Didn't look like 'nothing' to me."

Amy nodded, as if they were holding a secret council, her tone dripping with exaggerated seriousness. "Mmm-hmm. No way someone like Luke Carter was here just for unloading duties. Right, Leah?"

"Right," Leah agreed with a grin. "There's definitely more to this story."

Wendy sighed, plunking the crate down on the countertop with a bit more force than she'd intended, as she turned to face both women. They stood like sentinels, epitomizing everything Wendy had come to expect from them when new gossip was hot on the horizon.

"Look, girls," she said, voice firm. "He's here to write. He's quiet. Reserved. Just renting the cabin and has asked for privacy." Wendy punctuated the last part, hoping to squelch their endless theories.

Amy tilted her head, that mischievous twinkle back in her eye. She shared a knowing look with Leah, and for a moment Wendy wondered if she'd just thrown gasoline on the fire.

"Sure, sis," Amy teased, stepping closer, her voice sweetly curious. "Renting, writing, and now...just helping out. Are you saying there's nothing more? Because, c'mon, men like that don't just appear in

Laurel Ridge, and they don't drop everything to help a damsel in distress by unloading a truck full of apples. At least, not without a little divine intervention."

Wendy bit the inside of her cheek to hold back the retort that leapt to the tip of her tongue. She would rather not seem defensive—it wasn't like that.

Wendy shook her head, fighting to sound measured. "He didn't say much," she replied, almost too quickly. But even Leah gave her a side glance. She continued, trying again for casual, "Just polite, you know? Not much of a talker, really. Focused. He was just helping me."

Amy clasped her hands together dramatically, as if announcing a shopping network special. "Oh—polite and helpful? And quite the fine-looking man. An author to boot who has a way with his words. Be still, my beating heart! A rare love miracle in real life!"

Leah grinned, nudging Amy. "And that, we all know, is the quickest way to Wendy's heart."

Before Wendy could summon a reply—or an apple crate to hurl—Ruth approached, her laughter soft and wise. She balanced a tray of fresh apple turnovers in one hand like some sort of domestic goddess.

"What's all this fuss I'm hearing?" Ruth's knowing twinkle creased her face as she set the tray down on the counter with expert hands.

Wendy's heart sank to her shoes. Oh, no. Here we go indeed.

Leah turned like she'd just been offered the stage under a spotlight, her whole expression practically shouting, "Wait until you hear this, Ruth! You're gonna love this one."

Amy clamped her hands across her chest like she was reading lines from a script. "Picture this: Wendy, outside unloading the truck. Apple crates galore. Then, enter stage right: our hunky hero, who just happens to be in the neighborhood. Cue the dramatic background music. The hero helps her unload the truck!"

Ruth blinked but didn't miss a beat, her eyebrow arching upward. "Oh, really?" Folding her arms across her apron, she tilted her head. "And who might this heroic figure be?"

Leah's eyes gleamed, timing her response like a drumroll. "The one and only. Luke. Carter."

Wendy tried to will herself into the floor, but no such luck.

"Ah yes. Saw it all from the kitchen window. The man looked like he'd done his fair share of work before." Ruth said. "Honestly, Wendy, you seemed like you were enjoying the company of our well-respected writer, hmm?"

Wendy threw her hands up in surrender. Every one of them—Leah, Amy, and Ruth—were all standing there with the same mischievous twinkle in their eyes, as if waiting for her to smash the piñata of juicy gossip goodies.

"He just wanted to help," Wendy said with an exaggerated sigh, her voice colored with full exasperation now. "We unloaded the truck. We talked. That's it. End of story."

Leah grinned from ear to ear, holding up her hand like an eager student in class. "But is it, though?" she prompted, eyes gleaming with nothing but devilish delight.

Ruth chuckled while Amy all but slapped her thigh in giddy delight, and said, "Well, it's always nice to help a neighbor in need!"

Amy folded her hands in mock prayer, closing her eyes as dramatically as possible. "Lord, forgive me for my thoughts, but if unloading apple crates is what it takes to find a man, I'll move every single one within a hundred-mile radius."

Wendy grabbed a notepad from the counter and swished it in front of them like a teacher scolding an unruly classroom. "You're all terrible!" she huffed. But her words were no match for the chorus of laughter that followed.

"Well, Wendy, my dear," Ruth said, wiping a warm tear from the corner of her eye. "You know we're only teasing, but isn't it lovely? Sounds like we've got ourselves a classic small-town romance in the making."

Wendy sighed in faux exasperation. Finally relenting, she muttered, "Fine. Speculate all you want, but I'm not going to feed the fire."

Ruth stepped closer, laying a gentle hand on Wendy's arm, with a smile that held both amusement and love. "It's all in good fun, dear. But next time... Maybe ask if he'd like to pick up a shift or two here at the store. We could always use the extra help."

Giggles echoed in Wendy's wake as she grabbed her clipboard and hustled to the stockroom at the back of the store. Although she was slightly mortified, there was something else making her cheeks tingle—a warmth, a lightness. If love was something Wendy had closed the door on long ago, it seemed Amy, Leah, and Ruth might just be camped outside, forcing it right back in.

Tucked in the quiet of the storeroom, away from their teasing eyes, Wendy allowed herself to breathe. Leaning back against the wall, she rubbed the back of her neck, Luke's face lingering in her mind. She couldn't help smiling a little.

Luke Carter. Quite an interesting man.

But whether or not that was a good thing, she couldn't decide.

As the quiet settled over her, the familiar, old hesitation crept in again. Luke wasn't David—but letting anyone get close enough to matter was how it had all started.

Chapter 8

Wendy sat behind the counter, her fingers flicking through vendor lists for the upcoming Apple Festival. Each sheet of paper represented weeks of meticulous phone calls, visits, and negotiations. Her tired eyes traveled over the words, taking in the list of tasks she was proud to see falling into place—food trucks, live music, and even the pie contest judges were all lined up.

"Everything is almost ready," she murmured, scanning down the last list, but her gaze landed on two glaring empty lines under volunteers, her brow furrowing.

"We're still short a couple of volunteers," she said, tapping her pen.

Amy, perched on a stool by the cash register, raised an eyebrow as she lazily flipped through an old magazine, her voice casual but sharp. "Don't worry," Amy waved dismissively. "We'll find them. Grandma says we've always had enough hands, even in years when half the town decided to go on vacation at the same time."

Wendy's lips twitched into a reluctant smile. "Yeah, well, Grandma also thinks we could put the rooster in charge of the pumpkin patch, and everything would still turn out fine."

Amy grinned, as she tossed the magazine on the counter and stretched her arms over her head with a slow yawn. "And she's probably right." She glanced around at the quiet store. A couple of customers wandered through the aisles, pausing to inspect the rows of cider bottles and the shelves lined with jellies.

"It's kind of a slow day," Amy added.

Wendy chuckled and shook her head. "You sound disappointed. Like you actually want it to be busy."

Amy flashed a grin—mischievous and carefree, as always. "Never said I didn't enjoy slow days. Might go check the pumpkin patch later if this keeps up. You know, stretch my legs and pretend I'm being productive."

Wendy hummed as she slid her focus back to her vendor lists. Her fingers tapped against the pen, her mind already settling back into the festival's details.

"Ohhhh, have mercy!" Amy drawled, the playful tone in her voice shifting to something more dramatic.

Wendy's eyes flicked up from her notepad. Following her sister's devilish gaze, she felt a subtle shift in the air—a presence familiar but hardly casual. Luke Carter had just walked in.

A string of tension tugged at the back of Wendy's mind as she observed him striding into the store with a kind of quiet purpose, his eyes locking onto the shelves of cider along the back wall.

Why was it always the quiet ones who seemed to get to her the most? Wendy chastised her own thoughts as if she should scold herself for even noticing Luke. Nothing about him was flashy or arrogant—just purposeful in a way that left too many cracks for her imagination to wander.

Her fingers drummed against her notepad. *He's nothing like David,* she reminded herself. *But you know better than to get too comfortable,* the familiar warning uncoiled in her mind like a reflex. *Luke was here for a reason, but it wasn't her.*

Wendy straightened her posture, forcing the thoughts to the back of her mind. He was just a customer. Just a renter in her cabin.

Luke lingered near the racks of local roasted coffee beans now, his brow knitting together in concentration—almost as though he was debating the merits of each choice. Without thinking it through, Wendy slid off her stool and made her way toward him, her voice light as she broke the silence.

"Need help deciding?" she asked.

Luke turned toward her, those guarded eyes of his finding hers for a fraction of a second longer than he intended.

Hesitation. There was always hesitation with him—or maybe it was discretion. Wendy couldn't tell... and that made her uneasy.

Still, after a pause, the corner of his mouth twitched upward just enough to be noticeable. "Yeah," he admitted, his voice calm in a way that only seemed to pull her in closer. "Your local selection's a little overwhelming—for a humble city guy like me."

Wendy chuckled, taking a step closer. "I get it. When we started stocking these blends, I found myself second-guessing my own morning pot of coffee every day for a month."

Luke's eyes flickered toward hers, his relaxed smile that calm facade again—guarded and unreadable. "Got any recommendations? I'm not much of a coffee connoisseur."

Wendy ran her fingers along the shelf, pausing over a familiar blue-and-white printed label. Plucking the bag off the shelf, she offered it to him. "This one's my go-to," she nodded toward the label. "Mountain Morning Blend. It's smooth and mild, but it's got enough kick to get you through if you're burning the midnight oil."

"I'll, uh, take your word for it then. Do you drink a lot of coffee?" Luke asked as he studied the bag in his hands.

Why does it feel so easy to talk to him? Her smile felt too thin suddenly, her casual armor slipping. "More than I should, these days," she said, trying to lace her tone with banter, but failing. "The festival's coming up, and—" Wendy paused, biting at her lip as her fingers ghosted over another bag of coffee.

Stop it, she reminded herself. Being polite doesn't mean getting involved.

Luke seemed to catch that faint hesitation, though he didn't prod it. He chuckled, warm and natural despite the subtle tension clinging to his shoulders. "Well, if it's good enough for a festival, I'm game. Hopefully, it'll keep me steady while I work through all this writing."

Wendy's smile returned, softer now, as she moved beside him. "Good choice," she nodded toward the cider shelves near the edge of the aisle. "Stocking up on that too, I bet?"

Luke followed her gaze, his lips curving once more. "You caught me," he admitted, lifting two glass bottles from the shelf and tucking them under his arm. "The stuff's remarkable—better than anything I can get back home in Columbus."

Wendy's chest swelled with warmth, his compliment a small but meaningful acknowledgment of everything her family had built. "We're quite proud of it," she said, letting that note of pride color her words. "I can set some aside for you before the crowds hit next week if you'd like."

Luke's brows raised, interest replacing his guarded expression. "Is it that bad when the festival gets going?"

Wendy nodded, her smile widening. "The festival can get pretty intense. People come from all over for cider alone. It's usually the first thing that sells out."

He tilted his head, a mixture of amusement and curiosity coming together in his eyes. "Well, this festival sounds like something I don't want to miss."

His gaze drifted to the stack of pumpkin bread nearby, lingering there for a moment before he turned back to her. "I'll take a couple of those now also, but I'm guessing the pumpkin bread goes just as fast after the festival starts?"

Wendy laughed. "It flies off the shelves. I can put aside a couple of loaves for you next week before things get too crazy." She grabbed two loaves for him now.

"I wouldn't say no," Luke replied, a hint of gratitude in his eyes.

"Consider it done. Come festival time, you'll at least have the essentials."

The more they spoke, the more Wendy noticed how Luke seemed a little less tense than before. But still... still, there was something beneath that calm exterior. Something he wasn't ready to give.

Behind the counter, Amy's eyes were glowing with delight—her lips pulling into a grin as she flicked glances between Wendy and Luke like a spectator at some small-town romantic comedy. Leah, meanwhile, hovered beside a shelf of candles, arranging them just so, but Wendy knew better. She could feel Leah's curiosity rolling off her.

"So, you said the festival starts next weekend?" Luke asked.

Wendy's eyes brightened at the mention of the Apple Festival. That excitement bubbling up within her. "Yep," she said, her voice lifting. "Next Saturday. We've got food trucks, live music, games—it's an all-day thing. And this year, we're bringing back the pie competition with some new twists."

Luke's eyes showed a flicker of genuine curiosity. "A pie competition?"

Wendy nodded, her smile growing. "Yeah—apple pies, pumpkin pies, even peach pies. And we added a whole new category this year for what we're calling art pies."

"Art pies?" Luke's brow furrowed as he repeated the phrase.

Wendy couldn't help laughing at the expression. "I know—it sounds ridiculous. But people get really into creating pie designs—leaves, flowers, you name it. Sometimes they're so pretty, no one even wants to eat them."

A soft chuckle left Luke's throat, his eyes still bright with amusement. "This festival really sounds interesting."

Wendy couldn't help but smile. "It's a big deal around here. Even Ruth—my grandmother—sometimes swoops in at the last minute with some grand recipe entry."

Luke's gaze grew distant for just a moment, lingering on the jars of apple butter lining the nearby shelf. Wendy felt the stillness stretch between them, comfortable but expectant. She might've filled the air with small talk under any other circumstance, but something told her to let Luke have the space to think.

After a beat, she cleared her throat, breaking the tension. "We... still need a few more volunteers for some of the booths," she offered, summoning her smile back. "Nothing too intense. Just things like pie-contest tables or helping the vendors out when they need a hand."

There was a flash of hesitation in Luke's eyes—almost like the very mention of involvement tugged at too many buried strings at once. For a second, just one, Wendy doubted whether she should've even bothered suggesting it.

What are you doing? She chided herself.

Luke let a small smile drift back to his lips, a teasing glint in his eyes. "Volunteering, huh?"

Wendy nodded, her smile softening with relief at the way he wasn't shutting the conversation down completely. "If you want a front-row seat to some small-town chaos, it could be... entertaining."

For a heartbeat, she thought he might say something—-something reflective, something meaningful. But there it was again—that wall. That hesitation. His expression shifted ever so slightly, the softness vanishing just enough to remind her of who she was talking to. After all, Luke was no ordinary person.

"I'll, uh..." He gave her a small nod. "I'll think about it."

"No pressure," Wendy answered, matching his casual tone.

Amy sidled up beside Wendy as Luke attempted to step toward the counter to pay. The gleam of mischief burned brightly in Amy's eyes as she plucked the coffee and cider from Luke's hands. "Looks like you're all set," she said, far too cheerful. "I'll ring you up."

Luke nodded, following her to the counter. Wendy joined them, placing his two loaves of pumpkin bread beside the register. Leah drifted over, pretending to clean the already dust-free display case, her side-glances toward the unfolding interaction, anything but subtle. Wendy ignored her.

"How's the writing going, Luke?" Amy asked with that familiar teasing lilt, her tone innocent but carrying far too much interest to be casual.

"It's coming along." Luke said.

Amy shot Wendy a sly glance before handing Luke his receipt, her lips pulling wider with amusement. "Well, we've got plenty of coffee to keep you going through those late nights writing your next bestseller."

Luke accepted the receipt, nodding politely. "I'll let you know how it turns out."

As he turned and made his way out, Wendy caught Leah's pointed grin and Amy's raised eyebrows as they watched him leave.

"Well, well, well," Leah said in full-on-exaggerated surprise, her voice brimming with teasing energy as she practically danced across the storeroom floor. "That was a refreshing little visit, wouldn't you say?"

Wendy bit back a groan, but the smile that found its way onto her face was impossible to hide. "Will you guys stop?"

Amy elbowed Wendy, her eyes bright with laughter. "Hey, you're the one chatting up the brooding novelist, lady. We're just here playing innocent bystanders, watching a romance in the making."

Wendy rolled her eyes. "Impossible."

"Not impossible. Invested." Leah swooped in, crossing her arms.

Amy clasped a hand over her heart as though she were caught in the throes of a juicy romance movie. "So, um, are you recruiting Luke Carter for the pie contest? Or is this just a ploy to get him into the cider tent?"

Wendy blinked, but couldn't prevent the laughter that burst through. "I mentioned volunteering, that's all."

Leah gasped, eyes wide. "Oh, scandalous! And what did Mr. Carter say?"

Wendy shook her head, rolling her eyes as best she could without completely losing her composure. "He said he'd think about it." She tried to keep her expression neutral, but that smile... it tugged at her lips despite her best efforts.

Amy clasped a jar of apple butter to her chest dramatically, pretending to swoon. "Well, do keep us posted if Mr. Famous-Writer-Sir decides to grace us mere peasants with his volunteer presence."

Wendy shot them both an exasperated glance, pleading for mercy. But neither Leah nor Amy looked like they had much compassion in store today.

Wendy sighed—bending as she thwacked her hands down against the counter with a playful huff. "You two need to get back to work, or so help me—you'll both be working extra shifts during the festival."

Amy and Leah gasped in unison, their eyes wide with exaggerated shock.

"Oh, we're working all right," Amy said with a wink, her eyes twinkling with mischief. "Just on a little... creative matchmaking, that's all."

Wendy rolled her eyes, but again, couldn't quite keep her laughter down. Her friends were hands down terrible, but still—they were hers.

Chapter 9

Luke walked down the gravel road, each crunch of stone under his boots amplified in the still evening air. His mind was in knots, tangled in phrases, paragraphs, and character arcs that refused to connect. The solace of the cabin had worked... for a while. But now, the words felt as if they belonged to someone else. The progress he made that afternoon felt staggered, hollow, like trying to nudge a boulder up a hill.

As he rounded the bend, a sound caught his attention—a soft hum carried by the evening breeze. Something about the tune made him pause, head tilted toward the source. It was a simple melody, one that blended with the natural sounds of the orchard.

His eyes found Wendy perched on a ladder, reaching up to pluck apples from the higher branches. Her movements were efficient, practiced. Her sleeves rolled up to her elbows, revealing sun-kissed skin from long days of work. Golden light, flickering in the fading moments of daylight, made her hair glow like fire, strands catching the breeze as they fell from where they'd been tucked behind her ear. Every inch of her spoke of a quiet confidence, the kind ingrained over years of tending the land.

Luke hesitated, standing in the shadows of the trees, caught between wanting to approach her or simply slip away unnoticed. They hadn't exchanged much more than friendly words and pleasant smiles over the course of his stay, but something about Wendy—the ease with which she seemed to handle any task—drew him in. His body felt a pull to walk over, but his mind told him to keep away.

In the silence that followed her hum, he heard himself clearing his throat—a decision already made before his mind could catch up. "Need a hand?"

Wendy froze for a half-second, one hand hovering just above an apple mid-reach. A flicker of something passed over her face. Quick offers like that—sudden, out-of-nowhere kindness—they always triggered something in her. A flash of memory. David. His too-easy smiles, the way he'd integrated himself back into her life, only to tug the rug out from under her. One minute, everything was simple—the next, everything was... complicated. She tucked the unease away.

"Well, look who's here," she said. "Out for a stroll?"

Luke shrugged, taking a step closer. "I guess you could say that. Needed a break from the cabin...and the four walls closing in." He hesitated, unsure if his presence was welcome. But Wendy's chuckle dissolved his doubt as she waved him over.

"Well," she replied, walking toward a basket nearly overflowing with apples, "if you want to make yourself useful, I'm not about to turn down an extra pair of hands. This basket's heavy."

Luke smiled and stepped up, taking one end of the bushel basket as Wendy grabbed the other. They began walking, slow and steady, the apples inside shifting, their skins brushing against each other.

"So…" she said, as the orchard stretched around them, the sun casting long shadows. "Taking a break from the writing?"

Luke sighed, feeling the tension loosen, then settle again. "Something like that. Or… more like giving up for the day. It depends on how you frame it."

Wendy gave him a knowing side-glance. "Giving up doesn't seem like something you'd do," she said. "More like choosing not to give yourself a headache for one quiet evening. Sometimes the best ideas come when you stop looking for them."

"I hope you're right," he said, his voice low. "Because right now, it feels like those ideas are buried under a massive pile of rocks."

Wendy's smile widened, her eyes crinkling at the corners. "Oh, I know all about things being buried under rocks," she said. "Ever tried planting a pumpkin patch on a rocky hillside?"

Luke raised an eyebrow, despite himself. "Can't say I have."

"Well, let me tell you, it's like pulling teeth. If the teeth were made of boulders that is," Wendy continued, "it's a challenge. Roots don't like rocks, and neither do tractors. But once you get past them, there's good soil underneath."

Luke couldn't help the slight curve of his lips.

They paused by a small pumpkin patch nestled near the apple trees. Wendy crouched, her fingers brushing over the round skin of one pumpkin, testing its firmness. Luke took in the scene—the mass of vines twisting over the ground, miniature pumpkins scattered like glowing orange lanterns.

"What do you think?" Wendy asked, glancing up at him, her eyes playful as she stayed in her crouch.

Luke pretended to consider as he squatted beside a pumpkin, inspecting it with exaggerated seriousness. "I'm no expert," he said, "but it looks… like a pumpkin."

Wendy let out a laugh, full and rich. The kind that seemed to come from somewhere deep inside her. It was the kind of laughter that made Luke wish it would last just a little longer.

"Olympic-level pumpkin inspection skills right there, Luke," she said, still chuckling as she stood.

Luke grinned, shaking his head as they resumed their walk. The basket swayed between them; the apples shifting with each step.

"So," Wendy said, her voice softer now, more curious. "Seriously, how's it going at the cabin? Finding any inspiration?"

Luke was quiet for a moment, his eyes on the path ahead. The words came slowly. "I'm... stuck," he admitted.

Wendy nodded, but she said nothing, giving him the space to continue if he wanted.

Luke exhaled, the evening air cool on his skin. The words felt thick in his throat, foreign after being kept inside for so long. "Might as well say it. It's been like that since my wife passed," he said, his voice barely above a whisper.

Wendy stopped, jarring Luke to do the same. Wendy set her side of the basket down, Luke following her lead. She turned to face him, her eyes filled with a quiet understanding.

He took a deep breath, his gaze drifting to the tops of the trees. The sky was darkening, stars just beginning to appear, scattered like dust across the twilight. "We used to talk about coming to a place like this," he said. "Coming somewhere simple and peaceful. Picking apples, small things like that. But we kept putting it off. Life got in the way. And then... she got sick. And just like that..." His voice cracked, unable to say more.

Wendy didn't rush to fill the silence. She let the moment breathe—let it be, her eyes soft as they stayed on him. When she spoke, her words were quiet, almost a whisper. "And you ran out of time," she finished for him, a thread of sadness there, enough to tell Luke she understood. She had run out of time once, too.

He nodded, feeling the sting in the back of his throat again, the weight of regret hanging between them like one of the apples clinging stubbornly to its branch. "Yeah." He swallowed hard, forcing down the tightness. "We ran out of time."

Wendy's expression warmed as she watched him, but her eyes flickered with something all her own. Something Luke wasn't sure he understood yet. He sensed she had her own burdens, her own wounds. But she wasn't quick to share them, just like him.

"I thought I could just... get back to where I was before. That I could still write effortlessly. That it was just... a phase I was going through." He shook his head, a hollow laugh escaping him. "But I haven't gotten there yet."

He didn't know why he was telling her all of this. But there was something in Wendy's eyes—something open and unjudging.

Wendy shifted her weight, her gaze meeting his. "Maybe it's not about getting back to where you were," she said, her voice gentle. "Maybe it's about moving forward."

Luke blinked, her words settling in his chest like a weight.

"That's the hard part," he said.

Wendy's lips curved into a small smile, her eyes holding his. "Yeah, it is," she said.

He gave her a lopsided smile, shaky but genuine. "I'm real cheerful company tonight, aren't I?"

Wendy let out a soft, genuine laugh. "You're only human, Luke. We all lose our way sometimes." With a sigh, she tucked a loose strand of hair behind her ear, her voice growing a touch gentler, pulling him in. "Losing someone—it never really goes away. That emptiness stays with you, but it changes. Over time, the pain dulls, it stings a little less.

Losing someone... it transforms you, and at some point, we have to keep moving. We have to rediscover the joy in life."

Luke met her gaze, something resonant passing between them. Her words seemed to click as they settled on his shoulders.

Changes you.

He could feel those words sticking to his ribs like glue.

"I... I haven't figured out how to move forward yet," Luke admitted. "It's like I'm trying to hit reset, but I'm completely stuck."

Wendy's eyes turned down for just a moment, her expression softening as she took her side of the basket. "I know the feeling. My parents..." she paused, taking a delicate breath — "they passed when I was still in high school. One day, they were right here with me... and the next? Gone."

Luke's heart tightened at the weight of her quiet words. He almost stepped forward, almost said something, but stopped himself, not wanting to assume. He knew what it must've been like for her. Hearing the quiet steadiness in her voice—the resolve—he realized her walls weren't so different from his own.

"And that?" Wendy continued, lifting her chin. "I guess it teaches you to sort through what's left. Figure out who you are after it happens? You grow up quicker when the people you depend on are gone." She said. "Everything shifts."

Luke nodded; no response would be adequate. In the silence that followed, Wendy reached for the basket again. "Come on. Let's get these apples back to the store."

The rest of the walk passed in a comfortable quiet—the kind that wasn't uncomfortable, just filled with the hum of shared understanding. When they reached the dirt path leading toward the barn's side entrance, Wendy looked over at him, something lighter filtering through her voice. "You know," she said, "you don't have to carry all that weight of grief on your own. Grief, burdens...they're heavy. But maybe it's worth remembering that God's ready to help with the weight. You don't have to do it alone. You just...have to let Him in."

Her words hung in the cool evening air, offering a quiet sense of peace—one Luke didn't even realize he had been searching for.

Luke's brows drew together, confused, and yet... comforted by the suggestion she made with those simple words. "Maybe," he agreed.

They walked the final stretch until the store's lights flickered overhead.

"How about some comfort food?" Wendy suggested with a warm smile. "I think we both deserve some pumpkin bread."

Luke tilted his head with a grin. "Pumpkin bread therapy? Sounds like something I could get used to."

Wendy rolled her eyes playfully. "It's West Virginia country magic, didn't you know?"

Luke chuckled as they headed inside the stockroom of the store together, the weight on his chest not quite lifted, but lighter.

Chapter 10

Wendy and Luke entered the Farmstead Store's stockroom through the side door, the echo of their footsteps bouncing off the wooden barn walls. They set the basket of apples down, their red hues blending with the harvest collection that already lined the room.

Wendy dusted her hands off on her jeans. A playful grin tugged at her lips as she glanced over at Luke.

"Wait here. I'll grab the after-hours special," she said, giving him a wink before heading toward the door that led to the front of the store.

Watching her move with that simple confidence, Luke felt something stir—something he didn't expect. Sure, Wendy was friendly, but there was an edge about her, a subtle barrier, like she was holding something back. He knew it because he did the same thing.

Maybe that was why he felt more comfortable around her than anyone else he'd met in a long time. She got it—that instinct to keep people at arm's length, especially since life had already taught them both a lot about loss.

His lips quirked into a wry smile as he stared down at his boots. He was slipping. Unraveling, maybe. He shook his head, a faint, defeated chuckle escaping him. There's nothing there to dissect, he reminded himself. She's just good company. That's all.

He ran his fingers through his tousled hair as his gaze wandered over the stockroom. Shelves stacked with produce lined the walls, the lingering scent of fresh apples hanging in the air. It was oddly comforting—a far cry from the sterile, cold order of his writing desk at the cabin.

"Alright! Got the essentials."

Wendy's cheerful voice pierced his thoughts. She reemerged, arms laden in a way that made her appear almost regal, as if returning triumphant from some grand excursion. One hand cradled a loaf of pumpkin bread wrapped in wax paper, while the other balanced a jug of cider. A plastic grocery bag dangled effortlessly from her arm.

"Follow me," she said, nodding toward the door with a smile.

Luke trailed behind, the corners of his mouth lifting as something warm spread across his chest. It was strange how just being with her calmed him. She didn't put on a show, just... existed. Maybe that was what unnerved him. Or comforted him. He wasn't sure which.

They walked to one of the picnic tables behind the store. It served as a resting spot for employees and customers, but currently, with the sky painted in soft purples and fading pinks, it looked like a perfect escape from the stresses of life. The sun hung low behind the mountains, casting long shadows that sprawled over the ground, and for the first time in months, Luke felt the tension in his shoulders begin to ease.

Wendy set the jug and loaf down and began pouring cider into Styrofoam cups. Her motions were practiced, deliberate, but her eyes held a twinkle. The kind that made you think she was enjoying this simple act.

She sliced the pumpkin bread into generous wedges, spreading a hefty layer of apple butter across the top, and handed him a slice.

"Good call," Luke murmured, accepting the slice with a smile tugging at the corner of his mouth. "Apple orchard therapy with a slice of pumpkin bread? It's what the doctor ordered."

Wendy chuckled, leaning back after handing him a cup of cider. "Pumpkin bread is practically a religious experience around here. Even bad writing days are no match for it."

Bad writing days. Luke almost laughed if it weren't for the ache that accompanied the humor. His smirk was half-amused, half-weary. "If only the solution was that simple."

Wendy glanced at him, that curious look back in her eyes—playful, warm, but... always a little guarded. "Is it really that bad? Writer's block, I mean?"

Luke let out a laugh, rubbing the back of his neck, unsure why he felt the sudden pull, to be honest. "It's like... staring at a blank TV screen, hoping the picture will come back if you just keep watching. But eventually, all you see is static. Sometimes, the static feels safer than whatever comes through once the signal returns."

Wendy studied him for a long moment, her cup cradled between her palms, understanding peeking through her narrowed eyes.

"So that's where my award-winning author friend is, huh?" Wendy broke the silence, her face split in a grin. "Lost in static, waiting for a good movie to start?"

His laugh this time was fuller, tugged from deep within him. "Maybe more like sitting in a dentist's waiting room hoping no one calls your name because you know what's coming might not be the best experience."

After finishing a bite of pumpkin bread, Wendy shifted gears, her voice light again. "Let me ask you something. Have you ever been apple picking?"

Luke blinked at the swift change in topic, caught off guard. "Can't say I have. Why?"

Wendy's eyes turned thoughtful, her expression reflective as she faced him. "People think apple picking is this serene, picturesque activity, right? You stroll through the orchard, pluck a few apples, and probably enjoy the day. But it's more than that. It's work. Branch by branch. You get scratched, covered in sticky sap, maybe get stung by a bee or two if you're unlucky. And sometimes, the best apples are the ones hidden, just out of sight. You've got to climb a little higher and reach a little further for them. It's a challenge."

"Let me guess," he said, raising his eyebrows. "Is this an allegory?"

Wendy returned his look with mock-seriousness. "Who, me? Riddles and hidden meanings? Perish the thought. Though, cross my heart, it doesn't hurt to keep some Benadryl on standby."

Luke shook his head, his smile betraying him. "And the moral?"

She grinned, her eyes sparkling as she leaned in a little. "The stubborn apples—the ones you've got to stretch higher for? They're always the sweetest and worth the extra trouble. Even if you're a little afraid to reach."

Luke sat back, her words settling uncomfortably close—too close. He didn't immediately respond, glancing down at his cider instead, trying to appear like he was mulling it over, when actually it'd hit home the moment she said it.

"Look, the truth is, it's work. But that extra work—whichever apple you're reaching for—it's gonna be worth it." Wendy said.

He sighed, his gaze drifting toward the darkening line of apple trees as a chill breeze draped across the orchard. "Yeah. I know you're right. It's just... difficult to do sometimes."

They both grew quiet for a while after that. Luke hadn't expected to feel this... seen or heard. That's what worsened it. The more time he spent talking to Wendy, the closer he wanted to step, to encourage more of it. He liked her company. Liked the way they could just sit here and talk without any heavy expectations. But this wasn't easy territory. He was enjoying real human connection again. And it terrified him.

Wendy poured herself a second cup of cider, then tilted her head back to look up at the emerging stars, her voice soft. "Ever just stare up at the sky and let all the noise fade away?"

Luke followed her gaze, the stars twinkling above them like distant promises, too far to grab hold of, but warm and steady all the same.

"My grandpa used to say, if you ever get lost, you can always find your way again by following the stars. They're like God's map for wanderers."

Luke smiled, running a hand across the stubble on his jaw. "Smart grandpa."

"Well," she continued with a half-smile, "he was also the kind to tell you to get lost every once in a while, for fun. So, you might want to take the whole following star's thing with a grain of salt."

Luke chuckled. They fell into a natural silence; the moment stretching like the stars overhead, neither of them needing to fill the space with chatter. The quiet wasn't stifling—it was peaceful. And that was what made it feel... real.

After a while, Wendy shifted, drawing her knees-up on the bench as she crossed her arms over them, her eyes glinting with mischief. "So," she asked, "any big culture shocks since arriving in Laurel Ridge? I know it can't be easy, leaving the big fast-paced city and visiting a small quiet town?"

He grinned and folded his arms as if deep in thought. "Let me think… definitely the food. It's ridiculously good. I didn't expect that. Every bite somehow tastes better than any food at home."

Wendy shrugged, her smile widening. "Well, you wouldn't be the first to return home full."

"And probably with a weight problem."

Wendy laughed. "That's the secret to tourism here. We fatten everyone up, make 'em feel at home, and—bam!—they come running back next fall. Suction-cupped to the nostalgia."

He laughed and realized how wonderful it was to talk and laugh again. How great it felt to be around someone who expected nothing from him.

"But seriously, you've been here a few days now. What's your verdict?" Wendy continued.

Luke's smile faltered for a moment—more out of his own surprise than hers. "Honestly?" He paused again. "I feel like I'm starting to live again, instead of just… existing. It's different and kind of… nice. I'm noticing things I haven't paid attention to in a while. I guess I'm relearning how to enjoy the simple little things in life."

Wendy nodded, her gaze lingering on him longer than she meant it to. "Yeah. I get that."

He didn't know why, but his eyes stayed on her for a moment as something quiet passed between them. Comfort. Connection.

Luke tilted his head, watching her. "What about you? What's it like running this farm and the store? I mean, it seems like everyone depends on you. If I had to guess, I imagine you must have some pretty good stories."

Wendy laughed, shaking her head. "Oh, I certainly have some stories. All this," she said as she glanced around the property, "it can be overwhelming, sure, but I wouldn't trade it for anything."

Luke leaned in, curious. "Why do you do it, though? I mean, it must be exhausting. The early mornings, the long days. Why not do something... easier?"

Wendy's eyes grew distant, her smile turning nostalgic. "It's in my blood, I guess. My great-grandparents started this place, passed it down, and I grew up watching it all grow. Even as a kid, I loved seeing the orchards flourish, planting new trees, watching the pumpkin patches expand year after year. It's a part of me."

"That's...beautiful," Luke said as he watched her.

Wendy's gaze turned to the horizon, her voice softening. "There's something about it. The seasons changing, the orchards blooming, the store filled with people—it makes you feel connected. Like you're a part of something bigger. And the customers, they aren't just customers. They're family. And seeing people come from out of town, watching them experience it all for the first time... it's something special."

Luke's lips quirked upward. "But there must be tough days, too. When everything goes wrong—the tractor breaks down, nothing goes right?"

Wendy laughed. "More often than you'd think! But that's just part of it. You roll with the punches because the work still needs doing. And when it pays off—when people love what you grow, when families come back year after year—that makes the tough days' worth it."

A silence stretched between them, comfortable and easy, until Luke spoke, his grin playful. "So, when do I get to spend a day in the orchard helping with the harvest?"

Wendy's teasing smile reached her eyes when she replied, "You sure you're ready for it? Because let me tell you, it's not for the faint of heart. You'll get dirty, curse the sun, possibly injure yourself... The real question is: Are you ready to be stung by bees the size of tractors?"

Luke grinned, the challenge not lost on him. "Fair warning. Maybe I've been missing that—something real, something I can touch by working with my hands. Perhaps that's part of why I'm struggling so much."

Wendy nodded, her gaze turning thoughtful. "There's something grounding about working on a farm. You lose yourself in the work, and suddenly, your problems don't seem so big. The land reminds you just how small you really are."

Luke paused, his gaze lingering on her for just a moment too long. "You should put that in a story."

Wendy wrinkled her nose, laughing. "Oh, no. I'll leave the story-telling to you. I'm sure you could spin it better than I ever could."

Luke chuckled, but as they cleaned up together, his mind replayed the quiet truths buried in their conversation. Something new was dawning in him—small and hesitant, but real.

Chapter 11

The rhythmic clatter of keys filled the quiet cabin as Luke's fingers flashed across the laptop. His jaw clenched in concentration, eyes fixed on the screen, watching the words spill from his mind like a river breaking through a long-standing dam. There was something in the air today—an urgency he hadn't felt in a long, long while.

He paused, letting his fingers hover over the keyboard, eyes tracing the last line he'd typed. The scene in front of him had stirred to life, as though the world he was creating had breathed on its own for the first time in what felt like years. The right piece fell into place, like solving a puzzle.

A small, hesitant smile tugged at his mouth. He couldn't remember the last time writing had felt like this—something close to easy and enjoyable.

But even in this quiet victory, the absence struck him like a freight train. At one time, he might have leaned back in moments like this, arms stretched over his head, a triumphant grin forming as he called out to Sarah with a quip about his "genius at work." He would have chuckled as she shot back a witty remark, her laughter echoing from the kitchen, joining his.

The perfection of a scene standing on its own felt a little... hollow without her laugh echoing back.

So much of his joy in writing had been tied up in Sarah's presence. She had been his first reader, his eternal cheerleader—the one who both challenged him and made the process thrilling.

Luke closed his eyes, letting out a deep breath. His fingers flexed restlessly.

A sharp ding filled the silence, breaking through his thoughts. Luke glanced down at his phone, reading the name across the screen: Bill Fagan.

Without hesitation, he swiped the screen and brought the phone to his ear. "Bill. You've got impeccable timing, my friend."

A deep chuckle rumbled through the line. "Aww, did I interrupt one of your creative genius moments? I can hang up and let you get back to brooding in the wilderness like a tortured soul."

Luke leaned back in his chair, not quite shaking the grin that clung to his lips. "Believe it or not, I think you actually caught me in a rare moment of brilliance."

"Whoa, hold the presses." Bill's voice brimmed with exaggerated shock. "Is that the sound of excitement I hear coming from Mr. Doom'n'Gloom himself? Alert the media! World tilts on its axis!"

Luke chuckled, tipping his head back, eyes tracing the wooden beams above. "Don't get used to it. It doesn't mean I've cracked the code or anything, but... yeah. Writing's finally happening."

There was a pregnant pause on the other end of the line—a silence that carried more weight than the usual laughter. Then Bill's voice came through quieter, the edge of humor softening. "Good. That's good to hear, bud. I was starting to think we'd lost you to the dark side forever, like some unspoken writer's void."

Luke shook his head, the smile lingering. "The dark side, huh? You sure you're not confusing me with some long-lost villain archetype?"

Bill's laughter crackled through the speaker. "Well, we both know you've got the lone brooding thing down pat, so it wouldn't be that much of a stretch."

Luke shook his head, smirking. "Gee, thanks. Nice to know my hermit persona's thriving."

Bill chuckled. "Seriously, though—is that fresh mountain air doing the trick? Or is it the lack of human interaction that finally made the words flow?"

He glanced toward the window once more, where the apple farm stretched before him in neat rows, the mountains casting long shadows across the land. Something in those silhouettes called to him—steadier, quieter. "Maybe it's both," he admitted. "Honestly, there's something about this place. It forces you to slow down... pay attention to things. Details."

"A slower pace. Simpler living," Bill mused. "Good. You'd been spinning your wheels for too long. You couldn't hear your own voice through all the noise."

There was truth in that, though the weight of Bill's words stirred something else within him. "Yeah, well. That noise started when Sarah left."

The line went quiet, and Bill let the words sit. Luke leaned forward again, elbows braced against the edge of the desk. "But I think—maybe—there's finally a light at the edge of the tunnel. Like... a window cracked open, and I can finally hear something on the other side. Guess that's worth something."

"Of course it is," Bill's tone was firmer now, encouraging. "And given everything you've been through, well... it's worth a lot."

Luke swallowed, those words sinking into his thoughts. Could it be that simple? Was it even possible to push through this grief? This writer's block? Or had it become part of him—woven into every word he wrote, every moment he lived?

Still, out here in Laurel Ridge, it felt... manageable. A little more distant.

"Alright," Luke said, shaking his head. "Enough about my existential crisis. How are you—"

"Oh, you know, same old. My book's doing fine, sales are okay..." Bill said. "Actually, I've been thinking about... you know, dating again."

Luke nearly dropped the phone.

"You? Mr. I'm-Happy-Living-In-My-Cave-of-Books wants to date again?"

Bill's laughter rolled through the speaker like thunder, low and surprised. "Don't act so shocked. Turns out, being a recluse isn't all it's cracked up to be."

Luke let out a strained chuckle, though something in Bill's words hit closer to home than he cared to admit. The mention of dating was like nails dragging across concrete—a sound he wasn't sure he could stomach even now.

Could he even do that anymore? After watching Sarah fight—and lose. After clinging and losing her grip in his arms. The idea of letting someone else into his life felt impossible—maybe even wrong. No one else could fill the empty place in him. How could another person ever quiet the noise in his head?

And yet... Wendy. The name carried a foreign sort of warmth—a fresh feeling that wasn't suffocating. A tiny fragment of hope.

Luke sighed. "Well," he said, "as your friend, I support the endeavor. But dating's not really... in my wheelhouse right now."

Bill's voice turned more serious. "Luke, man, the world doesn't pause just because things go wrong. The world keeps moving, and eventually, we should, too. It doesn't mean we forget or leave behind the ones we loved—it just means stepping in a different direction."

Wendy had said something similar. And now Bill. It felt like the universe was trying to tell him something—nudging him to step out of the shadows and embrace whatever came next. Life moves on—it had to, didn't it?

"Yeah," Luke said, his voice quieter than before. "I hear you. Loud and clear."

Bill's tone lightened. "Okay, enough serious talk. You gotta tell me more about this masterpiece you're working on. Any hints? Or are you keeping it close to the vest this time?"

Luke laughed, shaking off the weight of their earlier conversation. "Ah, where do I start? I'm not ready to jinx it, but... something finally clicked. Feels real for the first time in a while. Like I've finally found something new again."

"Well then," Bill said, "you'd better keep pounding out those chapters before your muse decides to skip town."

"Yeah, yeah. I'm trying, trust me."

There was something comforting about Bill's teasing, a familiar dynamic they'd shared for years. But even more comforting was the sense that Luke wasn't doing this alone anymore. Not entirely. Maybe he still had people on his side—even if he wasn't always sure he deserved it.

"Luke, you're going to be alright," Bill said. "And when you hit number one on that bestseller list again? I'll be the first to say I told you so."

"And I'll put your name in the acknowledgments," Luke replied, amused.

"I'll hold you to that!"

They shared more jokes, the kind only lifelong friends could toss back and forth without pretense or hesitation. And as their voices found their way through the easy rhythm of conversation and laughter, Luke realized he was... okay. At least, for now.

Before hanging up, Bill's voice softened once more, turning more sincere. "Hey, man. Remember—faith's a funny thing. Sometimes, when you least expect it, life shows you something you didn't even know you needed."

"Yeah," Luke said, nodding. "I guess I have to believe that."

"You got this, brother. Take it one day at a time."

"Thanks, Bill. Talk soon."

As the call ended, Luke let the peaceful silence fill the room again. It wasn't as heavy this time. Somehow, Bill's words—and maybe Wendy's too—had lifted the weight that rested deep in Luke's chest. His loneliness wasn't gone, just a little muted.

He glanced back at the laptop. The words on-screen stared back at him, full of new life. Each sentence flowed as naturally as breathing. They felt real. Alive!

Luke smiled, saving his work, and leaned back in his seat. His stomach gurgled in protest, a growl resonating through the silence.

Glancing at the clock on the mantle, he realized it was already past noon. No wonder the hollow pit in his stomach demanded attention.

He stood up, heading toward the tiny kitchen, but faltered halfway. He stared at the stove warily. The idea of cooking didn't sound appealing. Sure, he could manage something, but... was it worth the mess?

He weighed his options for a solid three seconds. Martha's Diner was just a few minutes down the road, promising a hot meal without the effort.

Turning on his heel, he grabbed his jacket and slid into his boots instead. "

Diner food wins today.

Chapter 12

Luke pushed open the door to Martha's Diner, the familiar bell above the door jingling as he stepped inside. His stomach growled, reminding him just how long it had been since he'd had a proper meal. The comforting scent of home-cooked food wrapped around him like a warm blanket.

The worn chrome stools at the counter were filled with locals leaning over their plates, chatting or catching up with the day's gossip. Nearby, a jukebox played an old country tune that twanged into the heart of the diner. The whole place had that warm, distinctly southern vibe, unpolished and timeless. He couldn't say he didn't enjoy it.

Scanning the room, he saw the place was buzzing with the lunch rush. Every booth was filled. By a window, in a corner booth, Wendy sat. Her hair was loosely pinned back in a way that suggested it might fall apart at any second, strands already slipping free to frame her face. She wore a flannel shirt over a tank top, looking effortlessly comfortable—as much a part of the place as the old photos on the walls.

As his mind debated whether he should approach or leave her to her peace, Wendy looked up from her menu. Her eyes locked with his, and almost at once, her face lit up like the sun breaking through a cloud. Her smile, soft and welcoming, seemed to pierce through his indecision.

Luke gave a small wave, and Wendy responded by motioning to the empty seat across from her. There was no need to think it over any further; his feet moved toward her as if of their own accord.

"Fancy seeing you here, city boy." Wendy greeted him, her smile curving into a smirk as he slid into the seat across from her. "Let me guess—you're making this a habit?"

Her playful tone was disarming, but for a second—just a flicker—he caught something behind her eyes. She's smiling, flirting even, but... there's a faint shadow there.

Luke chuckled, allowing the moment to carry him. "I wouldn't say it's a habit yet, but..." He glanced around as if he were surveying the food scene like some high-profile critic. "It's getting there. The food is difficult to resist."

Before Luke had a chance to get too comfortable, Martha, in full energy mode, swooped in with the grace of a hawk eyeing prey—if hawks were known for wearing brightly colored aprons.

"Well, well! If it isn't my favorite city slicker and my farm queen!" Martha's eyes twinkled with pure mischief as she planted her hands on her ample hips. "Y'all planning on making this a regular occurrence? 'Cause I could sure get used to seeing you two together—kinda like when country gravy and biscuits meet for breakfast."

Luke raised an eyebrow, playing along. "I'm assuming I'm the country gravy in this scenario?"

Wendy smirked and pretended to think about it. "Well, you are from Ohio, so it's hard to say."

"Oh please," Luke grinned.

Martha let out a loud belly laugh that shook her shoulders. "I'll leave that for the two of y'all to figure out. But, in the meantime, what'll it be today?"

Wendy, entertained by the banter, handed the menu back to Martha with an easy smile. "Grilled chicken salad sandwich and a sweet tea, please."

With a wink, Martha scribbled the order down and turned toward Luke, still grinning. "And for the city gravy—I mean, city boy?"

"I'll go with the special—turkey sandwich, extra pickles. And coffee, black, and some water, too." Luke responded after a good bell laugh.

"Consider it done." Martha winked again. "Sit tight. I'll be back with the goods in a few minutes," she said, bustling away like someone who had the entire town's secrets stored under that apron.

As soon as Martha left, the energy between them shifted, almost an uncomfortable quiet. Wendy began fiddling with her napkin, folding it and then smoothing it out again, the action methodical, like something to keep her hands busy. The soft light streaming through the window caught the errant strands of her hair, giving her face a light glow. Luke felt something catch in his chest as he watched her.

"You look more relaxed today. Is our magical mountain air working its charm on you?" Wendy asked.

Luke offered a small, genuine smile. He leaned back into the booth, stretching his arms. "Yeah. Made some progress on the writing side of things."

Wendy's brows shot upward in pleasant surprise, her green eyes brightening. "Really?"

He nodded, letting out a small laugh that surprised even himself. "Not saying I'm cranking out a masterpiece or anything, but I found a good groove this morning. It's like I've been chasing something for a long time, and now it's... starting to come back."

Her smile inched wider—almost making it to her eyes this time—but something still held her back. Luke wasn't sure if it was habit or hesitation, but he recognized the dance she was doing; he'd been doing the same. Wendy felt it, too. That pull not to get too close, not to trust too easily.

She took a light breath, pushing her hesitations aside, and said, "See? What did I tell you? Sometimes you've just got to step away, take a breath. Let some of that pressure ease up."

Luke nodded in agreement, a soft chuckle escaping his lips. "Yeah. I guess I owe you some credit for that."

Her eyes sparkled with a mixture of pride and warmth. "I'll take it." She said, aiming for a touch of humor as she added, "I'll be expecting to see my name in the dedication, though."

Luke grinned, sensing a change in the air between them as much as in himself. "Every brilliant word you've spoken will be immortalized. How's that sound?"

"I'll hold you to it," Wendy said, her eyes crinkling with amusement. She hesitated then, her tone softening in a way that edged closer to vulnerability. "But honestly, I'm glad you're finding your way again, Luke. You—" she paused, staring down at her napkin, folding it tight, "you deserve that."

Luke blinked, wanting to brush off the sincerity but realizing, for once, he didn't want to. "Thanks," he said, the weight of her words working through him like the midway point of a good story—quiet, necessary, and unassuming.

They fell into peaceful silence again. The clinking of cutlery and the murmur of conversations around them set a gentle rhythm.

"So," she said, her curiosity shifting the energy between them once more, "give me a sneak peek. What's this story about?"

Luke chuckled, shaking his head as he rubbed his hand over his jawline. "Oh, you want insider information, do you?"

"Hey, after all my wisdom," Wendy said, pointing a finger at him, "I think I've earned it."

Luke let out a genuine laugh, readying for his response. "Alright, alright. It's still rough, but... it's about a guy, kind of stuck, using his work to avoid... dealing with things. He's a writer, but he's not sure if he's even a writer anymore. Everything feels... locked up." He hesitated before adding, "He ends up in this town away from his normal routine and meets people who help him see there's more to life than he's let himself believe."

Wendy tilted her head, the slight narrowing of her eyes making her grin all the more. "Hmm. Sounds familiar. Pure fiction, I'm sure. No parallels at all?"

Luke smirked, letting out a breath that sounded almost like a laugh. "Not a single one."

"Totally fictional," Wendy repeated, her grin growing.

They shared another laugh, this one full and genuine. For Luke, it was the kind of laugh that caught him off guard, like rediscovering a part of himself he had lost, and he liked it.

Martha returned soon after, her voice booming. "Here we go! One grilled chicken salad sandwich with all the fixin's and sweet tea for our farm queen, and one turkey sandwich, extra pickles, with coffee black and a glass of water for our city gravy author!" She set the plates down with an exaggerated flourish.

"Thanks, Martha." Wendy smiled.

Luke could only laugh as he nodded his thanks.

Martha stood there for a moment, hands planted on her hips like some wise, all-knowing oracle. "You two make quite the cute pair," she said with a knowing wink, her eyes twinkling with amusement and something deeper—like a bit of wisdom peeking through. "My gran used to say, 'Life's best moments are like meals—you've gotta share the good ones with someone who appreciates 'em just as much as you do.' Now, I ain't one to meddle, but it seems to me you two make good company for each other."

Wendy flushed, her eyes widening in mild horror. Luke, meanwhile, focused intently on his coffee, as if the cup were holding the answers to life itself.

Martha just chuckled, unfazed by their awkwardness. "Don't go gettin' shy now. Sometimes the best things come from the most unexpected places." With that, she floated off to tend to another table, leaving behind a quiet, tingling tension that neither Luke nor Wendy moved to fill.

Luke cleared his throat, forcing himself to look up, though his lips twitched with the urge to laugh. "Well... that was..."

"...Typical Martha," Wendy finished with a light laugh, shaking her head. "She means well. Just... not always subtle."

Luke chuckled in agreement, relaxing a little now that the awkwardness had been diffused. "What's on your agenda for the rest of the day? More apple picking?"

Wendy chewed, swallowing before she answered. "Back to the grindstone. The store was busy this morning, so I'm sure there's restocking to do, plus with the festival coming up, I need to make more apple butter and jam."

Luke nodded, taking a bite of his sandwich. "Sounds like a lot. Do you ever get a day off?"

Wendy laughed. "A day off during harvest and festival season? Not really. But Sundays are always family days. We all step away from the work, no matter how busy it gets. We go to church and relax. Sundays are the best."

Her eyes seemed to brighten as she continued. "Honestly, I love my work. There's something about seeing people find joy in the simplest things—like the perfect pumpkin or their first sip of cider—that makes the long hours worth it."

"It's admirable. You can tell you love what you do."

"Thanks," Wendy said, her voice warm. "What about you? What's your plan after this?"

Luke sipped his coffee, considering. "Actually, I thought I might stop by the bookstore. Figured it'd be a good time to see what it's all about."

"Oh, The Book Nook? Mitch and Loretta's place is an absolute treasure. I swear, Loretta has this uncanny ability to recommend the perfect book for everyone who walks in. And get this, not only do they own the store and the Laurel Ridge Inn here in town, but both Mitch and Loretta are authors themselves. Pretty impressive, right?"

Luke's eyebrows raised with genuine interest. "Really? What kind of books do they write?"

"Well, Mitch writes these incredibly detailed cozy mysteries set in the Appalachian region. They're full of rich characters, and he uses Laurel Ridge as his setting. Loretta, on the other hand, pens these heartwarming historical romance novels that always manage to capture the essence of small-town life. They're quite the literary power couple."

Luke nodded, impressed. "Wow, that's fascinating. I'll have to check out their work while sometime."

"You definitely should. And who knows? Maybe you'll find more inspiration for your own writing."

Their conversation flowed easily, punctuated by bites of food and sips of their drinks.

"I know you're busy, but I wondered—would you want to come with me to the bookstore?" Luke said.

Wendy blinked, then smiled. "Sure. Why not? Leah and Amy can manage the store without me for a while longer."

"Really?" Luke tried not to let his voice betray how pleased he was. "That's great. I mean, it'll be nice to have some company."

They made their way to the counter, and despite Wendy's polite protests, Luke insisted on covering the bill, leaving Martha a generous tip before they pushed through the diner's door and headed down Laurel Ridge's quaint Main Street. Sunlight brushed across rooftops, casting the small town in a warm yellowy hue, and their conversation shifted to books as they walked, the afternoon traffic and light bustle of pedestrians creating a gentle background hum.

"So," Wendy said with a playful gleam in her eye, aiming to spark some light-hearted conversation, "what's your guilty pleasure to read, Luke?"

Luke let out a bark of laughter as he ran a hand through his hair, resisting the urge to hide his face in embarrassment. "Ah, you're really going to make me admit it, aren't you?"

"Hey, no judgment here," Wendy assured him, though the glint in her eye told a different story. "I once spent an entire weekend binge-reading a series about vampire cowboys. Nothing can top that."

Luke stared at her, incredulous. "Vampire cowboys?"

Wendy nodded. "They were trying to reclaim the Wild West. With fangs."

Luke burst into laughter, doubling over a little, much to Wendy's delight. "Okay, okay, you win," he said, still chuckling. "But if you must know, I have a bit of a soft spot for cheesy spy novels. The kind with ridiculous gadgets and over-the-top villains."

Wendy grinned. "I knew it! You've got a secret James Bond fanboy inside that serious writer exterior."

"Guilty as charged," Luke admitted, holding his hands up in mock surrender. "But at least my heroes aren't vampires... on horseback."

Wendy rolled her eyes, nudging him with her elbow. "Ugh, not going to let that go now, are you?"

Their laughter echoed down the street, easy and genuine, and Luke realized just how much he'd missed this kind of interaction—effortless, unguarded. As they reached the bookstore, Luke held the door open, the scent of new books and coffee wafting out.

Loretta looked up from behind the counter, her face lighting up when she saw them.

"Well, well, isn't this a pleasant surprise? What brings my favorite farm girl and Laurel Ridge's visiting author in here today?" Loretta's eyes sparkled with genuine warmth as she motioned for them to come closer.

Luke smiled back, charmed by her ease. "Wendy's been telling me about this place, thought I'd check it out for myself."

Loretta beamed, clearly delighted. "Well, we writers always love crossing paths with fellow wordsmiths! Look around. And don't hesitate to ask if you need any recommendations—Mitch and I handpick almost everything we carry."

"Actually," Luke said, an amused twinkle in his eye, "rumor has it you've got a knack for matching readers with the perfect book. Think you've got something for a guy like me?"

Loretta's grin widened, as if she had been waiting her whole life for this exact challenge. "Oh, I certainly do. Let me see." She tapped her chin thoughtfully, scrutinizing him as if trying to peer into his soul. "You strike me as someone who appreciates depth and complexity in their reading. Am I right?"

Luke raised a brow, impressed. "You've got me pegged. But, I have to admit, I like a fun, easy read just as much."

Loretta nodded, disappearing down one aisle only to return moments later, clutching a hardcover book with simple yet evocative cover art. "Here you go. This one's a recent release. It's a beautifully crafted story about rediscovering yourself in the midst of upheaval, with characters who feel like old friends by the end. Trust me, you won't be able to put it down."

Luke turned the book over in his hands, raising a skeptical brow as he glanced at the blurb. "Are you saying I need to rediscover myself, Loretta?"

Loretta winked. "Well, if the shoe fits..."

Luke smirked. "Pretty sure I don't wear rediscovery shoes."

Loretta shrugged, but her eyes gleamed. "Maybe you just need to break those bad boys in first. Don't worry, the store has a return policy—on metaphors and otherwise."

Loretta swatted Luke's shoulder as Wendy wandered the aisles, looking every bit like someone enjoying a rare moment of relaxation.

Later, as Loretta rang up Luke's purchase, she leaned in, lowering her voice so that only he could hear.

"It's nice seeing Wendy take a break, you know? She works far too much."

Luke glanced toward Wendy, who was examining a cookbook on Appalachian heirloom recipes, her expression distant yet content.

"She mentioned things get pretty busy during harvest season." Luke said.

Loretta nodded. "Yeah, and she carries most of that burden herself. There aren't many people she lets into her circle, but it's good to see her letting her guard down a bit. You two seem to get along well, or so I hear."

Luke blinked, feeling heat creep up his neck. "Oh, well," he began, careful to keep his voice even, "Wendy's been really kind." The words felt inadequate, but he couldn't quite figure out how to articulate the strange, unspoken connection between them—so he left it at that.

"Mmm-hmm," Loretta replied, smiling. "Well, I hope you're finding Laurel Ridge to be... hospitable."

He didn't miss the emphasis in her words, just as Wendy returned with her heirloom recipe book.

"I found what appears to be a perfect book for me and Grandma!" Wendy beamed, holding it up for them to see. "Heirloom Appalachian recipes. Some of these are from the 1800s."

"Good choice," Luke said, his imagination picturing Wendy in a cozy kitchen, flour in her hair, testing out those old recipes. The scene played out so vividly in his mind, he found it almost... comforting.

"Well," Wendy said as they stepped out of the store, books in hand, "I should probably head back to the farm. There's still plenty of work to be done before the day's gone."

Luke nodded, though he felt a niggling disappointment that surprised him. "Of course. Thanks for this afternoon, though," he said, offering a genuine smile. "It was... nice."

Wendy hesitated, her green eyes softening in return. "It really was. We should... do this again sometime."

"I'd like that," Luke replied, surprised by how much he meant it.

"Well, I guess I'll see you around, city boy."

Luke chuckled. "Count on it, farm girl."

Chapter 13

Wendy tugged at the dark green apron strings, tightening the knot around her waist as she walked across the stockroom, heading to the front of the store. The soft clinks of utensils being set back into their drawers and the rhythmic sound of something being stirred in the kitchen filtered into the air, mingling with familiar scents—cinnamon, butter, and pastry fresh from the oven.

Yet Wendy's mind wandered to a different sweetness.

Luke.

If she were being honest, something about him had struck her today. Something intriguing in the way he spoke, in that calm, thoughtful air he carried around like a well-worn book jacket. Not that she'd never met someone who seemed comfortable or easy to be around—but in her experience, most people put on a front. Luke, though, wasn't pretending. He was... steady. Complex but simple. And despite those subtle barriers he put up—ones she noticed because she wore similar armor—he still had a way of being open, like he was trying to let her in.

The problem was that unnerved her.

A little comfort? Sure. But too much, and she could feel the walls she built so carefully starting to slide.

She found herself wanting to peel back the layers of this quiet man, to lean in closer. But wanting more was dangerous. She'd thought she saw more with someone else before—David—and that had ended with more broken pieces than she could count.

Her mind ran back to that day—finding the emails, hearing the truth from David's dismissive lips.

Wendy, it's just a farm. You'll thank me later.

She'd never thanked him. Only told him to leave without so much as another word.

Luke felt... different, she realized—but maybe too different. The kind of different that made her heart try to race forward, even though her brain screamed to hit the brakes. What if this could be something, and she was too wrapped up in her past hurts to see it? And worse—what if it was just history repeating itself? Was she ready to go down that road again?

No. She shook her head, as if to clear away the budding thoughts of what Luke might mean to her. There was no need to leap into overthinking—not now.

"Wendy! I know you're back there fiddling around." Ruth's familiar voice cut through her careful musings, jolting her back into the present. "You better not sneak out without giving these pies your stamp of approval!"

Wendy exhaled, a sheepish smile tugging at her lips. "Alright, alright!" she called back, pushing through the swinging door that led from the stockroom into the heart of the kitchen's warmth.

Ruth stood at the central island, her arms dusted in flour as she kneaded a dough mound that somehow seemed to obey her every command. Flour particles mixed with the afternoon light, and the entire scene felt so familiar, so right—like the traditions of generations could all be found in the work Ruth did with her hands.

Her sharp eyes glanced up, and with just one look, it seemed her grandmother was already preparing to ask a million questions.

"Well, now," Ruth began, her voice lilting with an edge of mischief. "Look who's strutting in here looking lighter than air. What's got you so peppy today, huh? Do I sense a spring in your step that doesn't come from apple-picking? You finish all your errands?"

Wendy tried to hold back the knowing smile, but it snuck out, tugging at the corners of her lips. She moved to the island, pretending to be interested in the dough, her fingers running along the edge of the cool counter in idle distraction. "Yeah, the usual. Picked up the chicken feed, got those groceries you wanted..." Then, trying to sound causal, she added, "Stopped by Martha's for a bite."

Ruth's focus didn't shift from her task, but there was no missing the glint in her eyes. Mischief was brewing, alright. "Martha's, huh?" Ruth pressed her weight deeper into the dough, her grin spreading across her face like caramel on a warm pie. "A little bite, you say. Was that quick snack enjoyed solo, OR... with a certain writer staying up in the cabin?"

Wendy's heart lurched into a traitorous skip. She tried to shrug, keeping her voice even despite the warmth prickling the back of her neck. "I ran into Luke there—"

"Mmm hmm," Ruth said, as she leaned into her work. "Just happened to run into him, is that it? Martha says you two shared the booth by the window. The good booth—the one everyone sits in during a... well, a date..." She let the sentence hang, teasing her like a cat batting at yarn.

Wendy sighed dramatically, rubbing her forehead with feigned exasperation. "Seriously, it was just a coincidence."

Ruth's chuckle was rich, reverberating around the kitchen. "Oh, honey, you can say coincidence all you want, but I'd say the good Lord had a hand in that timing. When Martha called me, you would have thought she had the news of the century—Wendy Lane seen having lunch with a world-renowned author."

Wendy rolled her eyes, though it was hard not to smile. "Grandma, it's really not what you're thinking. We just had lunch, talked a little—"

Ruth, covered in dough and flour, paused long enough to let her hands rest as she studied her granddaughter. Whatever playfulness was in her earlier teasing had seemed too quiet now. Her eyes stayed on Wendy, full of wisdom wrapped in softness.

"Sweetheart, listen to me," she said. "Whether it's Luke Carter or someone else, you deserve more than just work. A little joy, a bit of fun." She returned to her kneading, soft but firm. "You're always working. And when you're not, you're here or at church or thinking five steps ahead for the farm. It's okay to take time for yourself, Wendy. It's ok to have some fun!"

"If I don't put in the work here on the farm, who will?" Wendy shrugged, but her voice came out softer than she expected.

Ruth studied her for a moment before lowering her voice. "I know why you've got that fence around your heart, sweetheart—it's because someone before didn't know how to handle it." Ruth's voice softened further, though something steady and strong remained underneath. "But you can't live the rest of your life expecting the same story, Wendy. Just because one person saw your heart as something to gain or lose, doesn't mean everyone will."

Wendy blinked, caught off guard by how quickly her grandmother cut straight to the heart of the matter. "What happened with David—that was different," she said, her voice quieter now. "He made me think we were on the same page, and then... you know how that turned out."

Ruth stepped around the counter, tenderness crafting out the sternness in her flour-dusted expression. "Yes, I do. And I also know you can't live every good moment fearing the bad ones."

Wendy swallowed, her throat thick and words caught somewhere she didn't quite like. "I know, Grandma. But maybe I'm just not ready for anything else right now. The farm's enough to handle."

Ruth's pause was thoughtful. "Keep working hard, yes. But a life full of only work is no life at all." She gestured toward the window, where the farm stretched beyond. The orchards were bathed under the late afternoon sun—apples ready to pick, fields alive with the late autumn harvests. "This farm was a gift passed down from your parents. It's part of you. However, it's not all of you."

Wendy remained quiet, her hands resting on the countertop. The air had grown heavier—less from Ruth's words, and more from her own internal battle.

She heard the wisdom. She knew it. But hearing and believing were two different things.

People could waltz into your life and sweep you off your feet with promises—until they turned around and called your dreams a "dead end." What if Luke was just like that? Someone in town for a season, only to leave when the winds shifted and his muse turned elsewhere? She wasn't ready to face that kind of hurt again—not after David had shredded the belief that their future had substance. Luke felt different... but then again, doesn't everyone feel different at first?

Her thoughts jarred when Ruth gave her a reassuring pat on the back. "Anyway, I'll leave it be for now." She paused, her eyes sparkling with familiar playfulness again. "But let's not forget, Martha is a pretty sharp lady. When she tells me you two sitting at that table looked like two puzzle pieces fitting together just right, well..." she winked. "She may be on to something."

Wendy laughed, breaking some of the tension that had tightened in her chest. She threw an exaggerated look over at Ruth, aiming to sound nonchalant. "Don't let Martha put any more ideas into your head. I don't need a repeat of what happened last year with Pastor Thompson's nephew."

Ruth looked at her in mock horror. "Good gracious, girl. You're never going to let me live that down, are you? That poor boy didn't know whether to praise the Lord or jump into the New River after that Sunday dinner."

Wendy grinned mischievously, recalling the sheer awkward hilarity of being set up on that particular date. "He nearly drowned."

Ruth stifled her laughter. "In cheesecake."

The two women shared another laugh, Ruth now brandishing her rolling pin like a conductor orchestrating a grand crescendo. "Mark my words, honey. One of these days, I'll get it right!"

"Sure," Wendy said.

"No, I mean it. You..." She lifted a brow with meaning. "...and that writer next door—you know, I'm just saying I got a hunch. I can feel it in my bones."

"Grandma—please."

"Oh, come on!" Ruth went on, her voice swinging into a sing-songy tune. "Play 'round with a little poetic romance, honey! I can see it now—him reciting Shakespeare out in the orchard, and you're baking pies with sonnets on your mind."

Wendy's cheeks warmed, but this time not from embarrassment—just from the pure, ridiculousness of it all. "Yeah, keep dreaming."

"If anyone could make romantic writer clichés charming, Wendy Lane, it's you and that handsome man in the cabin!"

Wendy rolled her eyes but grinned. "You keep dreaming, Grandma."

The playful exchange stayed with her all the way to the front of the store before she was pulled back into the daily hustle. A customer asking about a bulk order, the hum of voices drifting in, and the routine of things calling her back into action.

Chapter 14

Wendy balanced on the wooden ladder, stretching to reach a bright Granny Smith apple. The crisp morning air touched her skin, cool and refreshing, and the surrounding leaves rustled with each gentle breeze. She twisted the apple from the branch, turning it in her hand, admiring its smooth, green skin. A small smile tugged at her lips as she placed it in her basket.

The familiar and simple sounds of the orchard surrounded her—the rustle of branches, the chirps from birds singing somewhere deeper in the trees. It was these moments, suspended in the orchard's stillness, that allowed the world to slow down for Wendy. She took a deep breath, feeling the quiet peace of the morning settle into her bones.

She reached for another apple when a familiar voice, deep and edged with humor, broke through the calm.

"So this is where you're hiding today."

Startled, Wendy nearly slipped. She glanced down to find Luke leaning against a nearby tree, arms crossed, a crooked smile lighting up his face. He looked every bit at ease in the orchard, like he had been there a hundred times before.

She arched an eyebrow, matching his smile. "I'm not hiding—I'm working," she said, lifting the basket a little, as if to defend her case. "Some of us earn our living with more than pen and paper, you know."

Luke pushed off the tree, his laugh rumbling low in his chest. He moved closer, his plaid shirt hanging open just enough to show a hint of tanned skin beneath. His sleeves were rolled up, revealing lean, defined forearms—a certain rugged edge to him that Wendy hadn't expected from a writer. It was catching her off guard more than she cared to admit.

"I can see that." He gave a pointed glance at the rows of apple-laden branches. "Need an extra hand?"

Wendy snorted, narrowing her eyes with mock skepticism. "Are you sure those writerly hands of yours can handle something other than coffee mugs and typing?"

Luke grinned, undeterred. "How hard can it be? You grab an apple, pull it down, and that's it."

She crossed her arms, studying him. "Not quite. It's not just yanking them down. You've got to twist it, keep it from bruising, or you mess with next year's crop. Think you can manage that?"

He shrugged, his smile widening. "I'm up for the challenge, farm girl."

She climbed down the ladder, dusting her hands off on her jeans. As she handed Luke the basket, their fingers brushed, a tiny jolt running up her arm. Wendy's heart skipped, and she stole a glance at his relaxed face. There was something about the way he looked at her—not too forward, but not distant, either.

No. She didn't have time for this.

"Alright, city boy," Wendy said, folding her arms again, a challenge clear in her voice. "Twist gently, don't pull. Keep the apple smooth—no pressure marks."

Luke nodded, reaching up. Wendy waited, expecting the rookie mistake—a yank, a bruise, something—but he surprised her. With careful precision, he twisted the apple until it came free, unblemished. He shot her a sideways glance, an eyebrow raised in triumph.

Wendy tried to suppress the grin that threatened to break free. "Not bad. Beginner's luck."

Luke gave her a look of mock offense. "Or maybe I'm just naturally good at this."

"You might make a decent farmhand," Wendy said, half-teasing, though there was a genuine surprise in her voice.

Luke raised an eyebrow, pleased with himself. "Could be I have a hidden talent. You know, back in the city, I'm considered more of a delicate, creative soul."

"Oh, you're delicate, alright," Wendy teased, her tone playful as she reached for another apple.

Luke got closer, so close she could see the amusement dancing in his hazel eyes. "You mean to tell me this farm life requires something I don't have?"

"Try again, Mr. Carter," Wendy shot back, folding her arms and mock-glaring at him. "You've picked one apple, moved apple crates, and seen a pumpkin patch during your brief stay here. There's more to farm life than meets the eye."

"And I've survived everything I've experienced so far," Luke quipped back, placing the apple into the basket with an exaggerated flair. "At this rate, I'll master this life in no time."

The laughter fell between them, as natural as the light filtering through the trees.

"So," Luke said after a while, the sun warming the orchard, "when you're not busy being queen of the orchard, what else do you do for fun around here?"

Wendy laughed, tucking a strand of hair back behind her ear. "Fun, huh? You mean this isn't fun enough for you?" she teased, her voice laced with mock seriousness. "What are you doing? Writing a piece on small-town life now?"

Luke's lips quirked into a grin. "Just doing my research, getting the inside scoop on Laurel Ridge."

"Well, then." Wendy matched his serious tone, her eyes glinting. "We've got square dancing on Saturday nights and butter-churning competitions when the moon is full..." She couldn't hold her expression, breaking into laughter as Luke raised his eyebrows.

Luke tried—and failed—not to laugh. "Do all the ghosts of old-time settlers attend those competitions too?"

"They make a mean butter," Wendy quipped back, leaning in just enough to let him know she was teasing him right back. "Honestly, though, there are community picnics, festivals, hiking, and a lot of river stuff—rafting or kayaking down the New River if you're the adventurous type. We keep each other busy and, honestly, we're all family here. People look out for one another. Of course, we have tourists coming and going most days, since the town draws so many visitors. It keeps things lively, but at its heart, this place keeps that close-knit feeling. Even with all the hustle and bustle, by the end of the day, we're a tight-knit community."

"Must be nice," Luke said. "A place where people care about each other."

Wendy nodded. "Yeah. It's comforting, knowing there are always people around who are there for you. It makes the hard days easier."

Silence settled between them as they worked, peaceful and warm. Wendy's arm brushed against Luke's every so often, and each touch sent a subtle shiver up her spine, reminding her just how aware she was of his presence.

Luke paused. "Tell me more about growing up here," he urged. "Ever dream about leaving? Going somewhere else?"

Wendy could feel his question nudge at the protective walls she had built over the years. But she didn't let it show, instead offering a gentle smile. "I thought about leaving once or twice—seeing unknown places, starting fresh somewhere else."

Luke's gaze was steady, not probing, but curious. "What made you stay?"

Wendy glanced down at the ground, her voice soft and thoughtful. "When my parents passed, this farm was all Amy and I had left to hold on to. It wasn't just land or work—it was our connection to them, to our past. I couldn't bear the thought of losing that, too. So, when I was a little older and took over the farm, I stayed. Sure, it was hard at first, trying to keep everything together. Running Nature's Gifts became more than just a responsibility—it became home. A much-needed joy in my life."

Luke nodded, letting the meaning behind her words settle between them. "That must've been a lot to carry... choosing to stay, taking it all on yourself like that."

Her throat tightened at the unexpected compassion in his voice. There was a sincerity in the way he spoke that made her feel acknowledged, as if he understood the weight of the choices she had made. "It was hard," she admitted, her voice quieter now. "For a long time, I was lost, confused about my path. But I held on to my faith. It's what kept me grounded. It still does."

Luke's expression shifted, something deeper passing through his eyes. "Yeah... I get it. Life throws you off course, and you're left just... trying to figure it all out."

He paused, his next words coming slower, almost as if they were being pulled from somewhere deeper inside him. "Faith, though? That's where it gets complicated for me. I've... I've lost some of mine along the way."

Wendy felt the weight of his confession. The air hung heavy between them, rich with unspoken words she didn't want to rush. She could sense there was more behind what he wasn't saying, things that mirrored some of her own struggles. She wanted to ask more, to understand, but something inside held her back, still wary of pushing too hard.

Luke cleared his throat, the mood too heavy for him, and gave her a teasing grin. "So, how's my apple-picking form so far?"

"Not bad for a city boy," she replied, tilting her head. "You might even make a decent farmhand."

"Maybe I'll leave writing behind and take this up full time. It could be my true calling."

Wendy's laughter filled the orchard. "You wouldn't last a week. You'd be back behind your desk with your coffee, brooding over characters."

"Touché," Luke replied, chuckling.

They looked at the surrounding baskets, now brimming with apples.

"Well," Wendy said, satisfied, "I'd call this a success. I think we have enough."

Luke wiped his brow. "I'll accept my accolades in the form of an apple pie."

Wendy smirked, brushing her hands off on her jeans. "Funny you mention pie. I've got to deliver these apples to the church. The Bible study group is baking pies to serve after church service tomorrow."

Luke's brow rose. "Need a hand with that?"

"Well," Wendy began, feigning contemplation, "I could always use an extra set of hands to load and unload the delivery van. And you've proven yourself capable."

They loaded the apples, their movements easy, laughter spilling over as Luke acted like the baskets were far heavier than they were, Wendy rolling her eyes at his antics.

Soon, they were on their way, Wendy behind the wheel with the windows down, letting the autumn air rush through.

"So," Luke asked as they cruised down the winding road toward Laurel Ridge, "the church... It sounds like a big part of your life?"

"It is," Wendy answered with ease. "It's where we come together to worship and enjoy fellowship. If I'm being honest, it's a home away from home."

Luke nodded, taking in her words. Wendy glanced at him as he stared out the front window, his expression soft, but there was a flicker of something else in his face—a curiosity, or maybe a struggle. Perhaps it was both.

When they arrived, the sun was higher in the sky, the stained-glass windows casting colors across the gravel lot. Wendy drove around the side of the church to the fellowship hall, where a group of women stood, aprons already dusted with flour.

"Wendy!" called Dolores, her voice warm. "Am I ever glad to see you, sweetheart! Thank you so much, dear, for bringing the apples. Store bought just don't cut it."

Wendy chuckled, exchanging amused glances with Luke as they began unloading the apples. Dolores took in Luke's face, her eyes sparkling with curiosity.

Another woman peeked around Dolores, eyes twinkling. "And who's this strapping young man helping you out today?" She looked Luke up and down, her grin widening.

Luke scratched the back of his head. "Just lending a hand—name's Luke."

"Well, aren't you a gentleman?" Dolores turned back to Wendy, raising an eyebrow. "Wendy, I didn't know you were hiding such a fine young man up in the orchard. I might have to come up there more often!"

"Dolores..." Wendy sighed, heat rising to her cheeks. "This is Luke Carter—he's renting the cabin, working on his book."

Another woman, whose apron sported bright pink peonies, poked her head from behind one of the other women. "A writer, you say?" Her eyes gleamed, assessing Luke with newfound interest. "Lucky you, Wendy. I imagine there's plenty he could write about you and that farm of yours."

"How about we get these apples inside?" Wendy said, attempting to distract the ladies.

The women's laughter echoed through the fellowship hall, radiating a soothing warmth that embraced Wendy and Luke as they brought in basket after basket of apples. The hum of conversation created a lively buzz as the ladies peeled apples, reminding Wendy why she treasured little moments like this.

As they set down the last of the baskets on the long wooden counter, Wendy wiped her hands on a towel and turned to the group of apron-clad women who were elbow-deep in apples. Their eager faces made her smile.

"Well, ladies," Wendy said, casting a playful glance at Luke, "we'd better not get in your way any longer. I have a feeling you're about to create some fantastic pies."

Dolores, ever the queen of sass, waved a hand in the air. "Oh now, Wendy, these aren't just any old pies we're making, darling. These will be works of art...worthy of a blue ribbon, even. And if Luke here is planning to stay in town for a while, he better get a taste of these masterpieces. It's a rite of passage, you know."

The other women chuckled, nodding their agreement. One of them, a feisty woman named Alice, added, "Better watch out, Luke. Once you get a taste of our pies, you'll never want to leave town."

Luke grinned. "In that case, I'll take an extra slice—to go," he quipped, casting a glance at Wendy.

"Honey, you're welcome back anytime. But don't think you're getting away with a regular 'ole slice. I'll be cutting you an extra-large piece—and none of this 'to-go' nonsense. You come tomorrow, enjoy the church service with us and then stay and eat some pie," Delores said.

Wendy stifled a laugh, shaking her head at their antics. She leaned toward Luke and mock-whispered, "See? I told you, these ladies don't mess around with their pies. They are downright serious."

Luke chuckled, holding up his hands in mock surrender. "I've been properly warned. I'll be back with an enormous appetite someday, I promise."

As the chatter quieted down, Wendy said, "Alright, ladies, it's been fun, but we'll leave you to work your magic. Thanks again for taking on all these apples. I'll see y'all in church tomorrow." She took a half step toward the door before pausing with a playful grin. "Save us a couple of slices, okay?"

"Oh, you know it, honey!" Dolores called after her. "Come hungry!"

Wendy waved as they left, Luke following close behind with a bemused smile. As they stepped outside, the door swinging closed behind them, Luke tilted his head, sliding his hands into his jacket pockets. "Did I just survive a pie initiation, or...?"

Wendy grinned, stuffing her hands in her jean pockets. "That was just a warm-up for them."

"Consider me warned," Luke laughed.

Pastor Eli Thompson came around the side of the church and waved his hand at them. Wendy and Luke paused.

As Pastor Eli neared, he said, "Wendy, hello my child," his deep voice boomed with warmth, his easy smile crinkling the corners of his eyes. "What brings you here today?"

Wendy returned the smile. "We brought apples for the Bible study ladies to use for the pies tomorrow. They're hard at it already."

Pastor Eli chuckled, shaking his head. "Oh... yes, that's right, I forgot about that. Mercy... Those women and their pies. Lord, help anyone who gets in the way once they've got a project like that going. Those ladies take their pies more seriously than most take my sermons. And who might this young man be, Wendy?"

"This is Luke Carter," Wendy said, turning to Luke with a warm smile. "Luke, I'd like you to meet Pastor Eli Thompson."

"Nice to meet you, Pastor," Luke said, extending his hand with a smile. "I hear I'm already signed up for a double slice of apple pie, according to the ladies."

Eli laughed, his deep voice ringing out. "Well, sounds like they're making sure you're introduced to Laurel Ridge the proper way. Apple pie is our town's unofficial currency. Next it'll be fried chicken at a church picnic, and then—well, you'll be one of us before you know it."

Wendy glanced over at Luke, enjoying the exchange between the two men.

"You coming back tomorrow for church service, Luke?" Pastor Eli asked, hooking his thumbs into his jeans pockets.

Luke shifted, his lips curling up into a thoughtful smile. "I hadn't thought about it, but..." He glanced at Wendy, then back to Eli. "Yeah, I think I will."

Wendy's heart gave a small jump at Luke's answer. Surprised, yet pleased.

Pastor Eli nodded, his smile gentle and reassuring. "Good, son. That's wonderful. We'll save you a spot—there's always room for one more, God willing."

Chapter 15

Luke stepped out of the cabin, the crisp mountain air biting at his cheeks. He took a deep breath, feeling the morning's coolness settle into his lungs. He squared his shoulders and slipped on his jacket, the fabric brushing against his skin as he moved. Today was different—a Sunday morning with its own quiet weight. He was going to church. Faith, church—it wasn't exactly his comfort zone anymore, but he was willing to try again.

As he drove his truck down the gravel road toward Wendy's farmhouse, Luke's thoughts drifted to Sarah. He could still see her beside him on those Sunday mornings in Ohio, her smile so certain as they walked through the church doors. There had been a time when his faith was unshakable, when Sundays were spent at service, praising God for the love and life they'd built. But that felt like a lifetime ago now—before illness had stolen her from him and shaken the very foundation of everything he believed in.

Yet here he was, attempting to start a new chapter in his life—uncertain, but determined to take a step forward.

Wendy waited on the wide porch, the wooden rocking chair swaying beneath her. Her dress, dotted with soft floral patterns, moving slightly in the breeze, her boots peeked out from beneath the hem. The sun caught her hair, and it seemed to add a shimmer to the freckles scattered across her cheeks.

"Good morning!" she called, a smile spreading across her face. "I was starting to think you might back out and spend the morning with coffee and your manuscript instead."

Luke chuckled, stepping onto the porch, the boards creaking beneath his boots. "I'd be lying if I said it didn't cross my mind."

"I'm glad you didn't."

She stood up, grabbing her hand-knit shawl from the back of her chair and draping it across her shoulders. "Amy and Grandma are already ahead of us at the church. They're busy getting things set up for coffee and pie after the service."

"Sounds good." Luke said as they walked toward his truck. "How large is the congregation? Is the church usually packed?"

He opened the truck door for her, and Wendy smiled as she slid into the passenger seat, buckling her seatbelt. "Oh, it's not huge. Maybe fifty to sixty people on a typical Sunday. It's small enough that everyone knows each other, but big enough to feel like a community. You'll probably see a few familiar faces from around town."

Luke nodded and closed her door, a jittery anticipation about him this morning. He climbed into the truck, started the engine, and they were on their way. "That sounds... manageable," he admitted, casting her a sidelong glance. "Not too overwhelming."

"Exactly." Wendy leaned back into her seat and stared out of the window as the truck rolled down the driveway, turning onto the main road. "We've had the same congregation for years. Generations, really. My family's been attending this church since long before I was born.

Honestly, it's like a second home—there's comfort in being surrounded by people who genuinely care about each other."

Luke's hands tightened on the steering wheel. He tried to imagine that sense of belonging—a community where everyone's faces were familiar, where everyone knew your name and treated you like family. The church he and Sarah had attended had been huge, well over a thousand members.

As they neared the church, Luke wrestled with the question that had haunted him since Sarah's passing: had God abandoned him, or had he just stopped listening? The answer, elusive as ever, hung somewhere between the crispness of the morning and the warmth of Wendy's voice beside him.

The white steeple of the Laurel Ridge Community Church came into view, the modest structure standing tall against a backdrop of changing leaves. Luke parked near the front entrance, got out, and stretched his arms, trying to shake off his nervousness. Wendy hopped out with a graceful ease he admired, looping the strap of her leather purse over her shoulder before he even had a chance to open the truck door for her.

"You ready?" she asked, giving him a gentle, searching look.

Luke took in the simple, whitewashed walls of the church, the worn steps leading up to its doors. He drew in a breath, steadying himself. "Not really," he admitted, trying for a smile that felt more like a grimace.

Wendy returned a soft smile—one that understood without judgment. "I get it. But don't worry, this isn't some grand cathedral with a massive organ and stiff pews. It's more... cozy." She waved a hand toward the modest wooden structure. "We're just a bunch of neighbors getting together to remind ourselves of what's important."

Just neighbors, huh? Luke thought. He could see that. There was no pressure in this space, but still, the gathering held a quiet significance. Sunday service. Church. It had been a long time.

They walked up the steps together, Wendy's dress brushing against her boots with each movement, Luke beside her.

Inside, several members were already seated and chatting among themselves. The church wasn't big—a simple nave with rows of oak pews and a raised sanctuary at the front. Light streamed through the stained-glass, making rainbows flicker against the walls. Wooden beams sloped high overhead, giving the place an airy, homey feel.

Pastor Eli stood near the back of the church, greeting people as they filed in. When his gentle eyes caught sight of Luke and Wendy, he shook their hands with a welcoming grin.

"Well, I'll be!" His voice boomed, filled with genuine delight. He stepped over, extending his hand first to Luke. "Good to have you with us, son."

Luke shook his hand, trying not to show the unease still sitting heavily on his chest. "Thank you, Pastor. Good to be here."

Wendy nodded at Pastor Eli, gesturing toward the pews. "We'll grab a seat. Don't let us keep you, Pastor."

"Of course, of course. And please remember, apple pie after the sermon," Pastor Eli added, his eyes twinkling as he gave Luke a wink.

Wendy led Luke down the center aisle. Luke took a seat beside her, the wooden pew cool beneath him. He couldn't help but feel a bit out of place, like an outsider in the middle of a warm living room, watching a family that wasn't his. He cast a glance at Wendy, who smiled. She seemed perfectly at ease.

The small church filled up quickly. Wendy waved and exchanged smiles with half a dozen people as they settled into their seats. Luke noticed how effortless it was for her—the way she slipped into gentle conversations, nodding and laughing with an ease that made it clear this was her home. Her community.

Ruth, Amy, and Martha arrived just in time, squeezing into the pew beside them, their greetings hushed but filled with warmth.

The service began not with a grand display, but with the gentle rise of a hymn, sung by voices that filled the room with a raw, resonant power. The harmonies wove together, rising toward the wooden beams overhead, where they seemed to linger before echoing off the stained-glass windows. It was simple, but the beauty of it felt sacred, almost overwhelming.

When Pastor Eli stepped up for the sermon, his tone was as familiar and relaxed as a conversation among friends. His message, however, carried weight—a reflection on faith in difficult times, and how true strength often came not from standing alone, but from learning to lean on others.

Each word seemed to find its mark, slipping past Luke's defenses and piercing through places he wasn't ready to expose. It stung. He wasn't sure if it was the truth in the message or the fact that he wasn't prepared to hear it yet, but it left him feeling raw, vulnerable in a way he hadn't expected.

The words lingered in Luke's mind, no matter how much he tried to shake them off. Pastor Eli's sermon, meant to offer comfort, had stirred something deep within—something he wasn't ready to acknowledge, let alone face.

After the service closed in prayer, the congregation slowly trickled out onto the sun-dappled lawn behind the church. Most made their way to the large wooden pavilion, where Pastor Eli had announced that coffee and fresh pies would be served shortly.

Luke stood back, watching the scene with quiet awe. Men and women moved seamlessly between the fellowship hall and the pavilion, balancing trays of homemade pies and carafes of steaming coffee with practiced ease.

He had never experienced anything quite like it before.

It wasn't just the act of bringing food to the tables that struck him—it was the way they did it. There was a rhythm, an unspoken choreography, to their movements, like a well-rehearsed dance honed by years of shared traditions and quiet understanding. The laughter that punctuated light-hearted conversations drifted on the autumn breeze, mingling with the smell of fresh-baked pies.

Some of the men, with powerful arms weathered by decades of farm work, carried multiple carafes at once, swapping easy banter as if they'd done this a hundred times. Women, aprons tied over their Sunday dresses, expertly balanced trays laden with pies, their smiles warm and familiar. The entire scene radiated a sense of belonging, as people flitted between picnic tables and the pavilion, sharing gossip and laughter like the lifelong neighbors they were.

For Luke, it was more than just a church gathering—it was a glimpse into a way of life he hadn't known existed. A strong community seeped in history. People who knew one another's names, stories, and hearts. There was no fanfare, no pressure. Just an effortless togetherness.

And for the first time in a long time, Luke found himself wondering if he could ever be part of something like this—if he could ever belong.

From where Luke stood beneath the pavilion's wooden beams, he could see the entire scene unfold like an intimate painting—a Norman Rockwell moment made real. Children wove between the adults, giggling and darting past legs with youthful abandon, their bright laughter punctuating the gathering. Some older men called after them with reprimands, but the soft crinkle of their eyes betrayed them.

What struck Luke most wasn't just the bustling activity, but the palpable sense of togetherness. These weren't performers going through the motions of some town tradition—they were friends and family, flanked by years of shared moments. It was in the way they greeted one another with warm handshakes and clasped shoulders, as though no amount of time could loosen the bonds forged among them. There was an intrinsic trust and comfort woven into every interaction.

To someone like Luke, who had spent so much of his life in the city and in solitude because of his work or lost in the shadows of a life he no longer had, it was fascinating. Alien, in some ways, that so many people could know each other so well, care with such ease, and—strangely enough—it made him feel both welcome and distant at the same time.

As he continued to watch, an older man with a ruddy, weather-worn face caught Luke's eye as he balanced a pie in one hand and gave him a nod with the other. Without saying a word, the man's expression held an invitation, a silent promise that there was a place for everyone in this gathering, even a stranger.

Luke smiled, unable to resist the pull of this unfamiliar scene that felt more comfortable with every passing moment.

"Go on," Wendy said, nudging him with her elbow. "You promised the ladies you'd give their pies a try, remember?"

Luke let out a soft, defeated laugh. "Yeah, I do. My mouths watering."

"Trust me," Wendy said with a grin. "Dolores will never let you live it down if you hesitate for too long and miss out. I promise, their pies are so good, they vanish quickly."

"Luke!" Dolores called, waving a pie server in the air from behind the tables. Her grin was wide and bright. "I've got your slice right here, honey. Come on now... Dutch apple pie—nothing beats it."

Luke chuckled as he approached the table, hands raised in surrender. "One slice is all I can manage—I promise you."

Dolores shot him a playful wink as she handed him a plate with the thickest slice of pie he had ever seen. "We'll see if you're still saying that after one bite."

When Luke returned to Wendy's side, she laughed, glancing around. "Don't look now, but they're all watching you, waiting for your reaction."

He forked a bite into his mouth, and his eyes widened in genuine appreciation as the flavors hit him. The tang of Granny Smith apples mingled perfectly with warm cinnamon and the buttery, flaky crust, melting together in a symphony of sweetness and spice. He gave Wendy a wide-eyed look, as if he had discovered something magical.

"Okay," he said, glancing at the ladies and offering them a thumbs up, which sent them into a fit of giggles. "This pie is dangerous."

Wendy shook her head, laughing. "Told you."

"You definitely weren't exaggerating," he agreed, taking another bite, savoring the moment.

Wendy and Luke stood side by side under the pavilion, watching as the rest of the congregation lingered in casual conversation. Families, couples, and old friends chatted while children wove between their legs or played tag across the field, their laughter ringing out like music on the breeze.

To some, it might have seemed like an ordinary scene, but it touched Luke in a way he hadn't expected. This was what community looked like—people coming together, sharing moments of small talk, laughter, pie, and coffee, as if, for a little while, the outside world didn't exist. It was simple, unhurried, and somehow... sacred.

He let the quiet contentment wash over him, grounding him in the moment—until his phone buzzed in his pocket, shattering the peaceful spell. Luke frowned as he pulled it out, the caller ID flashing an all-too-familiar name: Priscilla.

His gut twisted.

The weight of everything he thought he'd left behind for the day suddenly pressed hard against his chest.

Wendy noticed her brow furrowing slightly. "Everything okay?"

"A work call," he said, glancing down at the screen. "I should probably take this."

Wendy nodded, her expression understanding but reserved, a quiet distance creeping in between them.

Luke forced a half-smile before stepping away from the pavilion, his footsteps crunching over the gravel path. The warmth of the congregation and the easy laughter faded as he answered the call.

"Priscilla," he greeted, keeping his tone neutral. "What's going on?"

"Luke, darling," Priscilla's voice came through, smooth and businesslike as ever. "I'll keep this brief. There's been a development."

He braced himself. "What kind of development?"

"Your publisher is eager to push forward with the book tour I mentioned. We need to lock in dates and solidify your engagement schedule. I've already fielded some interest from venues stateside, plus international locations—Paris, London, Tokyo. The works."

Luke's stomach tightened. He had been dreading this conversation, the inevitable tug back into a world he wasn't sure he belonged in anymore.

"And the manuscript deadline?" he asked, already anticipating the answer.

Priscilla's tone didn't waver. "That's the thing—they've moved it up. When you signed the contract, there was wiggle room, but now... they're ready to lean in. They want the manuscript by the original deadline."

Luke rubbed a hand over his face, trying to push away the frustration rising in his chest. The writing had been flowing more easily recently, but it was because he'd been here—away from the constant pressure. Now, that pressure was closing in again, and the distance between the creative freedom he'd rediscovered and the demands of his career felt impossible to bridge.

"Okay," he said, the word thick in his throat. "I'll send over what I have so far, but I really think I'll need more time."

"More time would usually be negotiable," Priscilla replied smoothly, "but not in this case. They're adamant."

Luke nodded, even though she couldn't see him. His eyes drifted back to the pavilion, where Wendy stood among her neighbors and friends, her laughter drifting toward him like a balm against the tension gripping his chest. She handed two plates of pie to some kids, her simple nature on full display, as if nothing in the world could rattle her.

He envied that—her ability to just be surrounded by people who seemed to know exactly who they were. And here he was, caught between two worlds, unsure where he fit anymore.

Suddenly, the fast-paced, frenzied world he'd left behind didn't just feel distant—it felt undesirable, like a weight he no longer wanted to carry.

But could he really turn down a golden opportunity like the tour? Could he afford to walk away from the very thing that had kept him afloat all these years?

"Priscilla," he said, forcing a steadiness he didn't feel, "give me a little more time to think about the tour. Tell them I'm working on it."

"Oh, Luke," she chided, her tone a mix of impatience and condescension. "Don't overthink this. You're a professional, remember? Besides, you could use the distraction. A year of jet-setting could do wonders for getting you back on track after... everything. This is a gift on a silver platter, and you'd be a fool to let it slip away."

A gift? Luke wasn't so sure anymore. It sounded more like a chain being slipped around his neck.

"I'll be in touch," he said, dodging the rest of the conversation. "Thanks, Priscilla."

Before she could respond, he ended the call, the weight of it pressing down on him like a vice. He stuffed the phone deep into his pocket, as if burying it could help him escape the decisions looming over his head.

As he turned back to the pavilion, he noticed Wendy's eyes flicker in his direction. Her sunny smile hadn't faded, but there was a subtle shift—a questioning glimmer beneath her easy warmth. Had she overheard? Or maybe she just sensed the change in him.

"Well?" she asked, folding her arms gently over her shawl as he approached. "Book business?"

Luke hesitated for a moment too long, then nodded. "Yeah. Just... work stuff."

Wendy's smile faltered, the light in her eyes dimming just slightly. The easy warmth they'd shared moments ago now felt fragile.

"You good?" she asked, her voice soft but careful, as if she were tiptoeing around the invisible wall he hadn't realized he was putting up.

Luke swallowed hard, forcing a smile that didn't quite reach his eyes. "I'll figure it out," he said, though the words felt shallow, even to him.

Chapter 16

A light breeze whispered across the porch where Wendy, Ruth, and Amy had settled for the evening, sweet tea in hand, watching as the day gave way to another beautiful autumn sunset. The house was quiet now, dinner plates stacked in the sink, leftovers packed away for tomorrow—a rhythm they all knew by heart, comforting in its simplicity.

The old swing creaked softly as Amy rocked back and forth, one leg tucked beneath her on the wide wooden seat. Wendy sat cross-legged near the porch steps, leaning against the polished banister, absentmindedly tracing the rim of her glass with one finger. Nearby, Ruth sat in an oversized rocking chair, her old, well-loved Bible resting on the small table beside her. Her eyes, ever soft and observant, watched the evening unfold.

There was peace between them, the kind that only comes from years of shared stories, laugh lines, and heartache. Yet, despite the calm, Wendy couldn't quite shake the faint sense of disappointment that clung to her tonight.

She hadn't expected to care so much that Luke had passed on her invitation for Sunday dinner. It had been a simple, casual offer—or so she'd told herself. But when he'd politely declined, explaining that he needed to finish up some writing, something in her sank deeper than she wanted to admit. Sure, he had work to do, and she understood the pressures looming over him—they'd talked about it during the ride home from church. But still... she'd hoped.

Hadn't she always been the practical one? The woman who knew when to rein in her feelings before they ran away with too much hope? But this... this was Luke. The man who had been quietly weaving his way into her thoughts since the moment he arrived in Laurel Ridge. The one with the haunted eyes that had started to soften bit by bit when he was around her.

Amy stretched out on the swing, her feet brushing the weather-worn wood of the porch as the seat swayed gently. She took a long sip of her sweet tea before throwing Wendy a mischievous glance, a spark of mischief glinting in her blue eyes. As always, Amy knew just when to strike—right when Wendy wanted to be left to her thoughts.

"So," Amy began casually, though Wendy could hear the teasing anticipation hanging off the very syllable. "You gonna tell me why Mr. Tall, Dark, and Brooding isn't sitting here with us, enjoying this fine evening? Or did you scare him off with your charming ways?"

Wendy shot her a look that could only be translated as don't start, but Amy remained undeterred, her lips quirking upward in an amused grin.

"I didn't scare him off," Wendy replied. "He's just got work to do. Writing, you know? Big important book deadlines and all."

"Mmm-hmm," Amy said, dragging out the tone with clear disbelief. "Sure, it's work. I mean, it's so much more enticing than sitting on a porch with the Lane women and enjoying a glass of tea," she added, shaking her head.

Wendy rolled her eyes and shrugged. "Honestly, Amy, I don't know what you want me to say. He had things to do. That's it."

Amy swirled the last of her tea in the mason jar, giving Wendy a side-eye. "Ah yes. The classic excuse—Sorry, I can't take time to chat and relax because I'm too busy writing in my lonely cabin by candlelight. Please excuse me while I brood poetically into the night."

Wendy cracked a smile despite herself. "You make him sound like he's one step away from throwing himself off a cliff for artistic inspiration."

"Well, you do bring out the drama in people at times," Amy teased, waggling her eyebrows. "Poor guy probably stares out his window muttering, 'Miss Wendy, the elusive apple-farm enchantress who haunts my every thought.'"

Wendy groaned. "You've been watching too many cheesy romance movies, Amy."

Ruth chuckled, her hands cupped around her glass of tea as she listened to the exchange. The gray in her hair caught the last golden rays of sunlight, casting a soft glow over her calm face. She had that way about her—knowing your heart before you even spoke.

"Seems to me," Ruth said, her voice warm and full of quiet wisdom, "like you wanted Luke here more than you're letting on."

Wendy set her glass down on the step beside her, the clink of it echoing faintly into the peaceful evening. Did she want him here? What kind of question was that? Of course, she did. Or didn't she? She had felt... something since the moment Luke had walked into her life—a pull she hadn't allowed herself to fully acknowledge just yet.

"I don't know..." Her voice wavered, the frustration and uncertainty making it harder to speak the truth out loud.

Amy, ever the instigator, leaned in with a grin. "Oh, come on, Wendy. All you had to do was ask him a little nicer, maybe flash one of those charming smiles of yours that he seems to like so much. Next thing you know, he'd be sitting here swooning into his sweet tea, making googly eyes at you."

Wendy groaned, laughing but also feeling the ache grow tighter around her chest. "Amy, can we not do this? Luke's just—"

"Just what?" Amy prompted, raising an eyebrow as Wendy faltered.

Wendy hesitated, her thoughts tangling between the practical excuses she wanted to give and the more complicated feelings she wasn't sure how to express. Her mind wandered back to David—the boy she thought she'd spend forever with in high school. The one who had reappeared in her life only to use their rekindled romance as a way to push her into selling the farm for profit.

Luke was nothing like David. At least, she didn't think so. But how could she be sure?

"He's got things to figure out," Wendy said, her words halting with caution. "And, well... so do I."

Amy's playful expression softened, curiosity replacing the amusement in her eyes. "What's that supposed to mean?"

Wendy glanced toward Ruth, her grandmother's weathered hands resting around her glass. Ruth's expression was patient, understanding—an invitation for Wendy to speak her truth, not just to them, but to herself.

"I like him," Wendy admitted softly, the words surprising even her. "I mean, who wouldn't? He's kind, thoughtful... even funny in his own way." A small smile tugged at her lips as she thought of Luke awkwardly picking apples, his charm sneaking up on her in ways she hadn't planned. "But... I'm not sure if I want to get into a relationship."

Ruth raised an eyebrow, waiting for Wendy to elaborate. Amy stayed quiet, her attention now focused, knowing when to listen instead of joke.

Wendy sighed, her thoughts swirling with past hurt and present confusion. "I don't know if I can handle it. Luke lives in Ohio, for one. Doesn't seem like a big deal, right?" She let out a humorless chuckle. "But it's more than that. He's still grieving. He's... stuck, in a way, since losing his wife. And then there's me." She paused, her words faltering as old memories surfaced. "I've only ever had relationships that... well, they never ended well. So, how do I know if I'm even cut out for this?"

The weight of her question settled between them, heavy with unspoken fears and past disappointments.

Amy was the first to speak, her usual banter tempered by genuine concern. "Wendy, come on. You, of all people, deserve someone who's actually...I don't know, good enough for you. Besides, look at everything else you've handled in life. An out-of-state guy with a little heartache?" She waved her hand, dismissive. "Sounds like a manageable project compared to running an entire farm and store."

Wendy laughed despite herself. "Not sure Luke would appreciate being called a project."

Amy grinned. "Maybe not, but you have to admit, you could probably handle him—just like you handle harvest season without losing your mind."

Wendy shot Amy a playful glare, but Amy just shrugged in response, as if to say, you know I'm right.

Ruth, who had been silent up to this point, cleared her throat. "Sweetheart," she began, her voice carrying the slow, soothing cadence Wendy had come to depend on over the years, "I know you're scared. But fear should never stop something that might turn out to be one of life's great unexpected blessings. It might delay it, sure, but it shouldn't stop it. Not if it's something worth having."

Ruth's words settled in Wendy's heart, heavy and warm all at once. Wendy met her grandmother's gaze, searching for wisdom in her soft gray eyes. Ruth had been her rock for as long as she could remember, stepping in when her parents had died, weathering their grief with a kind of grace Wendy had always admired.

"I just don't want to get hurt again, Grandma," Wendy admitted, her voice trembling. She looked down, her eyes fixing on a chipped piece of wood on the porch floor. David's face flashed in her mind—his charming smile, the way he'd made promises about their future, only to see the farm as a dead-end. "I was so sure with David... thought we were building something real. But he wasn't in it for me. He was... using me. And I didn't even see it coming."

Ruth reached over, taking Wendy's hand. Her grip was soft but firm, a reminder that she had endured more storms than Wendy could imagine.

"Oh, honey. David was a lesson, not a conclusion. You're stronger now, wiser. You can't let someone like him keep you from opening your heart again."

"But what if Luke's the same?" Wendy said. "What if he's chasing something I don't even understand yet? He's still grieving. He's got his own wounds. I can't go through the pain of disappointment again, Grandma. I wouldn't survive it."

Ruth gave her a knowing look, her eyes full of understanding. "That's the thing about love, Wendy—it's always a risk. But you're not the woman you were back then, and Luke isn't David. You won't know what's waiting on the other side until you step out in faith, until you risk your heart a little."

Amy leaned in, her voice softening with sincerity. "Just don't rush anything, Wendy. You don't have to figure it all out right now. But... this man makes you smile. Not in that polite way you smile at customers in the farm shop, but the kind of smile that hits deep. Like, maybe, you're starting to feel something real."

Wendy's heart clenched, her mind swirling with conflicting emotions. Could she handle being in a relationship again?

The conversation shifted after a while, moving away from Luke and back into the mundane warmth of small talk—stories about the apple festival, memories of years gone by. Ruth even shared a tale about how one festival had nearly been rained out, only for the clouds to part ten minutes before guests arrived.

Amy sprinkled in jokes so sharp and spot-on, she had all three of them laughing until their sides hurt. The sound of shared laughter was comforting, and it tethered Wendy back to the moment, bringing a semblance of peace that had been missing during her earlier reflection.

But as the night deepened, and the stars twinkled overhead, Wendy couldn't ignore what Ruth had said earlier.

Life's unexpected blessings.

Could Luke be one of those?

She stared out over the darkened fields that lay before her, a place she knew better than she knew herself—a place where she had planted pieces of her heart, watched some grow fruit, others wither with the changing seasons. It was home. But was it... enough?

Ruth let out a soft sigh as she stood up, shaking her head at the cooling air. "Well now, girls, that's enough talking for one night. I'm off to bed before this cool air sets too deep in these old bones."

"Night, Grandma," Amy called after her, giving Wendy a knowing smile once Ruth had crossed the yard toward her cottage. "You okay?"

Wendy nodded, her thoughts still tangled but somehow lighter than they had been before. "Yeah. I'm okay."

Together, she and Amy gathered the empty mason jars and took them inside, Amy chatting about some new recipe she wanted to try this coming week. Wendy was quieter, thoughtful.

After they turned in for the night, Wendy stood at her window for a moment longer, gazing out at the dark hills that rolled into the horizon, the silent silhouette of Luke's cabin tucked among them. She wondered if he was still up, lost in his words, or if his mind was elsewhere, maybe even thinking of her. Wendy smiled at the thought, letting it linger for a moment.

She whispered a prayer into the quiet—one for clarity, for guidance, and for her heart to remain open to whatever lay ahead.

Could Luke be a blessing...or just another changing season in her life?

Chapter 17

L uke stretched back in his chair, taking his hands off the keyboard for a moment to glance out at the rolling hills. The leaves had slowly turned into every imaginable shade of red, orange, and gold, painting the landscape. His world had been reduced to moments like this since arriving—small breaths of beauty and quietness, unbroken by the hustle of deadlines or the noise of the city.

He had been working since before dawn, trying to chase down the feeling he had yesterday during and after church. An unexpected sense of clarity now clear in his writing. After so many months of nothing, there was a movement in his writing, and he couldn't afford to let it slip away. But it wasn't just the story that had sprung to life. Yesterday at church... something there had stirred in him.

Pastor Eli's words still lingered, tucked into the back of his mind: It takes strength to lean on others, to allow community to support you when you feel weak. It was a gentle reminder from the universe—or maybe more—something Luke had spent plenty of time resisting. For so long, he had been numb, detached, buried under the weight of what his life had become.

But then there was Laurel Ridge.

And there was Wendy.

Luke's fingers tapped restlessly on the edge of his laptop. Wendy Lane. Her face surfaced in his mind unbidden, her smile vivid and warm, as if she were right in front of him. He couldn't shake the image of her from church yesterday, the way she carried a quiet, unassuming light that seemed to reach everyone around her.

Something about Wendy touched him, too, in a way he hadn't expected.

She wasn't like Sarah. Not in the same way. It wasn't a comparison, not that Luke would ever dare make one. Sarah had been a soft, constant in his life...something steady that gave him a place to land. It wasn't until she was gone that he realized how much she had grounded him. Her faith, too—quiet but so sure—was a presence that stitched together the holes in him, holding him together during her illness. When Sarah was with him, he knew who he was. He knew where he belonged. After she left, he was like a tree cut loose, roots swaying helplessly in shifting winds.

Wendy's faith was different. It wasn't something tucked gently into moments—it was blazing, bright and open and spilling over into everything she did.

He breathed out slowly, leaning back in his chair, reflecting on the woman who had been on his mind so much. Wendy was a puzzle—not overtly unfolding herself before him, but pulling at him with every interaction. She had this strength—a confidence in the simple, everyday moments that he found himself drawn to despite himself.

But why did it feel so... complicated?

And then came the guilt—the gnawing feeling that letting someone else in, even slightly, was a betrayal. Could a person really love again? Was it even possible? Could there be room in his heart for Wendy without losing his memories of Sarah?

Luke rubbed a hand down his face, trying to untangle the looping thoughts.

Wendy was gentle and kind and seemed to understand the silence that still plagued his days. When he was with her, the ache for Sarah became less pronounced, less consuming. The guilt stung because part of him wanted more of that. Was it wrong to feel that way?

A low vibration rattled rattled across the desk, pulling him from his thoughts. His phone buzzed, Priscilla's name flashing across the screen. He glanced at the name, but let the call go unanswered, his focus unable to settle on anything related to work right now.

Luke slouched back, letting his hands fall into his lap.

Work... Sarah... Wendy...

It was all tangled together like chains wrapped too tightly. One pulling at the other. The thought of juggling it all, of trying to find the right balance between honoring Sarah's memory and permitting himself to feel again, was overwhelming. More than overwhelming. Exhausting.

But here, in this town—in this quiet, laid-back place—he was beginning to think he could find something new. Maybe even happiness. What if there was something waiting for him down the road that wasn't about loss, but about possibility?

Luke leaned forward in his seat, the wood creaking beneath him. Could you hold on to both—the past and the future? Could you keep the memory of someone alive while still nurturing hope for what's ahead? Even asking the question felt wrong, like betraying something sacred. But the longer he stayed in Laurel Ridge, the harder it was to ignore. The questions had crept up on him like the early morning fog rolling down the mountains—slow, inevitable, and thick with meaning. A desire for something more. A desire to move forward.

He wasn't certain where that left him with Wendy, not yet. But he felt something. For the first time in a long time, he felt something. Was it loneliness? Was it missing a human touch or connection? Maybe. Or maybe it was simply—her. Wendy. Her laughter. Her joy. Her way of making the world brighter.

A grin tugged at his lips as he thought about her smile from the day before. No. It wasn't just loneliness. It was her.

What about his faith? Was he ready to trust and believe again, the way he once had? That question lingered in Luke's mind, heavier than the rest. Faith used to feel as natural as breathing, guiding him through every rough patch, sustaining him when nothing else made sense. But after Sarah—after losing her—it was different. He found it difficult to lean on God the way he used to. It wasn't anger, exactly, but a quiet withdrawal, as if the steady ground of his belief had shifted beneath him. Burying himself in work had been easier. Retreating into a life where there was no room for anything unpredictable felt safer, a way to avoid facing the deeper wounds left behind.

Yet here he was... sitting in a mountain cabin, trying to piece together fragments of his old life with something new. Could Wendy—this bright, hopeful woman—be part of that something new?

Luke sighed, resting his elbow on the desk and rubbing his temples.

"Maybe," he said, though an undercurrent of doubt tugged at his thoughts.

He sighed and ran a hand through his tousled hair.

His phone buzzed again, this time with Bill's familiar name flashing on the screen. Luke swiped to answer, eager for the distraction.

Chapter 18

"Hey, man," Luke answered, leaning back in his chair. "What's up?"

"Just checking in on my genius author buddy," Bill's voice boomed through the speaker. "How's the writer's block treating you? Are you staring at blank pages, or have the mountain muses continued to grace you with their presence?"

Luke chuckled, running a hand through his hair. "Actually, they are. Something shifted yesterday. I figured out where I want this story to go."

"Oh?" Bill's tone became more serious. "What's the new direction?"

"It's... well, it's difficult to explain. It's more than just the plot. It's like the whole tone, the characters, their motivations—it all feels more... authentic, more real, I guess. More connected."

"Well, okay then. I'm following. Sounds like this mountain retreat is really working for you," Bill said.

"Well, something's working. I actually wanted to talk to you about the worldwide, yearlong book tour issue. Priscilla dropped that bomb on me again yesterday. I'm not sure if I want it."

"Seriously?" There was surprise in Bill's voice. "Luke, that's a wonderful opportunity. A year-long tour? That could be the next big step in your—"

"I know, I know," Luke interrupted, rubbing his forehead. "But something doesn't feel right. Not anymore. I'm actually rethinking the entire contract thing, too. The whole traditional publishing deal. I'm starting to think I've had enough."

"Whoa, hold on a second there, buddy," Bill said, his voice laced with caution. "That's a pretty big step. You sure you're not just... I don't know, running away again?"

"Possibly," Luke admitted. "But this isn't about avoiding grief. It's not about avoiding work anymore, either. It's about what's right for me. For what I want my life to look like next."

"Okay," Bill said. "Talk to me. What's going on in that head of yours?"

"I don't know exactly," Luke started, his thoughts tumbling out. "I'm looking at this town, at the people here, at the way they live, and... I'm starting to see something different. Something simpler. More... real for myself."

Luke paused, searching for the right words. "I don't know how to describe the way they live here other than there is a lot less focus on the next big moment or, better yet, opportunity. They focus more on the here and now. Spending time with each other, being involved with a church and within the community, being available for their neighbors. Being there for family. Just the simple things. The simple things that really matter. You know?"

"Yeah, I get it. A slower lane. It's appealing, for sure." Bill's voice was thoughtful. "Especially when you've been in the fast lane for so long."

"Exactly," Luke agreed. "And I'm thinking about the writing, too. What if I could just... write? No deadlines, no pressure. Just tell the stories I want to tell, connect with readers directly, build my career the way I choose?"

"Well, you could," Bill said, his voice gaining a new energy. "That's the beauty of self-publishing. You're in control. You make the decisions. It's not easy, but it's definitely liberating."

Luke hesitated. "But is it realistic? I mean, you're an exception, Bill. Not everyone can make it as a self-published author. I don't know exactly what to do without a publisher doing numerous things for me."

Bill chuckled. "Dude, you're Luke Carter. You've got a built-in audience. Do you think readers care who publishes your books? They care about the stories. And trust me, the freedom... it's worth the extra work. It's worth more than you can imagine. Until you step out on your own, you'll just never know the feeling?"

"Tell me more," Luke said, feeling a spark of genuine excitement flicker within him.

Bill launched into an enthusiastic explanation of the self-publishing world, sharing his experiences, the challenges, the rewards, the sense of ownership that came with controlling his own work. He talked about building a platform, connecting with readers, creating a community around his books—a community that felt more genuine, more connected than anything he'd experienced in the traditional publishing world.

As Bill spoke, Luke pictured himself here, in Laurel Ridge, writing his stories, setting his pace, building a life that felt authentic. He thought of Wendy, of the warmth in her eyes. The infectious joy she brought to everything she did. He envisioned a future where he wasn't chasing deadlines or book tours, but where he was creating a life that mattered, a life filled with purpose, love, and the joys of a small-town existence. He could start over, on his terms, and build the rest of his life the way he chooses to.

Luke glanced around the cabin, at the simple furniture, the worn wood floors, the view of the mountains through the window. It wasn't much, but it felt more like home than what was waiting for him back in Ohio.

"Look, we've had this conversation before, but I'm gonna lay it out plain. Self-publishing isn't just a fun little side option these days; it's a career. You keep playing the way the traditional publishers want—you're locked. You dance to their tune, or as I call it, the 'Sell Your Soul for Marketing' waltz. But if you go out on your own, you take back something the traditional world never gives you—control," Bill said.

"Control," Luke repeated under his breath, the word sitting heavy in the air.

"That's right," Bill continued. "You get to tell the stories you want to tell, market them how you want them marketed, and you're not caught in a web of contracts that make you a piece of their corporate machine. It's freedom, Luke. And trust me when I say—there's nothing quite like it."

Luke tapped his fingers against the desk, his mind racing. "How'd you know when it was time to leave the traditional publishing world?" he asked.

Bill didn't miss a beat. "Oh, I didn't. I was never absolutely certain, in case you're thinking there's some eureka moment where the clouds open up, and someone hands you a business plan on a silver platter.

But I took a step back and realized I was losing my love for writing. My life then had been about hitting deadlines and chasing the next advance, but the stories—I wasn't telling them for the right reasons anymore. I was doing it for some publisher's spreadsheet. And that didn't sit right."

Luke took a deep breath. That hit closer to home than he cared to admit. All these months—and even years, if he was honest—he hadn't just been battling grief. He'd been running on empty, churning out words onto pages because that's what he did. It was his job. It was his role. Chasing a number on a contract, rather than a story that stirred him the way writing once had. But the more Bill talked about self-publishing, about the freedom that came with it, the more distant his present world started to feel.

Freedom. It echoed back to what he was grappling with emotionally. The freedom to feel again. The freedom to choose how he wanted to live—outside of grief, outside of running from the life he used to know.

Was that Wendy's effect? The town? Or his own heart tugging him toward something genuine he hadn't yet fully recognized?

"It sounds like you've got some big ideas and decisions swirling around in that head of yours," Bill said, breaking into Luke's thoughts. "Are you sure you're thinking about them for the right reasons?"

Luke leaned back in his chair, his fingers tapping lightly on the wooden armrests. "I'm not sure," he confessed with a heavy sigh. "It's like...I'm starting to realize I don't need the things I used to think were essential. The contracts, the big book tours, the huge advances—all these things I thought would make me feel accomplished, or whole again. But maybe—what I really need is something simpler. Maybe I just need to... live. Live the way I want to, and stop chasing what doesn't matter."

He paused, his gaze drifting to the mountains outside his cabin window. Why had everything become so clear here? The world seemed to stretch out before him—pure, unhurried—as if he'd been blind to its beauty for too long.

"And?" Bill prompted.

Luke hesitated, biting his lip. "Honestly?" He shifted in his seat, still trying to untangle the knots of his thoughts. "I don't know yet. I'm trying to sort all of this out, but I don't know what my next move should be." He hesitated again, feeling a tightness in his chest as another face flickered into his mind—someone who wasn't Sarah.

Bill didn't let the silence drag on. "Something else?" he asked, the curiosity in his voice crackling across the phone. "Come on, man. Spill. What else is on your mind?"

Luke ran a hand over the back of his neck, letting out a nervous laugh. He hadn't told a soul about what had quietly been growing inside him. But after seeing Wendy at church yesterday, or hearing her laugh while working on the farm, there was no point denying it anymore.

"There's this woman," Luke began, his words slower, more cautious, as though each one was unfamiliar territory. "Wendy. I met her here in Laurel Ridge."

A brief pause, then Bill let out a low, amused whistle. "Well, that's a surprise. Go on."

Luke couldn't help but smile a little. "It's not like it's... anything serious. Not yet anyway. I don't really know, Bill. There's just something about her. She's different." He leaned forward, resting his elbows on the desk. "She's been on my mind, more than I expected. She's funny. Grounded. She's got this quiet kind of strength that makes me feel like I can actually—breathe, when I'm around her. I want to keep hearing her laugh and..." He trailed off, a flicker of guilt settling in his chest.

"And?" Bill pressed gently.

Luke sighed. "And... I'm not sure where it's going. It's complicated because—well, there's Sarah." Just saying her name weighed heavily, reminding him that even with all the time that had passed, his feelings for her—the ache of missing her—had never fully faded.

Bill's voice softened. "Yeah. Sarah... I understand completely. It's difficult to move on. I went through it when my sweet Connie passed away, but one day I just decided I needed to at least try to find happiness again. I had to take part in life again. It's tricky for sure. Your mind plays these games on you...it's just tricky."

Tricky was an understatement. "Yeah, exactly. I mean, part of me feels like these feelings for Wendy shouldn't even be happening. It's like... isn't it wrong to start something new? To feel something for someone else?" Luke's voice dropped quieter. "Like maybe I'm betraying Sarah somehow."

There it was—the fear he hadn't wanted to acknowledge out loud. The fear that moving forward with someone new meant leaving Sarah in the past in a way he wasn't prepared to do.

"Luke." Bill's voice was steady, offering the kind of reassurance only a good friend could give. "It's not wrong to feel again. That's human. And it doesn't mean you're erasing anything about Sarah. It doesn't mean your time with her ever stops mattering. You can carry those memories and still give yourself the chance to be happy."

Luke swallowed hard, the truth in Bill's words sinking deep, even if they didn't feel like enough to quiet the confusion. Still, since arriving here in Laurel Ridge, something in him had shifted. The feelings he was developing for Wendy—the need to see her smile and hear her voice—weren't something he could brush off anymore.

"Maybe," Luke relented. "But I feel like I'm at war with myself. I miss Sarah. Every day, I miss her. And Wendy... she's like this light I didn't know I needed. But part of me wonders—what if it's too soon? What if I'm just... filling the emptiness?"

Bill hummed on the other end. "Luke, you're not filling a hole of emptiness. Not if it feels like this. You're lonely, yes—but you're also alive. And that pull toward Wendy? That's real. It's not about replacing Sarah or filling in some missing piece that's been haunting you."

Luke sighed. "Maybe. She's... amazing, though. I don't even think she knows it. That light she carries? It's genuine, Bill. It's not just a show or something people put on. She's like sunshine on a day you forgot you missed."

He could hear Bill chuckling. "Well, sounds like you're halfway in already."

"I don't know... I mean," Luke said. "I'm still trying to figure things out. Trying to balance things between missing Sarah while not shutting Wendy out."

There was a brief silence, then Bill's voice came back, calm but firm. "All I'll say is this, Luke—you don't have to have it all figured out right now. But don't close the door on something good just because it's unfamiliar. If Wendy's making you smile, if she's lifting those heavy parts of your heart, maybe it's worth exploring. You don't have to fall headlong into anything. Let it unfold. Take your time."

Luke let Bill's words settle over him like the breeze filtering through the window. Maybe for now, the best thing was just... to keep inching forward. Being open to whatever his life could become.

A faint smile ghosted over his lips as he murmured, "Yeah, Bill. You might be right."

"So," Bill continued. "Want to send me your manuscript so far? I'd love to take a look at your work in progress."

"Yeah," Luke said, a sense of relief washing over him. "Yeah, I'll send it over."

"Alright, man. Looking forward to reading it. And hey, whatever you decide about the publishing thing, or Wendy, I'm here. I'll help you figure it out."

"Thanks, Bill. I sincerely appreciate it."

After ending the call, Luke stared at his laptop, but his mind had already wandered again. Thoughts of Wendy filled the space where once there had only been grief. This pull toward her—toward a life that seemed more real than the one he'd been living—was almost overpowering. Yet, nestled alongside it, was the quiet ache for Sarah and the life they had shared.

What am I supposed to do?

Luke stood, grabbed his jacket, and headed outside without a clear plan in mind—but maybe that was for the best. The autumn air welcomed him, sharp and cool, pushing thoughts away as he wandered through the trees.

He walked for a while, letting the path guide him, until the woods thinned, bringing the view of Wendy's farm into clear sight. His steps slowed as he neared the edge of the orchard and saw Wendy in the distance, her unmistakable laugh rising along the breeze as she worked with a few of her employees.

Luke stopped. Just watching.

There was a pull toward her. There had been since day one, but recently, it felt stronger—something magnetic and undeniable. He liked how easy she made things, how the weight he carried inside him seemed to dissolve whenever she was near. Was it too soon to think like that? Or had been long enough?

Could he feel one thing for Wendy and still hold on to what he felt for Sarah? Could he let the two feelings exist at once, without betraying either? Should he?

Wendy smiled at something one of the workers said, her laughter bubbling out across the field. Luke couldn't help the grin that spread across his face. Maybe... maybe there was enough space in him for both—his past and something new.

Chapter 19

Wendy absentmindedly twirled a worn pencil between her fingers, her gaze flicking over the cash register receipts scattered across the counter. Though her eyes traced the orderly rows of numbers on her ledger, the figures barely registered in her mind. The steady hum of the day had finally quieted, leaving the store cloaked in the serenity of early evening. The last customer had walked out just moments ago.

Sales had been brisk, driven by the growing anticipation for the upcoming Apple Festival, which seemed to bring more people into the store with each passing day. The preparations for the event were well underway—every detail falling into place exactly as planned.

But no matter how smoothly things were going, a persistent restlessness gnawed at Wendy beneath the surface. It hovered at the edges of her consciousness like a thin veil of fog, distorting her usually sharp thoughts and leading her down unfamiliar, tangled paths.

With a soft, weary sigh, she put the pencil down and leaned back, momentarily abandoning the numbers in front of her.

Wendy told herself it was just exhaustion, nothing more. But deep down, she knew better. Her thoughts had drifted—again—back to Luke.

No matter how hard she tried to push him from her mind, he always found his way back in. She could still see the way his hazel-green eyes softened when he talked about his writing, hear the quiet amusement in his voice. And then there was that smile—the one that barely curved at the edges, crooked and subtle, but powerful enough to unravel everything she had been trying to lock away.

She glared at the pile of receipts scattered across the counter, annoyed at how straightforward numbers were compared to the tangled mess of her emotions. Why him? Of all times. Here she was, drowning in the chaos of planning one of the biggest events of the year, barely staying afloat. And yet, Luke lingered at the edges of her consciousness, unwanted but persistent.

In her mind, she saw him again, standing at the edge of the orchard, his presence unwavering. There was a quiet strength in the way he moved, graceful yet solid. And it was that very combination—something both vulnerable and resilient—that pulled her in, no matter how tightly she tried to guard her heart.

Wendy brushed a stray lock of hair behind her ear, her gaze drifting back to the numbers in front of her. Numbers were simple. They didn't complicate things. They didn't twist her insides into knots.

But the pencil hesitated between her fingers, and a faint smile ghosted across her lips. When had it started—this endless preoccupation with him? Without even realizing it, thinking about Luke had become a habit she couldn't shake.

You shouldn't be thinking about him this much, she scolded herself.

Her teeth grazed the inside of her cheek as she stared blankly at the stack of receipts. The Apple Festival was looming, with its own avalanche of tasks demanding attention. The constant needs of the farm, the store, the growing list of to-dos—all of it should have filled her mind. And yet, Luke somehow wove his way into every stray thought, every quiet moment.

Frustration building, Wendy pushed herself away from the counter with a huff. Rising to her feet, she crossed the room to the ice cream cooler—a well-practiced routine when her thoughts became too tangled. Her hands moved automatically, seeking the familiar comfort of her little indulgence.

Without a second thought, she scooped pumpkin ice cream into a bowl waiting nearby, then reached for the jug of apple cider she kept in the mini-fridge. The cider splashed over the ice cream with a satisfying fizz, the contrast of deep autumn flavors mixing perfectly. From a cabinet overhead, she grabbed a small bag of pretzels, crushed them in her palm, and sprinkled the pieces over the frothy creation.

The sweet, the tart, the salty. A strange combination she loved, something that felt just right when she needed a distraction when things felt too complicated.

And for a moment, as she looked down at the bowl, everything else—even thoughts of him—faded away.

Perfect.

Leaning against the counter, she dug her spoon in and lost herself in the familiar flavors. Comfort food—her brand of therapy when life got crazy. She took another bite, letting the sweetness swirl across her tongue, hoping some semblance of clarity might come with it.

But it wasn't working. Not this time. Her thoughts kept circling back to him—his eyes, that crooked smile, the inexplicable sense of safety she felt when he was near. And yet, with that comfort came the undeniable fear, creeping in, warning her about getting too close.

She had barely managed a few more bites when she heard the light shuffle of footsteps behind her. There was no need to turn around; the voice that followed made it obvious.

"Well, well... there it is," Amy remarked. Her tone carrying a teasing edge.

Wendy kept her gaze fixed on the melting swirl in her bowl, stirring it idly. "What are you talking about?" she mumbled, though part of her already knew.

Amy gave Wendy a gentle nudge, her voice light but tinged with genuine concern. "Oh, please. Apple cider, pumpkin ice cream, and pretzels? That combo can only mean one thing."

Wendy sighed and finally looked up at her sister. "Don't start," she muttered, weary of the conversation she knew was coming.

Amy lifted her hands in a playful gesture of surrender, though her eyes sparkled with knowing amusement. "Starting something? I'm not starting anything. Just calling out the obvious." She nodded toward the mixture in Wendy's bowl. "That little concoction only shows up when your mind's spinning. So... care to share?"

Wendy fiddled with her spoon, her gaze drifting to the messy swirl of ice cream and cider. "It's nothing. I've just got too much on my plate—the festival, the store—everything feels like... too much."

Amy raised an eyebrow, folding her arms across her chest. "Right. And Luke has nothing to do with any of that, huh?"

Before Wendy could protest, Amy reached over, plucking a crushed pretzel off the top of the chaotic dessert. "Wendy, come on. We both know I'm right. When you whip this up, it's not just about the stress. Something's eating away at you." Her earlier teasing softened, concern creeping into her voice. "Is it him?"

Wendy groaned, setting the bowl down with a little too much force. "I don't know," she muttered. "I don't know if it's him, if it's me... or if it's just everything."

Amy's expression softened as she looked at her sister. "It's okay not to have all the answers, Wendy. Luke... he seems like a good guy, but that doesn't mean you need to rush into anything. Just give yourself the space to explore and enjoy it. Get to know him."

Wendy exhaled deeply, her shoulders slumping. "I know. It's just... I didn't plan for this. I didn't expect him. And now, I feel like I can't stop thinking about him. What if it's too soon? What if it's just..."

"What if it's exactly what you need?" Amy interrupted gently, her smile full of understanding.

Wendy stared at the half-melted pumpkin ice cream in front of her, the weight of her sister's words beginning to settle in.

What if?

Amy nudged her, playful yet kind. "One step at a time, Wendy. Start small. Let him in a little more, even if it's just over an apple pie. Invite him over, spend more time together. You don't have to figure it all out in one go."

Wendy snorted, but a trace of a smile tugged at her lips. As usual, Amy was right. Maybe taking a chance wasn't as terrifying as it felt.

"Maybe," Wendy mumbled, leaning back on the counter and taking another spoonful of her cider float. There was a flicker of something—hope?—in her voice. "Maybe."

Amy's grin widened, proud of her sister for even entertaining the thought. "Knew you'd come around," she said with a wink.

Leah emerged from the back room, balancing a box of apples in her arms, while Ruth trailed behind, wiping her hands on a dishtowel.

The moment Leah's eyes landed on Wendy, they went wide.

"Oh no," she said, adopting a mock-serious tone, "we've reached DEFCON One levels." Her brows shot up in dramatic exaggeration as she set the box of apples onto the counter.

Ruth, always quick to catch on, shook her head with a knowing chuckle. "Pumpkin ice cream and pretzels dunked in apple cider?" Her wrinkled face softened into a bemused smile. "Wendy Lane, I haven't seen you eat one of those odd creations since... well, let's not dig up the past."

Wendy avoided their gazes, slurping conspicuously on the last bit of her float. "It's good, okay? Just what I need right now. Don't judge."

Leah leaned an elbow on the counter, her auburn hair bouncing as she cocked her head to one side. "Mmm-hmm, sure. So good that you only break it out when you're seriously stressed." She gave Wendy a playful nudge on the shoulder. "So, is this about what—or who—I think?"

Wendy let out a frustrated huff, tossing her spoon down with a clatter. "You guys, it's just an ice cream float. Everything does not have to be about Luke."

Ruth's soft laugh echoed through the room. "Oh, honey," she said gently, "when you start mixing pumpkin ice cream with cider, it's clear something's really weighing on your mind. And from the looks of it, Luke seems to be at the center of it."

Leah crossed her arms, her smirk only deepening. She was just about to start in on her next round of teasing when the soft jingle of the bell above the door cut her off. Instinctively, all four women turned toward the entrance at the same moment, eyes landing on Luke as he stood framed in the doorway.

"Hi," he said cautiously, his gaze fixed on Wendy. "Is this a bad time?"

Leah, ever quick on her feet, shook her head, her smile growing even wider. "Oh, not at all. Perfect timing, actually."

Amy chimed in, her own smile like the Cheshire Cat's. "Hi, Luke."

Slowly, Luke stepped inside, his initial hesitance easing as his eyes swept across the room. The warm, homey scents of apple butter, cider, and candles seemed to relax him even more as he took a deeper breath. A small smile tugged at his lips. "This place always smells amazing."

But soon enough, his attention locked back onto Wendy, and something shifted in the air. His tone softened, more tentative. "I know you're busy, but I was wondering... would you like to have dinner with me at Martha's Diner?"

Wendy's world seemed to stutter in that moment. Dinner? Was he really asking her out?

"Dinner?" she echoed, her voice a touch uncertain, as if her mind was struggling to catch up. "You mean... right now?"

Luke shifted on his feet, a flicker of vulnerability crossing his face. "Yeah. I've been writing all day, and I just realized I haven't eaten since this morning." A faint chuckle escaped him. "Thought it might be nice to get out for a bit."

Wendy blinked, her mind scrambling to catch up.

Dinner?

Like, an actual date?

At Martha's?

With him?

Before she could properly react, Amy sidled up beside her, practically glowing. She looked like she had just taken home a blue ribbon from the county fair. "Oh, I'll finish closing up the store," Amy declared with a not-so-subtle grin. Without missing a beat, she turned to Leah, adding, "And so will Leah, right?"

Leah flashed a knowing smile. "Absolutely."

Wendy's pulse quickened. "Thanks, but really—"

"Oh, please," Amy cut in, placing an exaggerated hand over her heart. "Go on; don't worry about us. We've got everything covered."

Ruth, standing by with her usual calm warmth, chimed in. "Dinner? Sounds like a wonderful idea. Wendy's earned a break after today." Her gaze softened as she turned to Wendy. "Go on now. Amy and Leah can handle the paperwork."

Three pairs of female eyes were on her, all brimming with care but teaming with mischief. She was outnumbered—and knew it.

"Well..." Wendy let out a breathy laugh, tinged with both nerves and resignation. "If you're all so set on it."

Leah's face lit up, positively radiant, her excitement too infectious to ignore. Amy, of course, was smirking like a cat with a bowlful of cream, clearly reveling in her matchmaking efforts. Ruth was smiling gently, her twitching fingers betraying her inner joy at the unfolding moment.

Amy couldn't resist one last parting shot. "And don't forget to save room for dessert!"

Wendy rolled her eyes, but there was no stopping the smile curving her lips. Throwing a final glance at the women, she followed Luke to the door, her heart pounding in her chest.

Chapter 20

Luke and Wendy stepped inside the diner as the bell above the door rang out in a familiar jingle, ushering them into the warm, inviting atmosphere. A swirl of heat greeted them, banishing the cool night air left lingering on their skin.

Cutlery clinked against plates, voices hummed in casual conversation, and the steady clatter from the kitchen added to the ever-present buzz of small-town life. It was the kind of background noise that nestled into you, unassuming and comforting.

"Oh, would you look at this!" Martha's voice boomed from behind the counter before they even had a chance to sit. Her eyes twinkled with unmistakable delight as she wiped her hands on her checkered towel and rested them on her wide hips. "I was wonderin' when I'd see you two lovebirds again."

Wendy shifted, feeling a sudden rush of heat flood her cheeks. She busied herself tucking strands of wind-tousled hair behind her ear, pretending to be entirely unfazed. Luke, however, seemed more amused.

"Lovebirds?" he echoed with a chuckle as he met Martha's teasing gaze, his smile pulling at the corners of his mouth. "I'm not sure we've gotten quite that far yet, Martha. But I'll take the warm welcome."

Unabashed, Martha laughed, waving him off. "Mmm-hmm, lovebirds, good friends—whatever you young folks are calling it nowadays," she said with a wink before jerking her head toward the booths. "Go on and grab a spot. I'll be right over."

As they made their way toward an empty booth near the window, Wendy's pulse galloped beneath her skin.

Sliding into the red-vinyl seat, she pressed herself into the corner, her fingers nervously tracing invisible patterns on the varnished tabletop.

"This place..." Luke said as he glanced around, taking it all in, before letting his gaze land back on her. "It makes a person want to stay forever, doesn't it?"

Wendy followed his lead and took in their surroundings. The vinyl stools at the counter were occupied by the usual patrons, some nursing cups of coffee, others deep in conversation. The walls, adorned with framed black-and-white photos of long-forgotten festivals and hometown heroes, hadn't changed in decades. It was all so familiar, so deeply rooted in who she was.

And yet, sitting across from Luke, the diner seemed different tonight—alive with some unspoken energy she couldn't quite place.

"Yeah," she said.

Luke's warm gaze locked onto hers, and the world stilled. There was something unspoken in the way his eyes lingered on hers, something that didn't need to be put into words.

Martha bustled over, eyes twinkling, behind a playful grin. She dropped off menus with a flourish, her brows lifting in amusement as she zeroed in on the two of them. "Well now, you two behave yourselves. This booth's extra cozy feeling tonight," she teased, her voice laced with both humor and affection.

Wendy flushed immediately, heat crawling up her neck as she glanced down at the laminated menu. "We'll behave..." she muttered, the blush on her cheeks betrayed her usual composure.

Martha, never one to let a moment slip by, threw a wink at Luke. "Don't you worry," she said with a smirk, "I'll be sure to keep an eye on her."

Luke's low, easy laugh filled the space between them. "I appreciate the backup," he quipped, casting a sidelong glance at Wendy, who was now studying the menu with great intent.

Martha didn't linger long, moving away to tend to other customers in her usual, efficient manner. But when she returned moments later, it was with her notepad poised and pen at the ready. "Alright, before you two lovebirds get any cozier, what'll it be?"

"I'll have the chicken pot pie special and a glass of sweet tea," Wendy said, her voice steadier than she felt.

Comfort food—it was precisely what she needed.

Martha's eyebrow arched. "And apple pie for dessert, right?"

"Of course," Wendy answered, smiling.

Luke, matching her choice, handed Martha the menu. "Same for me, but I'll trade the sweet tea for one of your thick milkshakes. Gotta indulge a bit, right?"

Martha snorted, scribbling down the order. "Indulge away. But don't come crying to me if you leave here stuffed to the gills."

Luke leaned back, flashing a boyish grin. "I've got someone making sure I don't overdo it."

Wendy couldn't help but laugh—really laugh this time.

Martha collected their menus and stepped away. The background chatter and clinking dishes melted into mere ambiance, and the only thing that seemed to matter was the presence of the man sitting across from her.

Luke leaned forward, resting his arms on the table, his expression soft. "So," he started, his voice gentle, "you've been knee-deep in festival prep. Have you had any time to slow down and catch a breath?"

"Barely," she admitted with a half-smile. "There's so much riding on it. The entire community shows up for the festival. The income keeps the farm going through winter, so... yeah, it's a big deal."

"I've never been to an apple festival," he said. "But it sounds like something I should've gone to a long time ago."

Wendy grinned at the admission. "You're forgiven. Just don't miss this one."

Luke chuckled, leaning back against the booth's worn, red vinyl. "Noted." he teased with a playful glint in his eyes. "But seriously, what should I be ready for? What's this festival really like?"

"Well," she started, "it's more than just fun booths with people selling their handcrafted items and hayrides, you know?" Her words came to life as she vividly described the excitement to come, the way everyone from Laurel Ridge and beyond gathered to celebrate. "There's cider, warm and spiced, flowing all day long. Kids running around with sticky caramel apples in their hands, laughter mixing with music from guitars playing tunes in the barn..."

As Wendy spoke, her passion was unmistakable, a quiet fire that burned beneath every word. This wasn't just an event for her—the festival was the embodiment of everything her farm and life had worked toward. The gravity of it fueled her energy, coloring her every detail with affection. "It's my favorite time of year," she said. "It's the core event of our community. People come together for the simplest things, and that simplicity? It's why it means so much to me."

Luke leaned in, captivated by her. Watching Wendy describe the festival—her world—so openly, he couldn't help feeling drawn in by her dedication, her connection. He understood, at that moment, that this wasn't just a story, an event spun from words; it was her life. One anchored deeply in family roots, stretching toward the future with quiet determination.

"This place," Luke said. "It's opened my eyes, you know? The traditions, the way people here live—how nothing feels rushed, forced. There's a rhythm... a pace that feels undeniably real. It feels like the complete opposite of what I've known—this authenticity, this grounded sense of what matters. It's rare. And it's priceless."

Wendy hesitated and studied him for a moment before deciding to push further, her mind finally catching up to the question that had lingered ever since she'd met him.

"So..." she paused, choosing her words carefully, "why are you here, Luke? Why Laurel Ridge? Why now?" She tried to sound casual, but couldn't quite keep the hint of curiosity from sharpening her tone.

Luke held her gaze, his expression shifting, as if her question caught him somewhere deeper than he was ready for. He exhaled slowly, weighing his response, and for the briefest of moments, his usual ease seemed to fade. When he spoke again, his voice was lower, sincere.

"Why here?" He tapped his fingers lightly on the table, as though mapping out his thoughts. "I guess because I needed this place—needed somewhere quiet, away from the noise. Everywhere I've been, everything I've seen... none of it felt real anymore. I've chased success, traveled, shared my stories with the world, but after a while..." He broke off, his hazel-green eyes soft but resolute as they locked onto hers. "After a while, I realized I'd lost the ability to just be—to hear my own thoughts. To feel alive, not just busy."

Wendy studied him in silence.

Luke leaned forward, his voice quieter, more deliberate. "I came here because I needed the quiet. I wanted to be somewhere I wasn't 'Luke Carter, author,' with expectations from everyone. I just wanted to be Luke. A place where people didn't look at me like I was on display, constantly performing for an audience—or trying to live up to some impossible standard." He paused, the weight of the words settling between them. "I needed to remember what life felt like, away from all that noise."

Wendy's heart thudded softly in her chest. There was more to Luke's escape to Laurel Ridge than she originally thought. Something deeper than wanting a change of scenery or a quiet place to write.

Luke paused, weighing his next words carefully. "I've been struggling for a while, not just with my writing," he admitted softly. "But coming here—it's like things are finally starting to make sense again. I'm seeing things more clearly."

Wendy felt a flicker of curiosity swell inside her. His tone carried a weight that went beyond just writer's block or needing peace and quiet. There was something deeper there, something still untold. "Struggling?" she prompted him to continue.

Luke's gaze faltered briefly before locking onto hers again. A subtle shift in his posture betrayed the vulnerability he was working to keep in check, but when he spoke, his voice was steady. "It's difficult to talk about," he began, running a hand through his hair as if the act might steady his thoughts. "And I get that bringing up the past, especially when a guy's interested in someone like you, probably isn't the smartest move." He breathed out a small, self-deprecating laugh, then shook his head, steeling himself. "But... I need you to know that I'm not stuck. I'm not lost in any one moment or event. Still, there's a part of me that's... healing. I lost my wife two years ago. I know we talked a little about this the other night, but... well. Where do I begin?"

Luke's throat tightened as he paused, searching for the words to continue. "Her name was Sarah. We met in high school," he continued, his gaze drifting toward the window, as if the darkness outside might cushion the memory. "She... she battled cancer, and watching her fight, watching her slip away despite everything—I don't know if I'll ever find the right words to describe what that did to me. It felt like my entire world had stopped. It was suffocating."

Luke released a slow breath, searching for answers—or perhaps just for the strength to continue.

"For a long time after she passed, I felt like I wasn't really alive," Luke admitted. "I poured myself into work, into writing. Not because it helped, but because it was the only way I knew how to keep going... without completely falling apart."

Wendy's heart ached at the candid honesty in his voice. "Luke... I know this is challenging to talk about. You don't have to go into details...."

He gave her a small, tight smile, gratitude flickering in his eyes. "I appreciate that," he said. "But I've realized, especially since I came here, that I need to say it out loud—remind myself that I'm still here, that life's still going on around me. I can't keep pretending it didn't happen just because it hurts."

"Thank you for telling me, Luke," she said. The words felt simple, inadequate even, but they were all she had.

Luke leaned back, releasing a deep breath as if preparing to uncover parts of himself he wasn't used to sharing. His voice softened, laced with sincerity. "I guess what I'm trying to say is... being here, with you, has made me realize there's more to life than the grind I've been hiding behind. The work, the deadlines, always chasing the next thing—even when it stopped mattering." He paused, searching her face, then added, "You've helped me see that. That I can keep going.

That life doesn't have to stop or feel stuttered... I can build something new if I'm willing to take the chance."

Wendy's heart fluttered uneasily, the weight of his words stirring something vulnerable inside her. It was too close—too raw. Her pulse quickened.

Luke leaned forward. He rested his hand, not on hers, but close enough on the table-top that she felt warmth radiating across the polished wood between them. There was no pressure, just a quiet nearness that made her breath catch.

"I'm not asking for any promises, Wendy," he said, his eyes trained on hers, full of hope and patience. "I just want to spend time with you, get to know you, see how this plays out. No expectations. I enjoy being around you."

A flicker of a smile tugged at Wendy's lips—small, hesitant—but real. She looked at him, feeling both drawn in and uneasy. "I like being around you too, Luke." Her voice wavered, softer than she intended, but there was something knotting up inside her. "It's just..."

"Just what? Talk to me, Wendy." Luke said.

She drew in a slow, steadying breath, her eyes searching his before she spoke, her tone carefully measured. "I don't do this lightly. Relationships, opening myself up... it has to mean something. If I let someone in, I need to trust that they'll stay. I can't—won't—go through another heartache."

She hardly needed to explain the rest. Luke's life was anchored miles away, in Ohio. He'd have to leave, eventually. That was inevitable, and she wasn't about to risk her heart for someone who might not be there for the long run.

Luke listened, intent, his hazel-green eyes absorbing her words. When he spoke, it was low and earnest, the weight of his sincerity palpable. "I get it. I've asked myself the same thing: why start something that could be complicated, long-distance? But the truth is… why not? If this feels real—if what we have is worth exploring—shouldn't we at least try?"

His gaze held hers, unwavering, as he added, "And honestly… there's nothing holding me to Columbus. That house, that life—it hasn't felt like home in a long time. If there's a reason for me to stay here… I will. I want to see where this could go. And I promise,"—he paused, his words more deliberate—"you don't have to worry about me leaving. Not unless you ask me to."

"I've never had a man be this upfront and honest with me before," she confessed, her gaze fixed on Luke. "It's… strange, in a good way. Refreshing, but part of me keeps asking—are you real? This isn't just some dream, right?"

Luke met her eyes with an unwavering gaze. "I'm as real as you, Wendy. What you see is what you get. And isn't that how it should be? Between two people, I mean? Open, honest, vulnerable." He hesitated for just a moment, as if weighing the depth of what he was about to say. "I never thought I'd want something like this again after Sarah. After she passed… I convinced myself I could live the rest of my life alone. That it would be easier." His voice softened, carried by the weight of grief. "I shut myself off from even imagining what it'd feel like to care for someone again—until now."

Wendy felt her heart tighten, the strength and gentleness in his words cutting through her defenses.

"But here I am," he said firmly. "And here you are. Whatever this is… I want it to be real. I want to build something meaningful with you in it."

As his confession lingered between them, Luke glanced down at the scarred table, taking a moment to gather his thoughts. When he looked back up, there was an unmistakable tenderness in his eyes. "Wendy," his voice was careful, deliberate, "I know you've been through your own horrible times. Losing your parents... That's something that changes a person. And I can see you've endured because you're strong. Stronger than maybe you even realize."

His gaze never wavered, and Wendy felt it.

"But there's more, isn't there? Something else you've locked away. You carry a pain with you—the kind people don't bring up. Who hurt you, Wendy?" he asked.

Wendy's breath caught. She hadn't expected him to dig so deep, so quickly. She turned her face away, momentarily rattled, unable to meet those penetrating eyes of his. This was uncharted territory, a place she rarely allowed herself to go with anyone. He wasn't skirting the issue, wasn't asking her to keep things light. He was cutting directly to what she'd spent years pushing down.

"You know, it's funny," she started, while forcing herself to meet Luke's gaze. "Earlier, you mentioned how weird it can be talking about the past with someone you're just starting to get to know... and that's where I am right now. This... this isn't a conversation I have often," she admitted, tone edged with mild discomfort. "David—he's in the past. I made sure of that a long time ago. But I'll say this much—I won't let anyone hurt me the way he did ever again." Her words, though not harsh, carried the unmistakable echo of wounds that had taken time to heal over. Trust was not something she gave freely anymore.

Luke didn't flinch. His eyes remained soft, patient, like he wasn't rushing for answers, didn't expect some grand revelation. Slowly, deliberately, he placed his other hand on the table between them, palm up—a quiet, open gesture. No pressure. Just an invitation.

Wendy hesitated, her eyes shifting from his face to his hand. Something in her cracked open. She slipped her hand into his, letting the warmth of his palm wrap around hers.

"David and I were high school sweethearts," she began, her voice holding an edge of nostalgia that quickly softened into something more fragile. "We dated through junior and senior year. He was... you know, the type. The guy everyone loved—charming, funny, magnetic. People just gravitated toward him."

Her hand tensed in Luke's grasp, though her eyes didn't meet his. She was somewhere far away now, tangled in emotions she wasn't sure she wanted to revisit.

"When we graduated, I stayed here to run the farm. That's always been my dream. The dirt, the apple trees, this place—it's in my blood. My parents and then my grandma... they gave me all this. It's always been home. But David had other plans." Wendy continued, and her tone darkened, shaded by old hurt. "He wanted more. Or at least he convinced himself he did."

Luke could feel the weight of her story before she even continued, the pain rising just beneath the surface.

"He went off to college in the city," Wendy's voice trembled. "But we had plans. We were going to make it work—long-distance, visits when we could. You tell yourself it'll be okay, that you can keep holding on. But deep down, I knew..." she trailed off, letting the silence fill the space. "I knew we were slipping away."

Luke tightened his hold on her hand.

"Then, one day, during his sophomore year of college, he broke it off." Her voice flattened. "He said things had changed. That we'd grown apart. I was heartbroken, of course—crushed. But I was also clinging to something that had already slipped through my fingers. I just couldn't see it."

Luke's chest tightened. He'd been there—different circumstances, different pain—but he knew loss. He watched Wendy carefully, unwilling to interrupt but wanting her to feel his presence, his under-standing.

"Ten years later, without a word in between, he showed back up here. Out of nowhere, he came strutting onto the farm like nothing had changed. Like he hadn't walked out of my life. Told me he missed me. Missed the simplicity—this easy, laid-back life. And he acted like he was ready... ready to settle down with me."

The bitterness that colored her voice was sharp, curling out like an old, poorly healed scar.

"He thought he could waltz back into my life like nothing had changed. Like I was just sitting here waiting for him." Her throat tightened against the bitterness of the memory, but she steadied her-self. "And I fell for it. He made it seem so real, like we would have a life here together, like we were building something lasting. We even started planning our wedding. I pictured everything—working on the farm together, raising kids, growing old the way my parents never had a chance to. But David..." Her voice wavered, bitterness creeping in. "David had other plans."

Her voice hardened, sharp with the sting of betrayal. "It was all a lie. He'd been working with some sleazy real estate company behind my back, planning to sell the farm—the farm my family has worked on for generations—to the highest bidder after we were married. He called what I do here a 'dead end' lifestyle." She scoffed bitterly. "He said I was wasting my potential."

Her words cut deep, not just for Luke, but for herself. He could hear the anguish, how deep the deception had run. It wasn't just a betrayal of love, but of identity—of everything that defined who she was.

Slowly, Wendy slipped her hand from Luke's. Not to push him away, but because she needed room to breathe. She stood and paced a few steps, keeping her arms wrapped around herself as though physically bracing against the memory's cold bite. Her voice cracked around the edges as she continued. "He lied to me. Every single day, he looked me in the eye, and I never saw it. When I found the emails, I felt like such an idiot. I felt... used."

Wendy rubbed her hands along her arms, trying to shake off the lingering chill of those lies. "When I confronted him, he didn't even deny it. He thought he was doing me a favor, helping me." Her expression darkened, shadowed by the memory. "He said I'd 'come around eventually,' like the farm was nothing more than a cage keeping me from some better life he had all figured out."

Her voice faltered, the words releasing the hold betrayal still had on her. "I called off the wedding that same day and told him to get out of my life. And he did." Her breath hitched again, more hesitant this time. "But the damage was done. I trusted him more than anyone, and in the end, I was just part of a plan. A means to an end. It... broke me."

"You're not broken, Wendy," Luke said, his voice steady, deliberate.

Wendy turned back toward him, the vulnerability in her eyes raw, naked. "Not now. But I've had no choice but to guard my heart since then."

Luke gave a slow, understanding nod. "After what you went through, who wouldn't?" he said. "It makes sense. You had to protect yourself."

She studied him for a moment, her walls still hovering somewhere between up and down. Yet here, with Luke, things felt a little less threatening, a little more possible.

Wendy raised her chin, her words carrying the full weight of past promises she had made to herself, her voice firm. "I will never let anyone make me feel small or unimportant again, Luke. Never."

Chapter 21

Wendy sat on her bed, the gentle hum of the night pressing softly against the farmhouse walls. She was cocooned in her favorite quilt—the one her mother had pieced together from worn flannel shirts long before Wendy could grasp the idea of treasures passed down. Now, each faded patch and delicate stitch felt like an embrace, a tender reminder of where she'd come from.

Her eyes had long since drifted away from the book in her lap, a romance she'd picked up from The Book Nook. The pages lay open, untouched, for what felt like hours. The heroine of the story had just realized she was in love, but Wendy's thoughts were far from the printed words. Her pulse quickened, but not because of the love story on the page.

Her mind refused to settle, wandering back to dinner with Luke. The way his voice held that quiet, unshakable strength, how his gaze lingered, like she was the only presence that mattered in the room. It wasn't just the conversation that had stayed with her; it was the ease between them. Every word they traded felt like a silent vow, another step closer to truly seeing each other.

Wendy couldn't deny it anymore—it wasn't just Luke's appearance that lingered in her mind. It went deeper than that, into a space that felt both dangerous and fragile. A space he had carved out with each passing day, filling her thoughts more and more, but one so delicate she feared it might crumble if she acknowledged it too much. This wasn't safe. It wasn't smart. And it certainly hadn't been part of her life plan.

She exhaled, sinking deeper into the safety of her pillows, trying to calm the chaos swirling inside her.

A soft knock broke through her inner storm. Wendy looked up just as Amy's head peeked around the door, her eyes sparkling with a familiar mischief.

"Hey," Amy greeted, using her hip to nudge the door open as she carefully balanced two steaming mugs of tea. A playful smile tugged at her lips. "Mind if I join you?"

Wendy quickly set aside the book she hadn't really been reading, placing it on the nightstand. She managed a small smile, grateful for the distraction. "Of course. I could definitely use some girl time right now."

"You look like your thoughts are running a full marathon in your head," Amy observed, sauntering into the room. She handed Wendy a steaming mug and plopped down on the edge of the bed without waiting for an invitation. "What's going on, Wendy?"

Wendy shrugged, taking a sip of tea to avoid answering right away. The hot, sweet liquid soothed her nerves, but the heat blooming on her cheeks wasn't from the tea.

"Mmm," Amy hummed as she blew her cup before taking a sip. She scooted further back onto the bed and crossed her legs beneath her, settling in comfortably at Wendy's feet, her face bright with that all-too-familiar look of playful curiosity. "So… dinner with our local literary heartthrob went well, huh?" She raised her eyebrows, her eyes sparkling with humor.

"Oh, my goodness," she muttered, "do you ever stop?"

"Not when the material's this good.," Amy said, leaning in like she was demanding a detailed report. "Come on, spill the details. Dinner at Martha's? You know, that's a big deal worthy of small-town gossip."

Wendy sighed and leaned back against her pillows again, holding the mug close to her chest. "It was a big deal for me."

Amy wiggled her brows. "Did you kiss him? Come on, give me something!"

Wendy shot her an exasperated look, as a small laugh escaped her lips. "You're impossible."

"Yes. That is a fact," Amy chirped. "Now. Tell. Me. Everything."

Wendy hesitated, her thoughts tangled, unsure if she wanted to go there—to admit to Amy how effortlessly Luke had bypassed her emotional walls, defenses she'd spent years perfecting.

"I don't know, Amy," Wendy mumbled. "It's just… it's complicated."

Amy's playful grin dimmed at the edges, her demeanor shifting to something more sincere. "Complicated how?"

Wendy tapped her fingernails against the mug, the soft tinkling sound filling the silence as she searched for the right words, a nervous cadence to her movements. "I like him," she blurted before she could stop herself. Her voice trembled just the tiniest bit. "And that's the problem."

"Uh, I'm not seeing the problem here," Amy said, eyebrow raised. "Last I checked, liking a guy—that's, you know, a good thing? It tends to be step one."

With a frustrated exhalation, Wendy raked a hand through her hair, the weight of her emotions cresting like a wave. "You don't get it, Amy. Liking him is the problem."

Amy bit her lip but said nothing.

Wendy leaned forward, her voice spilling out in an emotional rush, like a dam on the verge of breaking. "Look at my life, Amy. I've built everything here—this town, this farm. It's what keeps me grounded; it's what I love. And then Luke... he just came into my life, out of nowhere, and hit something deep. Like this force, I didn't even know I was waiting for. And as crazy as it sounds, I don't want to ignore it anymore."

Amy raised an eyebrow, her expression skeptical but curious. "Well, he's kind of difficult to ignore. So, what you're saying is he's different?"

Wendy exhaled, her gaze distant. "Yeah, he is different. Tonight wasn't just small talk or playful banter. We got real, Amy. Like, the kind of honest conversations where you lay everything out. No pretending, no hiding behind polite words."

Amy's lips curved into a half-smile, her intrigue growing. "That sounds serious. So what's got you all knotted up then? You know you can tell me."

Wendy hesitated, her eyes drifting toward the window, searching for some kind of clarity outside in the orchard. "It's this place, Amy... it's my entire world. The farm, our family history—it's everything. I'm not leaving that behind. But Luke... he has a life back in Ohio. Everything he's built is there." She paused, her hands tightening in her lap. "He told me tonight that Columbus means nothing to him anymore. That if this—whatever this is between us—means something, he'd stay. And I keep wondering... why? How can I believe that? No one just walks away from their entire life."

Amy blinked in surprise. "Are you sure about that?"

Wendy raised her eyebrows, crossing her arms defensively. "Of course, I'm sure. He's a bestselling author with deadlines, contracts, fancy publishers breathing down his neck. Why would he stay here in this sleepy little town? How could I ever compete with a life like that?"

There it was. The truth, out in the open.

Wendy wasn't sure if she felt better or worse having said it, though. It was a bitter piece of reality that stung every time she thought about it.

Amy, on the other hand, didn't seem the least bit shaken. "Okay, first off, I wasn't aware your self-esteem is living out a solid decade behind where it should be."

Wendy glared at her with frustration.

"I'm serious, Wendy," Amy said, uncrossing her legs. "You need to stop seeing yourself as just some small-town farm girl. You're not 'just' anything. You've built this remarkable life for yourself, and this farm wouldn't be what it is today without you."

Wendy's eyes fell to the floor, her chest tightening. She knew her sister was right.

Amy reached over and squeezed Wendy's knee. "And don't act like Luke hasn't noticed how amazing you are. You know he has. You're not competing with his life somewhere else—you're offering him something different. Something new. Something with you."

Wendy swallowed hard, trying to push down the emotions clawing their way up her throat.

"You're the strongest, most selfless person I know. And if Luke doesn't see that? Then he's a fool." Amy shook her head, her voice filled with conviction. "What if he stays? What if he wants to see where things go with you?"

Wendy's voice came out barely above a whisper. "And what if he doesn't stay, Amy?"

Amy nodded, her expression softening with understanding. "I know, Wendy. David really hurt you, and I'm so sorry you had to go through that."

She shifted closer on the bed, her arms gently wrapping around her sister's shoulders.

"You've lost so much in your life," Amy continued, her voice calm but full of empathy. "I know how hard it's been for you—how hard you've fought to keep everything together, to hold on to the things that matter."

Amy had always admired Wendy's strength, a strength she knew her sister had built out of necessity, not choice. But behind that tough exterior, there were fragile, hidden parts of Wendy's heart—bruised pieces locked away behind walls of solitude and years of enduring loss.

A long silence stretched between them before Amy spoke again, her words gentle yet filled with conviction. "I get that it's scary. You've built these walls...these defenses...because you're terrified of losing someone else... and I can't blame you for that. But Wendy, you can't hide from love and still expect it to find you."

She took Wendy's hand in hers, squeezing it tightly. "I don't know what's going to happen between you and Luke. I'm not going to pretend I've got this love thing all figured out, or that I have the right answers for you. But if you keep waiting for everything to be perfect—for some guarantee that you won't ever get hurt—you'll end up waiting for something that doesn't exist. Love doesn't work like that."

Wendy sat in silence, staring at the gentle tendrils of steam rising from her cup of tea, lost in thought.

"Wendy, I'm sorry to say this, but I believe you've convinced yourself that you don't deserve love. You've told yourself that the farm is all you're meant to have, and nothing more."

The words hit her like a blow, stealing her breath. Was it true? Had all those years of throwing herself into the orchard, into the land, been less about passion and more about building walls to keep love out? Had she truly convinced herself that she wasn't worthy?

"You're a good person, Wendy. Maybe Luke doesn't need someone from the big city. Maybe he needs someone exactly like you," Amy said.

Wendy swallowed, her chest loosening ever so slightly as Amy's words sank in. She was so different from what Luke was used to—her life here was small and simple compared to the bright, fast-paced world he came from.

Amy gave Wendy's shoulder a gentle, reassuring squeeze. "Look, it won't hurt to see where this leads. Maybe it works out, maybe it doesn't. But... don't you at least want to try?"

"I don't know if I'm brave enough," she admitted.

"You don't have to be brave all at once," Amy said. "It's just one step at a time. And who knows," she added with a mischievous grin, "Luke might be more terrified than you."

"I doubt that," Wendy said, the corners of her lips pulling into a smile, "but I guess anything's possible."

Chapter 22

Wendy wiped the sweat from her brow and glanced toward the small pile of pumpkins gathered in the pickup's bed. A weary sigh escaped her lips.

"How many kids are supposed to come tonight?" Amy asked, brushing dirt from her hands as she surveyed the field.

"Pastor Andrew said there would probably be 15 kids and maybe a few of their parents. Plus, we might as well pick a few more while we're out here for the store." Wendy said as she glanced around the vast pumpkin patch, ripe with a sea of plump, orange globes.

"Fifteen, huh? I think the kids will have fun with these this evening." Amy remarked, crossing her arms with a sly grin. "I can practically feel the gears turning in that head of yours, Wendy. What's up?"

Wendy sighed, wiping a hand across her forehead, and leaned on the side of the pickup. She knew Amy could read her like a book, and there was no sense in pretending otherwise.

"Same old, same old." Wendy muttered, reaching for another pumpkin. "I'm just thinking about... well, everything."

Amy raised her eyebrows. "Everything meaning Luke? Or everything meaning the festival, the pumpkins, the farm? Come on, Wendy, I know that look. Spit it out."

"It's just... everything with Luke has gotten into my head, front and center? It's distracting," Wendy said.

"Distracting? No. It's your brain telling you what's most important. So quit fighting it, step up and be the strong woman I know."

Wendy shot her sister a glance. "You are so blunt sometimes."

"Hey, I'm just your friendly local truth-teller," Amy shrugged.

Wendy glanced across the field, towards the barn, looking for something to focus on that wasn't the bright, glaring eyes of her little sister.

"Speak of the devil—or rather, the... handsome writer." Amy said with a chuckle.

Wendy turned her head, and sure enough, there he was, sauntering down the gravel road toward them.

Luke wore a flannel shirt, unbuttoned over a plain white tee, and his jeans had that lived-in, effortless softness that only came from years of wear. His chestnut hair, tousled just enough to look intentionally carefree. The sight of him, backlit by the evening light, was almost unfair—disarmingly handsome in a way that made it difficult to look away. And that crooked smile of his didn't help matters.

"Hey," he called out, voice warm and familiar as he strolled over. "Thought I'd take a break from staring at a Word document. Saw you two down here and figured I'd offer a hand."

Amy exchanged a knowing glance with Wendy, a mischievous grin tugging at her lips. "Well, isn't this perfect timing? Wendy was just saying how much we could use some extra help."

Wendy wiped her hands on her jeans, arching a skeptical brow in Luke's direction. "You sure about that? This isn't pretty work. You'll be covered in dirt before you know it, and that shirt of yours might not survive the day."

Luke laughed as he casually shrugged. "A little dirt won't kill me. Besides, staring at a blank screen wasn't doing much for my creativity. Maybe some farm work's exactly what I need to get the ideas flowing."

His simple grin tugged at Wendy's resolve, and despite herself, she grinned. "All right, but don't say I didn't warn you. Farm life isn't as laid-back and easy as it seems."

Luke winked. "I like a challenge."

"All right, then." She bent down, sliced another pumpkin clean from the vine, and handed it to him with a smile.

Luke accepted the pumpkin with ease, placing it in the truck bed. "Are these for the festival?"

"No, these are for the youth group this evening," Wendy said. "They'll be painting them, and while they wait for everything to dry, they'll enjoy a Bible study right here on the farm. It's always a fun event. The kids really get into it, and it's a nice way to mix a creative activity with a little bit of reflection."

Luke raised an eyebrow, his expression playful. "Oh, pumpkin painting? Count me in. My artistic abilities with a brush have definitely been underutilized."

Wendy folded her arms, half-grinning. "You? Paint?"

"We all have hidden talents, Wendy," Luke said with mock seriousness.

Amy leaned on the truck bed, placing her chin in her hands. "Well now, this just keeps getting better. Luke painting pumpkins. This I've gotta see."

Luke latched onto Amy's tone of playful banter. "Hey, don't underestimate me. I might surprise you."

After the final pumpkin was secured, Amy spread her arms out dramatically, as if she were leading an orchestra. "Alright... to the picnic tables!" she announced, her voice full of excitement.

With a quick leap, she slid into the driver's seat, while Luke and Wendy clambered into the truck bed to sit among the pumpkins.

When they reached the pavilion behind the store, Amy parked the truck, swiftly turned off the engine, and hopped out with her usual lively energy, her smile as bright as ever.

The picnic tables were already prepped, each draped in plastic. Paints, brushes, glue, glitter, and aprons were laid out in anticipation.

As the youth group spilled out of cars and gathered around in clusters, their chatter filled the air. Wendy couldn't help but smile as she watched them approach. Wide-eyed kids ready to take on the world, or in this case, turn pumpkins into masterpieces.

One particular boy, around ten years old, shuffled up to the tables, looking intently at the pumpkins like they were serious competition. His eyes narrowed in concentration, and Wendy suppressed a laugh. This was a battlefield, and he clearly wasn't here to mess around.

Just as the excitement around the tables began to bubble over, Pastor Andrew, the youth pastor at Laurel Ridge Community Church, came strolling up with his usual pleasant smile and an easy wave.

"Thank you so much for having us out at the farm, Wendy," Pastor Andrew greeted. "It's a real treat to be out here in this beautiful setting—and I'm sure these kids are ready to dive headfirst into some creative chaos."

Wendy shook his hand and flashed a warm smile. "Well, they're in the perfect place for it," she said with a chuckle. "They're going to have plenty of time to let those imaginations run wild."

The pastor gave her a knowing nod before turning toward the gathered kids, rubbing his hands together with a grin. "Alright, gang! Pick your pumpkins, grab some brushes, and let's make art!"

The kids erupted into a flurry of excitement, scrambling to claim their pumpkins as though they were treasure. Some dove in headfirst, splashing different colors together like mini Picassos. Others were a bit more careful, holding their brushes in midair with the seriousness of seasoned artists contemplating their next stroke.

Wendy stepped back and noticed Luke already helping a few of the kids sort through their paint supplies, chatting with them like he'd been doing this forever. His relaxed presence blended with the energy of the moment, and she couldn't help but marvel at how naturally he fit in.

A young boy with sandy-brown hair was sitting with his arms folded in frustration beside Luke, staring down at his pumpkin with an unenthusiastic sigh.

Luke arched his brow. "What's the matter, buddy?"

"My pumpkin is boring," the boy said, scrunching his nose. "Everyone else has better ideas."

Luke folded his arms, standing over the boy in mock seriousness, as though assessing the pumpkin's creative potential. "Hmm... Better ideas, huh? How about an alien?"

"An alien?" the boy's eyes gleamed with interest.

"Yup," Luke replied, bending down to level with him. "You know, with antennae and googly eyes. Oh, and maybe some goofy teeth."

Wendy leaned against the table, smiling at the exchange.

The boy grinned, grabbing a paintbrush. "I think I can make an alien pumpkin."

Wendy spotted Amy already up to her usual antics—allowing one of the younger girls to "accidentally" paint a streak of orange across her arm instead of the pumpkin. Their laughter was contagious, and Wendy joined in as she moved from table to table.

When she glanced over her shoulder at Luke. He was surrounded by kids, helping another with a tricky design.

Maybe Amy was right. Maybe he could fit into her world.

***

After the final touches were added to their pumpkins, Pastor Andrew called the group to gather on the lawn nearby. The kids, some still sticky with paint and glitter, shuffled into a circle, settling in as the day slipped into dusk. Above them, the sky blazed with the final hues of sunset, soft oranges, deep purples, and pinks. The cool night air brought with it a sense of calm, as if nature itself was leaning in, ready to listen.

Pastor Andrew stood at the center of the circle, his Bible resting in his hands.

"All right, kids," Pastor Andrew said, his voice calm and steady as the breeze ruffled the surrounding trees. "Let's be still for a moment. I want to share a piece of scripture with you tonight. It's something simple, but really important."

The kids, still buzzing with creative energy from earlier, began to quiet down.

"Tonight," Andrew continued, "we're going to focus on something we all need—a reminder of why we come together and set aside time like this. Proverbs 27:17 says, 'As iron sharpens iron, so one person sharpens another.'"

He paused, letting the words settle. "What we're doing tonight isn't just about painting pumpkins or having fun. It's about something bigger. It's about helping each other grow stronger and become the people God wants us to be."

As Andrew spoke, Wendy felt the significance of the moment deepen. She glanced at Luke, who sat quietly beside her on the tailgate of the truck, his attention fixed on the youth pastor's words just as much as the children's. But there was something more—a weight in his expression, like someone poised on the edge of a revelation.

The way his fingers flexed against the tailgate drew her in, as though the message had stirred something buried, something raw and unspoken.

Sensing her gaze, Luke turned and met her eyes, a quiet understanding passing between them. Without hesitation, he reached for her hand, his fingers intertwining with hers—his touch warm, grounding, and full of unspoken meaning. Something in that simple act felt like a promise, one that wasn't rushed or demanding, but patient and steady—as if whatever burdens they carried had become just a little lighter.

Pastor Andrew continued, his voice filled with meaning but still gentle. "It's easy to get wrapped up in our daily routines—school, chores, homework—and sometimes forget about moments like this, where we slow down and spend time together. While we're here tonight, painting pumpkins and laughing with friends, we're reminded of how important the people around us are. We're meant to share life together, not just go through it alone."

The rustling leaves blended with his words, creating a peaceful backdrop. "The Bible tells us that God wants us to grow, not just by ourselves, but with one another. We're here to help each other, to share our worries and our joys. This," he said, motioning to the group, and the pumpkins scattered around, "this is what it looks like when people come together. It might seem simple, but it's also really special."

He closed his Bible and smiled at the kids. "God's love is in these moments—moments where we gather, create, laugh, and support one another. We're all part of something bigger, and we grow stronger when we remember that. Now, let's take another look at those pumpkins."

The kids burst into excited chatter, each eagerly showing off their creations with a mix of pride and laughter. There were pumpkins with wobbly googly eyes, haphazard streaks of glitter, and eccentric designs that defied any traditional harvest imagery—and that made them all the more delightful.

Amy, never one to waste an opportunity for fun, seized the moment. Draping an imaginary scarf around her shoulders like a seasoned art critic, she proceeded to pace dramatically around the tables. With exaggerated gestures and a faux-posh accent, she delivered grandiose appraisals.

"My, my! What vision! Such bold use of glitter here!" she exclaimed, leaning close to examine one wild creation before widening her eyes and gasping. "A pumpkin Picasso in the making, no doubt!"

Her over-the-top praise, paired with her serious expression, sent the kids into fits of laughter. Even Wendy couldn't suppress a grin as Amy continued her ridiculous reviews, lifting a pumpkin as if it were a fine sculpture in a museum.

Not to be outdone, Luke joined in the antics. Placing his hands on his hips, he assessed an especially chaotic creation—a lopsided pumpkin with neon green splatters and pipe-cleaner antennae. He cleared his throat, putting on his best authoritative tone. "Ladies and gentlemen, I present to you... the illustrious recipient of the Intergalactic Design Award! For sheer creativity and bravery in pushing pumpkin art to daring new heights." He lifted the pumpkin high like it was a cherished trophy, earning hoots of laughter from the kids.

It didn't take long for the entire group to be caught up in the joyful momentum, giggling at their works of art as they bantered back and forth. Wendy's heart warmed as she watched their excitement. Laughter echoed through the air, knitting them all together in the simple joy of the moment.

"Well," Amy said with a grin, sidling up to Wendy, "looks like our boy Luke is fitting in just fine."

"Are you shocked?"

"Nope."

Wendy laughed before turning back toward the table, where Luke had just put the finishing touches on his own masterpiece. The pumpkin now sported an absurdly large and somehow endearing smiley face, complete with crooked eyes and a heavy coating of glitter.

"What exactly is that?" Wendy asked, folding her arms and raising an eyebrow as she walked his way.

Luke stepped back, appraising his pumpkin with mock seriousness. "I like to think I'm pushing the boundaries of pumpkin art. You're welcome to challenge it, but I have a feeling this one's a winner."

"Pushing boundaries? It looks like you poured glitter on that thing and called it a day," she teased, her heart doing a strange little flip at the smile now playing on his lips.

Luke stepped closer, his eyes locking on hers. "Be honest. It's at least a little impressive, right?"

Wendy scoffed, but couldn't hide her smile. "It's... well. Something, all right."

They stood there, the sound of the kids' chatter becoming distant background noise. Their eyes lingered a moment.

"You did good tonight, Luke," Wendy said.

"Truth is, Wendy, being around you... It's good for me. More than you know."

Chapter 23

Luke stared at the blinking cursor on his laptop screen, a familiar sensation spreading through his chest—a mix of relief and excitement. He leaned back in the creaky wooden chair and stretched his arms above his head.

Words had flowed easily today, the story rushing out of him like water from a long-clogged faucet. Whatever barrier he had been slamming his head against for the last several months had cracked wide open, and now it was all just... there. Pouring out.

It wasn't just the peace of Laurel Ridge, the silence of the cabin, or the stunning scenery and small-town rhythm that had fueled this. It was Wendy.

She always seemed to creep into his thoughts when he least expected it. He hadn't meant to think about her so much today, but there she was between the lines of dialogue, the warmth of her smile sneaking into the creases of his characters. Whether it was her laugh, that easy, open sound, or the way her hair would come loose from her ponytail by mid-afternoon—dangling strands that framed her face in a way that made her look carefree.

Wendy grounded him.

Balanced him in a way that made sense, even if he couldn't quite explain how.

Luke glanced at the clock on the mantle. Almost six. Maybe he would take a walk out to the orchard again, let the crisp air clear his head before tackling his book once more.

But before he could push away from his desk, his phone buzzed to life on the edge of the table. The screen lit up with Bill's name and picture.

Luke chuckled as he swiped to answer. "What's up, Bill? You're not about to give me another lecture on enjoying my rural sabbatical, are you?"

"Hey, I would never lecture." Bill's voice held his usual sarcastic charm. "Just calling to make sure you haven't gone full mountain man on me yet. I can totally picture you in flannel, slaying that cabin-Timberland-boot Instagram aesthetic. All manly, chopping wood, and—let me guess—writing a new bestseller by the fire?"

Luke smirked, leaning back in his chair. "I'm not that predictable." He paused, his lips quirking as a laugh threatened to escape. "Okay, fine. Maybe I have worn some flannel. But I'm still fully shaved, at least most days, thank you very much."

"Ah, shaving too? You've gone soft on me, Carter. And here I thought you'd emerge from the wilderness with a beard full of wisdom and a completed manuscript."

"Well, I can't give you the full mountain-man look," Luke said, a glint of humor in his voice. "But as for the manuscript... I'm making progress. Today was a good day."

"Yeah?" Bill's tone shifted, the usual teasing taking a back seat. "How good are we talking? Words flowing like a tap turned loose? Or more like a slow drip?"

Luke glanced at the jumble of papers stacked on his desk, proof of his productive day. "We're talking flowing. I got about ten chapters down since noon. I haven't had a day like this in—well, let's just say this retreat is doing its job."

"I knew it," Bill replied, smug pleasure dripping from his words. "I told you, didn't I? There's just something about escaping the noise, trimming down all the distractions. Next, you'll be swapping your laptop for a typewriter and really getting in touch with nature."

"Easy there," Luke warned, though he couldn't suppress the laugh. "I'm not quite ready for the full Hemingway aesthetic yet."

"I'm telling you, man. This book's gonna be your best one yet. I can feel it. Not just because of what I've read so far, either," Bill continued, his voice calmer now, more thoughtful. "It sounds like you're living again, Luke. Really living."

Luke let Bill's words settle for a moment, his gaze drifting out the window to where the orchard's treetops brushed the edge of the horizon. Living. Not just pushing through each day, not just filling hours with obligations or deadlines, but actually letting himself breathe, letting himself want things again.

"I guess so," Luke admitted. "I'm figuring some things out."

"Yeah?" Bill's voice held no judgment, just curiosity. "Work things? Or life things?"

"Both, I guess."

Silence stretched over the line for a moment before Bill broke it, humor creeping back into his tone. "Okay, full disclosure—how much of this is small-town good vibes and how much is a certain someone by the name of Wendy?"

"I knew you'd bring her up." Luke said.

"Come on!" Bill's laugh floated through the phone. "You can't expect me to resist this kind of material. I mean, a reclusive, brooding writer goes off the grid, well almost, and meets a small-town farm girl who's, what, half sunshine, half spitfire?"

"Bill—" Luke started, but he couldn't help the smile spreading across his face.

"I'm serious! This is straight out of one of those romance novels you used to make fun of. Next, you'll be telling me you're gonna save the farm from foreclosure or something."

Luke shook his head, still grinning. "First, the farm is doing just fine, from what I can tell. And second, it's not like that."

Luke was silent for a few seconds.

"I don't know what's going to happen between Wendy and I," Luke admitted. "I'm not even sure if I want to think too deeply about it. I'm just wanting to let whatever happens, happen."

"Just live life and enjoy the ride," Bill said.

He had a point, and Luke knew it. He didn't have to overthink where everything was headed, didn't have to map out the future of his relationship with Wendy.

"Thanks, Bill," Luke said, genuine appreciation settling into his tone. "I mean it. I needed a push these past few days...well, months really, and a listening ear. And you're always there for me."

"Always here to push, my friend. Now go live life, but don't forget to get that novel done somewhere in between." Bill said.

Luke chuckled. "Yeah, yeah. Talk to you later."

As he stood up from the chair, he glimpsed movement outside the cabin window.

There was Wendy. Golf cart bumping its way down the gravel road toward him, her hair blowing in the breeze as the little machine jostled over the uneven terrain.

Luke felt a familiar tug in his chest again. The same tug that happened every time he saw her. Her smile was welcome after the long day, and as she parked her cart and hopped down with practiced ease, Luke stepped out onto the porch.

"Fancy meeting you out here," he said.

Wendy grinned.

"To what do I owe the honor? Need more hands for pumpkin picking or something?"

Wendy shook her head, but her teasing smile held. "Maybe tomorrow. Right now, I've got a better idea."

"For?"

She gave him a wink. "Ice cream. Homemade. Grandma's been at it in the kitchen again, so I thought maybe you could use a break from all that writing genius and come enjoy something sweet."

Luke's stomach growled in response, and his lips curved into a grateful smile. Something sweet after a day of writing sounded beyond perfect.

"My hero," he joked, pushing away from the railing. "Lead the way, Miss Lane."

Chapter 24

"This... this is something else," Luke said, his voice muffled as he took another blissful bite. Creamy vanilla blossomed on his tongue, followed by chunks of delectable peach, both sweet and tart, that dissolved into pure heaven. "I'm not even sure I have the right words."

"You're a writer," Amy piped up from her spot across the porch. "If you're at a loss, imagine how the rest of us function."

The group erupted into laughter, joining in on her playful jab. Luke chuckled, shaking his head as he scooped more ice cream into his mouth with exaggerated delight.

"I'm serious. This is the best ice cream I have ever eaten in my life. Is this what you've been hiding from us city folk all along? I might have to move here just for the ice cream."

Ruth, seated in the chair beside him with a satisfied smile on her face, waved a casual hand in mock modesty. "This recipe's been in my family for generations. We had little growing up, but what we lacked in wealth, we made up for in dessert. It's our duty to fatten the ones we love."

Martha chimed in, grinning. "Although, don't get too comfortable—churning ice cream has a price. Next time, we'll make you work for it. Heaven knows, you city boys could use a good workout now and then."

Heads bobbed in agreement as the porch rang with more laughter.

Luke held up his hands in surrender. "Okay, okay, fair enough. You show me how, and I'll churn as much ice cream as you want."

Wendy, seated on the lower step with her bowl balanced on her knees, shot him a teasing smile. "You'll be a man of many talents, Luke. Soon you'll have ice cream making to add to your list, but let's not forget about farming. I need to get you out in the orchard and put you through farmhand boot camp."

Amy snorted around a spoonful of ice cream. "Oh, he wouldn't survive. Your boot camps have been known to break lesser men."

Luke shot a sideways glance at them, playing along. "You're talking to a guy who's survived book deadlines, reviews from people who didn't even bother reading the entire book, and once—believe it or not—a full-on blizzard in upstate New York during a book signing. I like to think that counts for something."

"Oh, sure." Amy waved him off. "Wendy, mark him down as Farmhand Material of the Year. We just found ourselves a keeper."

Wendy rolled her eyes, but her smile stayed in place as she scooped another bite of ice cream. "You're ridiculous, Amy."

"She's got a point, though," Martha said, raising her own spoon as if to make a serious point. "There's something to be said for a man who's willing to stick it out, even when things get messy. Just like ice cream making, come to think of it. You never know who's really up for the job until the churn breaks down halfway through."

Ruth hummed her agreement. "That's right. Had a neighbor back when I was first married who thought she was clever with her brand-new electric churn. Told me it was the answer to everyone's problems. Well, wouldn't you know it? Two minutes in—and the kitchen lights flickered, she screamed, and we almost had to call out the fire department. That's why I stick to the old ways."

More laughter ensued, so infectious that even Luke couldn't hold back. His shoulders shook, his bowl tipping in his hands before he caught himself and set it down on the porch.

Luke's gaze drifted toward Wendy. She grinned up at Ruth with that touch of childlike affection—the kind that made it clear she'd grown up wrapped in genuine love. He realized how much history there was between these people. He had barely scratched the surface of it.

Ruth's gentle laugh brought him back. "Oh, I suppose making ice cream is part of being a good grandmother. And it always amused me how little Amy would sneak behind Wendy's back and steal half of her bowl after emptying her own."

Amy had no shame. "What can I say? I had a weakness for your ice cream. Still do, come to think of it."

"I think I understand why you all turned out so well. Must be the ice cream," Luke said.

"And the faith," Martha added, slicing a glance toward Luke, winking just as she finished her bowl. "But yeah, mostly the ice cream."

Another round of chuckles circled the porch—a merry blend of voices drifting along with the falling night. Conversation dipped in and out of easy, familiar rhythms and light teasing. Each playful jab, each smile, felt effortless. It all made Luke feel... welcome.

No, more than that, Luke thought, watching Wendy as she laughed at something Amy had said. This feels like home.

Every day here seemed to pull him in a little further, wrapping him tighter in its embrace—even though it wasn't his town, his farm, or his life. The sense of belonging had been creeping up on him since he arrived. The shared laughter, the comforting rhythm of the days, each casual conversation, from something as small as pumpkin picking to something as sweet and simple as homemade ice cream. All of it felt like it was leaving a deeper mark on him than he'd expected. Like this place, these people were becoming a part of him.

"You look like you're a million miles away," Wendy commented. He hadn't even realized she'd moved closer. "Still deciding how to win farmhand boot camp?"

Luke shook his head, smiling. "Nah. I think I'm ready for whatever your boot camp throws at me. Mentally, at least."

She gave him a skeptical look. "You sound confident."

"Confidence is key," he replied, his voice casual, but something in his gaze softened as it stayed on her. "Besides, if it involves being around here—with you... I think I'm up for it."

Wendy flushed, trying to ignore the tiny flutter that ignited in her chest. She shifted her focus to the porch railing instead. "We'll have to see if you make it through the festival first."

He chuckled. "Challenge accepted."

Ruth, who had overheard the exchange, leaned forward in her chair, a glint of mischief in her eyes. "If you survive the festival, you'll really be part of the family."

Amy grinned. "Definitely. If you help this coming Saturday and survive, we'll get someone to print you up a little 'Honorary Lane Family' certificate. Framed and everything."

Luke pretended to consider it, leaning back in his chair. "And here I thought there were more hoops to jump through."

"Oh, there are," Martha chimed in, inspecting her nails as if it were the most serious matter to discuss. "Can't hand out titles too freely, ya know."

Luke raised an eyebrow. "And what's the next duty?"

Before anyone could respond, Ruth cut in, "Now, don't be asking questions like that. We don't want to scare you off."

As another round of laughter filled the air, Luke could picture himself spending more evenings just like this, surrounded by good people and laughter. He soaked it in; the sound wrapping him in a sense of comfort that felt deeper than just a fun evening. He wasn't just an observer on the outside, but part of something—a shared connection, a lighthearted closeness he'd been craving.

As he glanced at each face, from Ruth's knowing smile to Amy's teasing grin, the thought struck him almost unexpectedly: I could get used to this. Spending quiet nights on the porch, surrounded by caring, genuine people, their laughter lifting the weight of the world from his shoulders—it felt like something out of a simpler, happier time, free from the pressures that had been hounding him for years.

And then, as his gaze settled on Wendy, sitting there with her head tilted as she laughed at something her sister said, the feeling deepened. It wasn't just the town or the sense of belonging that was nudging its way into his heart. It was her. The way her presence seemed to ground him, to draw him out of his own insecurities, and make him believe that a life like this could be his.

Could this be home?

Was it the simplicity? The family feeling? Or Wendy, sitting there with her quiet warmth?

Maybe a little of everything.

Chapter 25

Wendy took a step back, hands on her hips, and surveyed the autumn display she'd been perfecting all morning in front of The Farmstead Store. The bales of hay stacked behind pumpkins and multicolored gourds formed a patchwork of color—burnt orange, pale green, buttery yellow—each one nestled precisely into the lay-out she'd envisioned. Around them, bundles of cornstalks rustled in the breeze, their dried leaves adding a golden warmth that practically smelled of fall.

She felt a flutter of pride as she took it all in—the mums she'd layered in bright hues of purple, crimson, and gold felt like little fireworks against the backdrop of hay. The pair of scarecrows stood on either side of her creation, their straw-stuffed arms hanging at crooked angles, as if they had some secret to share whenever the wind picked up.

Wendy swiped the back of her hand across her forehead, brushing aside a rebellious strand of hair that had slipped out of her ponytail. From this angle, it felt right, more than she'd hoped after such a hectic week of festival prep. Even so, tension nagged at the back of her mind. Would it be enough? Had she missed some detail, forgotten something critical in the chaos of it all? Managing everything—the farm, the store, the festival—sometimes felt like trying to juggle too many fragile things, each one threatening to crash if she wasn't careful.

The rhythmic crunch of gravel met her ears before she saw the truck rounding the bend. Luke's red pickup pulled to a stop nearby with a soft rumble.

Luke stepped out, his effortless smile already curling at the corner of his mouth, and for a moment Wendy felt her heart flutter in response. She tried to ignore it, but it was a losing battle. His worn jeans and unbuttoned flannel set against a simple tee gave him the most casual look—rugged, yet magnetic, without even seeming to try. He had an ease about him, something she envied in moments like this, moments where her worries clung too tightly.

"Well, look at this." His voice, with that teasing warmth, slipped around her like the comfort of flannel on a chilly evening. He gestured at her display like an admiring art critic. "I'm sensing a theme here. Something to do with pumpkins?"

Wendy laughed, feeling her shoulders relax. "Just trying to give a proper welcome for everyone coming to the farm this weekend."

Luke cocked an eyebrow, stepping closer. "Impressive. I'd say this display has apple festival queen written all over it." He lifted a hand, showing the brown paper bag he'd been holding. "But before you're crowned with all the glory, I come bearing something far more important—lunch."

Her stomach betrayed her first, growling in response before she could think of anything clever to say. Luke's smile widened, and Wendy could see the slightest hint of satisfaction in his eyes.

"I didn't ask for—"

"I know," Luke interrupted, waving off her protest with a flick of his hand. "But I'm also guessing you haven't thought about it yet. And I'm willing to bet you probably skipped breakfast, too."

He was right, of course. And while Wendy would have usually kept on working, ignoring her hunger, something about the soft, familiar challenge in his smile made her stop.

She sighed with a little shake of her head. "Okay, maybe you've got me there."

Luke stepped a little closer, eyes glinting with teasing warmth. "So? Lunch? Strictly picnic-table style. Completely harmless. Promise."

Wendy bit back her smile, and tried to resist the way her heart warmed at his offer. There was no reason to keep denying what was right in front of her, especially when she'd been looking forward to these lunches, these moments of shared company, more than she cared to admit. Not long ago, she would've brushed him off, told herself there wasn't time for things like this. But everything felt different with Luke around. His presence was this steady, surprising rhythm that cut through the weight of her responsibilities, making her realize just how much she missed being carefree.

"Alright," she said, with a mock sigh of defeat. "You wore me down. Let's see what kind of fancy meal Martha packed this time."

Luke's eyes sparkled with a triumph that made her blush as she wiped her hands on her jeans. It felt like more than just a casual lunch, but Wendy decided not to dwell on what more might mean.

"Follow me," he said, gesturing toward the rows of picnic tables like he was a tour guide leading her through a five-star dining experience. They walked down the gravel path to the open-air pavilion behind the store, a small breeze rolling through the orchard.

Luke sat the bag down and began unpacking it with a deliberation that was far too dramatic for sandwiches. "Today's special: turkey sandwiches with cranberry mayo, coleslaw, and—wait for it—caramel apple bars for dessert." His attempt at sounding nonchalant didn't hide the quiet delight he seemed to take in this.

Wendy sat back as he arranged the containers, flashing her a grin before sliding a sandwich toward her.

Wendy took that first bite, the tart cranberry mixing with savory turkey in a way that lit up her taste buds. She let out an unfiltered groan of contentment that had Luke looking at her with appreciation.

"If you keep bringing me food this good," she said, half-joking, "I might have to nominate you as the true MVP of this year's festival." She wiped the crumbs from her lips, unable to keep the smile from her face.

Luke gave her a playful nod, looking all too proud of himself. "I'll add that to my list of growing festival accomplishments," he said.

As they settled into quiet companionship, Wendy found herself soaking it all in more than words could convey. It was easy being with him. He didn't force conversation. He didn't need to. Just sitting there, sharing food with him, felt like a break she didn't realize she'd been craving for so long. She kept catching his gaze from the corner of her eye, though—like he was studying her, wondering what she was thinking.

After a moment, Luke broke the silence, lifting his sandwich in mock seriousness. "So, what's next on your festival prep-to-do list? Everything set, or have you hit full panic mode yet?"

Wendy grinned. "I like to stay organized, thank you. It makes things run smoother."

"Organized?" Luke raised an eyebrow, amused. "You are way more than organized. You're practically a walking efficiency machine."

She laughed then, fully and unabashedly. "And what about you?" Wendy shot back, curious. "You've been wielding that laptop like it's a sword all week. How's the writing?"

For a moment, Luke's expression shifted. The lightness in his smile dimmed just a little, and there was something more vulnerable lurking behind his hazel-green eyes. Wendy noticed the way his shoulders tensed ever so slightly.

"Better. A lot better, actually," he admitted, but there was no celebration in his voice. "I've written more in the last week than I have in months."

Wendy, ever perceptive, frowned. "That sounds like progress. So, why doesn't it feel like it?"

Luke let out a long breath, setting his sandwich down as if concentrating on something invisible just beyond reach. "Writing... it's complicated," he said, as if he were only just unraveling his own thoughts. "It used to be an escape, you know? My way of finding something bigger. College, family... life. The stories gave me something else, a place to go when everything felt too messy."

He paused, gaze drifting out toward the orchard as if the trees might answer him. "But somewhere along the line, the joy disappeared. It became about deadlines and expectations, about sales and hitting goals. Writing stopped being... mine. And before I knew it, I was just going through the motions."

There was such raw honesty in his voice. Wendy knew, all too well, the burden of carrying something you loved until it felt like a weight rather than a gift.

She reached out, her fingers tracing the grain of the picnic table. When she spoke, there was no hesitation, just genuine understanding. "I think I know what that's like... When something you care so much about starts slipping through your fingers. No matter how hard you work, you always feel like it's about to break underneath the pressure."

Luke shifted toward her, his gaze soft and attentive, as if he could see right through her confession.

"This farm is everything to me," Wendy continued, her voice quieter now, as though confessing to a fear that had long been buried. "It's been my whole life. After my parents passed... I took it all on because it felt like that's what I had to do. Some days, though, no matter how much I plan or organize, it just feels like it's slipping away. Like failure is one wrong step away, and I can't stop it."

Luke was watching her, his expression serious and full of understanding. "You're not failing, Wendy," he said. "You work harder than anyone I know. And I promise you, even if you took a break, even if everything wasn't perfect... you wouldn't be letting anyone down."

Luke leaned back, pausing for a beat, before sharing, "I think... I've always been running from the feeling that if I stop pushing, everything I've worked for will fall apart. That if I disappoint someone along the way, that'll be the end." He met her eyes, his gaze deeper now, as if it held something fragile he'd never shared before. "But being here... it's different. The farm, the town... you. It's like it's giving me back something I didn't realize I'd been missing. A reminder that there's more to life than just meeting expectations or chasing success."

The sincerity in his eyes was almost too much to take in, and yet she leaned into it—welcoming it, even.

"That's... beautiful, Luke," Wendy said, her thoughts turning over like leaves finding their place in the wind.

For a long moment, neither of them spoke. They simply sat there, the world around them soft and golden in the afternoon light, a gentle breeze rustling through the trees. It was comfortable; it was easy, but mostly, it was real.

Before she could say more, Luke broke the lingering silence, his voice gentle.

"I guess what I'm realizing is... the things that matter most aren't the ones we can plan or measure. They're the moments we let ourselves live in... the ones we don't see coming."

Wendy swallowed hard at the way his gaze held hers. How the quiet truth he spoke mirrored her own feelings more closely than she ever thought possible.

And, in that perfect moment, there was nothing else she needed to say.

<h1 style="text-align:center">Chapter 26</h1>

Luke sauntered toward Wendy from the flatbed truck, hands tucked casually into the front pockets of his worn jeans. He had a mischievous, lopsided grin on his face, as though he hadn't just spent the past several hours lugging enough pumpkins to fuel at least three kid-friendly fall festivals.

He rolled his shoulders, like he was shrugging off a hard-won fight, and said, "You sure we're not done yet? Feels like we've moved enough pumpkins to feed a small army. I could think of about a thousand better ways to spend an evening than orchestrating a pumpkin revolution."

Wendy stifled a laugh, shaking her head as the magnetic ease of his humor washed over her.

"We've still got a few things left on the list, city boy," she teased, tucking a strand of her rebellious hair back into her ponytail. "I need your help setting up the photo booth stage. It's kind of a big deal around here."

Luke raised an eyebrow, following her gesture toward the unassembled booth. "The photo booth? Now, that's practically a vacation. You make it sound like we're about to climb Mount Everest or something."

"Trust me, it's more work than you think," she said.

Luke clapped his hands together with mock seriousness. "Alright, then, boss. Lead the way. I'm ready to obliterate some photo booth aesthetics."

Wendy shot him a side glance, unable to suppress the smile creeping across her face, and began walking toward the display area. "So enthusiastic for someone who, not five minutes ago, looked like he needed a two-week nap."

"What can I say? My drive for perfection is my undoing." His smirk widened. "Plus, I've recalibrated my strategy. Keep working, and I won't collapse from exhaustion. And anyway, snacks are my primary motivator. Keep feeding me, and I might just make it through this festival of yours."

"Oh, snacks again?" Wendy quipped, leading him to the area where stacks of hay bales and scarecrows waited for assembly. "And here I thought you were here for the company."

A flicker of surprise danced across Luke's eyes, that easy smile returning, as if it never faltered. "Well, now that you mention it," he said, the warmth in his voice so soft it felt like hot cocoa on a crisp autumn day, "the company isn't too bad either."

Wendy bit back the small flutter his words stirred. Clearing her throat, she kicked a hay bale into place. "If you're so invested in the company, you'd better help me get things just right. This photo booth is serious business," she said. "No half-done displays are allowed."

Luke picked up one of the scarecrow props, twirling it, like he was Michelangelo about to sculpt a masterpiece. "Oh, don't worry, Wendy. You're looking at a certified fall festival decorating expert."

Wendy crossed her arms over her chest and raised a brow, staring at the scarecrow now flailing in Luke's grip. "Certified... by whom, exactly? Pinterest?"

He balked, clutching the scarecrow dramatically to his chest. "Wow. Underestimating me already? That hurts, Lane. I'll have you know, pumpkin Feng Shui is a highly respected art. Requires years of secret training you wouldn't believe."

Her lips twitched at the corners, refusing to surrender the grin that threatened. "Pumpkin Feng Shui, huh? Didn't know that came with the city-boy package."

"Oh, absolutely." Luke's eyes gleamed with mock sincerity. "And this is no ordinary Feng Shui. This is seasonal Feng Shui. I could turn this booth into a sophisticated masterpiece of autumn Zen with strategically placed pumpkins—unless, of course, you prefer mediocrity?"

Wendy leaned closer. "Mediocrity's fine for today, Feng Shui master."

Luke grinned, pleased with himself. He placed a single, bold pumpkin on top of one of the haystacks and positioned the scarecrow nearby. "There. Perfect. Spontaneity. Dear harvest queen, don't be afraid to embrace the bold flavors of fall."

Wendy took a step back, eyeing it. Sure, it was completely out of her carefully planned symmetry, and not where she would have put them.

Before she could form a response, the scarecrow he had positioned on its haystack throne toppled over with a dramatic swoop.

Luke gasped, rushing toward it like he was a doctor called to emergency care. "Scareboy!" he yelped, his voice oozing exaggerated distress. "Hang in there, buddy. You're gonna make it."

Wendy blinked at him, then her laughter burst free, uncontainable. His hopeless dedication to a ridiculous endeavor brought humor to the moment. "Scareboy?" she asked in between giggles. "You named the scarecrow?"

Luke gave her a sly wink as he repositioned the floppy figure. "Every artist talks to their work. Picasso probably had names for all his sculptures. You're gonna make it, Scareboy. Stay strong."

Wendy crossed her arms over her chest again, staring at him. "You need help over there, Picasso?"

"Nonsense," he waved her off with a mock air of authority, still grappling with the scarecrow's limbs. "I've got this completely under control. Scareboy and I are simply refining our technique."

Sure enough, moments later, the scarecrow toppled again, legs in the air like a ballet flop gone wrong. Wendy's laughter intensified as she threw her hands up. "Refining the technique, huh?"

"Bold doesn't always play it safe," Luke muttered in good humor, wrestling poor Scareboy back upright one last time. "There. Standing tall. We're back in the game."

Smiling, Wendy wiped away an errant tear of laughter and refocused on the hay bales. "Well, Picasso, if you're done performing surgeries on helpless farm decor, we should probably finish up here before Amy walks by and takes even more pictures of our masterpieces."

Luke stepped back to stand beside Wendy, squinting at the arrangement as though appraising a work of fine art. "You've got to trust the process, Wendy. All great decorators were misunderstood in their time."

She shot him a mock-serious look and observed the arrangement again. It was definitely out of the usual symmetrical balance she liked, but... there was something fun about its randomness. Bold, indeed.

Wendy's hand slid into his with ease—a natural, effortless motion she didn't second guess, her fingers curling around his in a solid, confident grip.

Luke's surprise was brief, subtle. He glanced down at their joined hands, his lips quirking into a soft smile. One that made her feel like this was precisely how it was supposed to be. No awkward withdrawal, no anxious second-guessing—just the two of them, holding hands without complication or fanfare.

The warmth of his palm pressing against hers sent little sparks up her arm, but not the kind that made her want to run. These were good sparks—the kind that made the world around them blur.

"Well," he said softly, his voice no longer playful but sincere. "Looks like you're pretty good at being spontaneous after all."

Wendy's heart fluttered in response, but her grip stayed steady. "I guess I've got the right teacher," she replied, the corners of her lips lifting into a soft smile of her own.

"Well, well, well," Amy's teasing voice interrupted from behind them. "It looks like you two are getting along well enough."

Wendy shifted back a step. "Just... putting the finishing touches on the photo booth area."

"Yep. Certified experts at work," Luke added.

Amy arched an eyebrow, not missing a beat. "Well. Bravo to both of you." She made a show of inspecting their work. "Wendy usually runs a pretty tight ship... but you're still standing, Luke. Color me impressed."

Luke chuckled, rubbing at his shoulder in mock agony. "Barely. I think I'll be feeling it tomorrow morning."

"Surviving Wendy's festival prep is an accomplishment in itself," Amy replied with playful smugness. "Let's just say your initiation to small-town life might be over."

Before either of them could respond, Amy turned on her heel, tossing them a sly wave. "I better get going before Grandma sends out a search party for me." She hesitated, though not enough to suppress her grin. "Don't doddle you two, I think she's planning round two of some fresh ice cream."

Chapter 27

Wendy and Luke stood side by side, surveying the rows of pumpkins that still needed to be arranged for the children's activities. Clusters of vibrantly colored pumpkins—some large and lumpy, some small enough to fit into the palm of a hand—dotted the grass like oversized beads strewn carelessly across the ground. Behind them, several volunteers moved about, finishing up the final touches for the festival. The soft hum of chatter carried over the fields, blending with the distant clank of tools and occasional bursts of laughter.

"I still think we need more pumpkins," Wendy said, twisting the end of her hair as she studied the endless rows of orange.

Luke, standing with his hands shoved into his jeans pockets, raised an amused brow. "You're kidding, right? I mean, should we just empty the entire field and use it all for the festival?"

"Well..." Wendy bit her lip in thought, letting her gaze drift across to the pumpkin patch. "If we don't have enough, it might not look festive enough."

Luke chuckled, leaning into the playful jab. "Festive? You could sell tickets just for this display alone. Come one, come all, town's largest pumpkin patch—bring your own wheelbarrow."

Wendy laughed, the sound soft and unguarded.

She glanced over at him, catching him squinting at a large pumpkin like it might try to bite him. "You're making fun of me now, aren't you?" she teased, crossing her arms over her chest.

"Wouldn't dare." Luke lifted his hands in mock surrender. "But seriously, Wendy, look at all this. The kids are gonna love it, trust me."

Wendy sighed, glancing back at the rows of pumpkins, hay bales lined up along the edges, and craft tables that were soon to be covered with tiny hands and splashes of paint. It was all coming together—the culmination of weeks, no months, of meticulous planning. And yet, there was still that small voice that whispered, Is it enough?

"I guess I just want everything to be... perfect," she admitted, though she winced a little at her choice of words. She knew all too well the dangers of aiming for perfection—it had been a thorn in her side for years.

Luke angled his body toward her, his teasing smile softening. "Wendy, it's already great. You've done a fantastic job. And tomorrow, when this place is packed with families and kids running in every direction, they're not gonna care if every pumpkin is perfectly aligned, or if one hay bale is a little crooked."

"I know." She let out a puff of air, trying to shrug off the lingering worries. But that was always easier said than done.

"Here," Luke's voice interrupted her thoughts as he crouched down to pick up one of the smaller pumpkins. With a mischievous gleam in his eye, he stood and held it up to her, squinting as if sizing her up. "You need to name this one."

Wendy blinked. "Name it?"

"Yep." He held it close to his heart, exaggerating the moment. "Every good pumpkin deserves a name. I'm thinking... Gary."

She raised a brow, unable to suppress a smile. "Gary?"

"Yeah, Gary has a nice ring to it."

Wendy shook her head, laughing. "You're ridiculous, you know that?"

"I live to serve," he replied with a bow, before placing the pumpkin back in its spot.

Luke's knack for bringing humor to any situation was refreshing.

"Alright, let's get serious," she said, picking up her clipboard and flipping through the last few items on her list. "We need to organize the art supplies. Will you help me unload those boxes?"

"Of course," Luke said, heading toward his truck parked nearby.

Wendy followed behind, casting a quick glance at the sky. The sun was lower now, and soon, the light of day would give way to the cool tones of evening. It was the perfect weather for the festival.

Luke swung open the tailgate and reached for a large cardboard box filled with bottles of paint, brushes, glitter, glue, and plastic drop cloths. "Think the kids'll be careful while decorating their pumpkins, or will these paints end up in places they shouldn't be?" he asked, giving her a wry smile.

Wendy smirked. "I'm going with the latter. Last year, we found paint in the oddest places. One little girl painted a smiley face on the back of her brother's head."

Luke grinned. "I knew it. Future artists, all of them."

They continued working side by side, unloading supplies from the truck and setting up the painting stations.

"Oh no," he muttered, eyes widening as a fine dusting of glitter wafted into the air, catching the light and turning the scene into some kind of autumn fairy tale explosion. "This isn't good."

Wendy looked up just in time to see him standing there, covered in shimmering gold specks, from his hair to his jeans. Try as she might, she couldn't suppress the laughter that erupted from her the moment their eyes met.

"You look... spectacular," she managed between giggles, trying to catch her breath.

Luke raised his brows, looking at his sparkling arms miserably. "Do you have any idea how long glitter stays on a person? I'm going to be a human disco ball for the next year." He brushed at his shirt, only making the situation worse as it spread further.

Wendy was laughing so hard now, she had to steady herself by holding on to the picnic table. But seeing Luke standing there, flashing her a sheepish grin despite his glitter predicament, made her heart stir. It was impossible not to be charmed.

"And now the real artist has arrived," Wendy said with mock seriousness, throwing her hands wide. "Luke Carter, professional painter of words and accidental sparkler of men."

Luke shrugged, accepting his fate. "Hey, Picasso reinvented himself all the time... maybe glitter is my new medium, or at least a good start for my next book cover. Glitter and harvest aesthetics—there's a niche market for that, I'm sure."

Wendy took a slow breath, still chuckling, as she stepped toward Luke, who stood there defeated by the shimmer of glitter that refused to leave him alone.

"Hold still," she said, biting her lower lip to keep her grin in check. She reached up with one hand, swiping at the streak of glitter that clung to his cheek. As soon as her fingers brushed his skin, that familiar spark flared between them again.

Luke's breath hitched, just the faintest intake of air, but it sent a ripple through the space between them. His hazel-green eyes watched her as she made another swipe at his other cheek, laughing as more glitter sprinkled down.

"You might be stuck with it forever," Wendy murmured, now brushing the stubborn specks from his shoulders.

"I guess there are worse fates," he said, his voice low. "You've got a little something... right there," he whispered, reaching up ever so carefully. His roughened fingers brushed just under her eye, sweeping away a speck of glitter. Wendy's heart tumbled in her chest as the world around them faded into a soft blur.

For a moment, she forgot it wasn't just them—forgot about the volunteers in the distance, the eager families that would arrive tomorrow, the festival itself. It was just the two of them now, suspended in a glance that made the autumn air feel warmer and alive.

"Better?" she asked, though her voice felt like it belonged to someone else.

"Perfect, Wendy," he replied.

The playful shout of a volunteer somewhere nearby broke through the trance, snapping the moment like a fragile thread.

"I guess we should, um, finish up here," she said, giving a small, nervous laugh as she rubbed her palms against her jeans. "The paint, the pumpkins, the... glitter."

"Right. Finish up," Luke echoed.

Chapter 28

Wendy sat at one of the picnic tables stationed by the barn's entrance, serving as the check-in spot for festival volunteers and vendors. It was the day before the festival officially kicked off, and while the vendors trickled in one by one, Wendy couldn't help but feel a flutter of excitement mixed with anticipation.

Beside her, Ruth sat with a steaming mug of freshly brewed apple cider cradled between her hands. The rich, comforting scent of apples and cinnamon filled the crisp air, blending harmoniously with the earthy sweetness of hay. The familiar sounds of activity surrounded them, vendors chatting, carts creaking under their loads, and the faint rustle of the autumn breeze weaving through the trees.

Wendy smiled to herself. Tomorrow would be a big and exciting day.

Inside the barn, the soft rustle of hay bales being stacked along the back wall mixed with the gentle clinking of instruments as the band tuned their fiddles and guitars onstage. The rising and falling hum of chatter spread from various corners of the barn. The open doors bathed the space in the warm afternoon sun, the light catching on the swirling dust particles, making the entire scene feel like something out of an old postcard—familiar, comforting, timeless.

Wendy tapped the eraser of her pencil against her clipboard as she scanned her list one more time. It felt strange—being ahead of schedule for once. With the festival beginning tomorrow, she was used to a last-minute scramble. But this year, everything seemed to be running smoothly, like a well-oiled machine.

She glanced over at Ruth, her hands wrapped around her mug, blowing on it to cool the cider. Ruth, always the calm amidst the whirlwind. Her grandmother's eyes danced as she watched the bustling activity, as if the day's perfection was just another one of life's pleasant mysteries—not something to be questioned, only to be savored.

"Seems we've got everything in place," Wendy murmured, shifting in her seat. Her eyes moved back to the clipboard, checking off yet another task. She hovered over the final few items but found little left to worry about. The hay rides for tomorrow were set, the pastries and other snacks and drinks she provided for the vendors had already been delivered. All the volunteers were in their designated spots, helping to set up booths or guiding vendors to their respective areas.

"We're actually ahead," Wendy said. "I don't know whether to be relieved or suspicious."

Ruth chuckled, "Well, when you've been organizing this thing for over a decade, it's bound to run like clockwork. Lord knows, you've made it what it is."

Wendy shot her a side-eye glance as she flipped a page on the clipboard. "Either that, or this is the calm before the storm."

Ruth waved off the comment, adjusting her shawl against the cool autumn breeze. "Oh, come on. Let yourself enjoy it, Wendy. Everything's falling into place. The band's setting up, the vendors are rolling in, and the town's been buzzing with excitement for weeks."

Wendy nodded, but her instinct to worry tugged at her. "It's just... a lot. This year feels different for some reason."

Her grandmother gave her a knowing look. "Maybe because you're putting too much on your own shoulders as usual, running the farm, the store, everything. You're a good leader, Wendy, but even the best need to let some of that stress go."

"I know," Wendy sighed. "I just want everything to be—"

"Perfect?" Ruth cut in with a sly smile. "Yes, I've heard that before. And while I admire your determination, my dear, perfection isn't always what's needed. Sometimes a little mess here and there adds charm."

Wendy chuckled despite herself, lifting her gaze to watch one vendor maneuvering his cart filled with supplies toward his assigned spot. "Well, if messy charm is what we're going for, we might just pull it off."

Ruth's laughter was gentle. She reached over and gave Wendy's hand a small pat. "You've done more than enough. Trust me, it's going to be a wonderful festival."

"Alright," she conceded. "For now, things seem okay."

"Oh, don't get too excited all at once," Ruth teased. "Wouldn't want you to crack a smile."

Wendy grinned and shook her head as she checked off another item on the list.

Just as she was about to make a note about one of the children's game booths, a familiar figure appeared. Luke, moving towards them with a casual, easy stride. His hands were tucked into the pockets of his jeans, and that rugged, tousled look he seemed to carry effortlessly made him stand out among the activity of the workers moving hay and setting up decorations.

Wendy's heart fluttered, but she pushed it aside, straightening her posture as Luke strolled over, his lips curling into a lazy smile.

"You look calm," Luke teased. "Aren't festival organizers usually running themselves ragged by now?"

"Funny," Wendy shot back with a grin. "I'm pretty sure I was supposed to run myself into the ground three days ago. But..." She checked her watch with a theatrical sigh. "I'm behind schedule."

Luke chuckled, glancing over at Ruth, who was watching them both from the corner of her thoughtful, observant eye. "And how's the queen festival grandmother doing?"

Ruth grinned. "Oh, I'm just supervising. Keeping the kingdom running smoothly, you know?"

"Nice to see your hard work is paying off," Luke replied with a grin.

Ruth gave a playful smile. "That's what grandmothers are for, Luke. We do the hard work of bringing people together and... keeping them there."

Luke grinned. "Well, ladies, I'm ready for whatever the next task is you throw at me."

"Alright, Mr. Ready for Anything," Wendy said, her green eyes sparkling with mischief. "Your next mission, should you choose to accept it, is an important one. It involves setting up some food tables here in the barn for the feast I've got coming from Martha's Diner. Every year, I host a special dinner for our volunteers and vendors. Kind of my way of saying thank you before the madness of the festival begins tomorrow. And I need your help to get everything arranged."

Luke raised an eyebrow, a slow grin spreading across his face. "A feast, huh? Sounds serious. I'm thinking I showed up just at the right time."

"Well, don't get too excited yet," Wendy teased, giving him a playful nudge with her elbow. "We've got a lot of work to do so you can earn your dinner. We need to set up the picnic tables inside the barn for those who want to sit down and eat as well."

Luke made a show of cracking his knuckles, enjoying the banter. "Food tables? Picnic tables? Easy. I've been training my whole life for this, Lane."

"Oh, I had no idea I was in the presence of a seasoned professional," Wendy replied, her lips quirking as she folded her arms. "Because last time I checked, you were more of a mishap with glitter kind of guy."

Luke mock gasped, placing a hand over his heart in feigned injury. "Low blow, Wendy. I'm still finding glitter in places I didn't even know existed." He shook his head and smiled. "But don't worry. I'm ready to redeem myself today. Lead me to the tables."

Wendy couldn't help but laugh. She motioned toward the barn behind them. "The picnic tables are stacked in the back. Let's grab a couple of those first."

As they walked side by side, Luke glanced at her, his voice lowering just a little. "You always do this, huh? The dinner, I mean."

"Yeah." Wendy nodded, a hint of pride in her tone. "You know, people give a lot of their time and energy to make this festival happen. It's important to me that they know they're appreciated. Plus, it gives everyone a chance to just... relax for a bit before tomorrow. It's like the calm before the storm."

Luke's steps slowed as he considered her words. "That's... really thoughtful of you," he said, his voice genuine. "Not everyone would go through all this trouble. You've put so much of yourself into this festival. It shows."

Wendy smiled, trying to brush off the warmth that spread through her chest at his words. "Well, I've been doing it long enough. It's second nature now."

"Even so," Luke added, "It's not just the effort, it's the heart behind it. That's what makes it special."

Wendy opened her mouth to respond but found herself speechless. There was something about the way Luke said it, the way he looked at her, that made her feel... seen and important. Not just as the festival planner or the woman running the family farm, but as a person. She cleared her throat and turned her attention back to the task at hand.

"So, what's on the menu for this legendary feast of yours?" Luke asked, lightening the mood again as they reached the tables near the back corner of the barn.

"Oh, only the finest small-town delicacies," Wendy said with a playful grin. "Martha's bringing her famous fried chicken—you know, the kind that makes you rethink every meal you've ever had? And don't even get me started on the mashed potatoes. Creamy, buttery, the stuff that dreams are made of. Plus green beans, cornbread that melts in your mouth, and her legendary desserts. Rumor has it she's been experimenting with a caramel crunch apple pie that could bring a grown man to his knees. Of course, she'll bring enough food to feed the entire town twice."

Luke's eyes widened in mock awe. "I think I'm in love. You had me at fried chicken. If that doesn't motivate a guy to move tables, I don't know what will."

Wendy stifled a laugh, shaking her head. "Well, if the way to your heart is through food, then consider this your personal training day. Let's get moving, city boy."

"Bossy," Luke teased, but the smile that tugged at the corners of his mouth was anything but begrudging.

Luke grabbed one end of a picnic table, and Wendy took the other, their movements in sync.

Luke shot her a sidelong glance, a lopsided grin already forming. "You know, I think we're getting pretty good at this. We could make a career out of festival setup."

Wendy chuckled, rolling her eyes. "Or we could save ourselves the trouble and stick to our day jobs."

They carried the table down one side of the barn.

"Alright, set it here," Wendy instructed, and together they lowered the table into position.

As soon as the table touched the ground, Luke stretched his back, faking exhaustion for comedic effect. "Phew, that's exhausting work. I don't know how much longer I can keep going."

Wendy scoffed. "Please, I'm the one who's been running this festival for years. You're just here for the heavy lifting and to look pretty."

Luke raised an eyebrow at her, amused. "Is that so? Looking pretty, huh? I didn't know that was part of the job description."

Wendy tried to suppress a grin as she motioned toward the next table. "Yeah, well, don't let it go to your head. There's more where that came from. Think you can handle another round?"

Luke's grin widened. "Oh, I'm in it for the long haul now, Lane. Just don't be jealous when people start calling me the king of festivals."

She laughed, shaking her head. "You've gotta earn that title. One picnic table at a time."

They continued their light-hearted banter as they worked, arranging the tables along both sides of the barn. The long folding tables in front of the band's stage area went up next, and they made quick work of it.

At one point, Luke stepped back and surveyed their progress, crossing his arms. "You know," he started, his voice softer now, a hint of sincerity threading through the usual humor, "I get why this festival means so much. Everything about it—how it brings the community together, the way it all just feels... right."

Wendy paused in her task, glancing over at him.

"Every person I've met here so far," Luke continued, his gaze drifting out beyond the barn doors, watching the flurry of activity unfolding outside. The soft hum of festival preparations filled the air. Vendors setting up, hay bales being arranged, volunteers laughing as they hurried between tasks. There was a comforting chaos in it all, a rhythm that felt alive. "They've made me feel like part of something. It's not like I'm just some outsider passing through."

"That's a small-town community for you. It gets under your skin when you least expect it," Wendy replied.

Luke returned her smile, that teasing glint still present in his eyes, but tempered now by something more heartfelt. "Yeah... I think I'm starting to see that."

Chapter 29

Martha's food truck rumbled up the gravel drive and rolled to a stop beside the open barn doors. The evening sun caught the red-and-white paint of the truck, bouncing off the worn metal with a soft gleam that spoke of years of hard-earned use. Dust swirled around the tires as the engine gave one last sputtered breath before going silent, as if the vehicle itself felt the weariness of a long day's work. A magnetic sign on its side, "Martha's Diner on Wheels".

Martha pushed open the driver's door with an audible grunt. The sun caught in the streaks of salt and pepper in her hair pulled back in a simple bun, her plump face flushed from hours spent behind the stove. She wiped her hands on her worn apron, the same faded blue one she had worn since dawn, a true badge of honor for the culinary queen of the town. She surveyed the gathering already starting to form around the barn's entrance, her sharp eyes missing nothing.

"Well, look at this!" Martha hollered, her voice carrying like a mother calling her children in for dinner. "I hope y'all are hungry—'cause trust me, I brought enough to feed a small army!"

Her words were greeted with a mix of laughter and genuine relief from the tired workers nearby. A collective exhale, as if everyone had been waiting for this moment. A shift from work to comfort, from preparation to replenishment.

Amy was the first to react, stretching out her arms, drawing attention with her usual flair. "Salvation has arrived!" she said, rolling off the nearest stack of hay bales where she'd been perched like a diva between scene takes. She dusted off her jeans with exaggerated movements, her face bright with gratitude. "I thought we were goners for sure. You're a saint Martha, we're all starving."

Leah chuckled, folding her arms and offering Amy a raised eyebrow. "Drama much?"

"Not drama. Truth," Amy corrected, though she was already halfway to the food truck, flouncing toward Martha as if her legs had suddenly regained full strength after hours of hard farm work. "Now, move aside!"

Martha, with a knowing grin, hopped down from the driver's cab. She removed an aluminum foil tray from the back of the truck. The smell of hot food—rich, salty, peppery—moved with her as she shifted the bulky tray in her arms. "Don't kiss my feet just yet, kiddo," she replied, shooting Amy an amused glance.

Amy groaned as she reached for the tray, the air filled with the scent of Martha's famous chicken.

Wendy, standing just inside the barn, couldn't help but smile as the scene unfolded.

Behind her, the barn was read, not only for this much anticipated dinner, but for the festival as well. The band was set up. Hay bales, picnic tables and other seating were in place. The wood floor of the barn clean and ready for dancers the next evening. String lights dangling from the rafters, twinkling in the growing dusk. It was a perfect picture of small-town warmth—humble and unassuming. Wendy took it all in, blinking against the sudden rush of emotion that tugged at her. Yes, the festival would be beautiful, she was sure of it. The unscripted camaraderie between her family and friends filled her heart with warmth and bliss, like rays of sunlight dancing on her skin, illuminating her world with love and laughter.

A familiar deep chuckle interrupted her thoughts. Wendy turned as Luke approaching, his tousled hair catching the soft breeze. Even with his relaxed demeanor and calm smile, there was a tiredness in his eyes, an obvious reflection of the effort he'd put in today.

"Looks like it's time for some grub," he said.

"Trust me, Martha's here to save the day. And I'd say you've earned it, too."

He grinned. "Yeah, let's just hope I survived the day with no permanent damage. Though, if today was any indication of how rough tomorrow's gonna be, I may need more than just food to get through it."

Wendy chuckled, but before she could respond, Martha hollered her way.

"Wendy! You and that handsome feller, get over here and help unload this food before my arms fall off. I don't have all day to coddle people. I feed 'em, I don't carry 'em."

Luke rolled his eyes and shot Wendy a playful look, lifting his brows in surrender. "Duty calls."

With an amused huff, they walked toward the truck brimming with bulky food containers.

"Mind if I carry this one?" Luke asked, stepping ahead of Wendy to grab the oversized tray. His hand brushed against hers as they both reached for it at the same time.

"All yours. I would rather not be responsible for dropping any food," she teased, stepping back, though her heart was racing from the small, unexpected touch.

Luke raised an eyebrow, picking up on her flustered tone but choosing to play along. "I'll take good care of it—promise." He shot a teasing glance over his shoulder. "Can't risk the wrath of Martha if food doesn't make it to the table."

Inside, the barn was busy with activity as volunteers, farmworkers, and vendors alike began lining up to enjoy the feast.

Martha bustled inside, barking instructions. "Amy, Leah! Start unwrapping the food instead of standing around acting like you're auditioning for a role in a movie. These folks are hungry!"

Amy groaned. "I've already clocked out, Aunt Martha."

"Clock back in," Martha replied. "No resting until I say so."

Wendy grinned, "Always the slave-driver, huh?"

"Someone's got to whip this lot into shape," Martha answered, placing an enormous container on one long table covered in a checkered red cloth. Amy and Leah made an exaggerated show of bowing to the queen of the diner food truck.

With the food now spread out into an unofficial buffet, the evening meal kicked off. Even with aching feet and bodies worn from the weight of the day's work, laughter bubbled through the barn. Plates were filled with everything from friend chicken, homemade mashed potatoes, vegetables, fresh salad, cornbread, and various desserts.

Luke, Wendy, Ruth, Amy, Leah, and Martha had all plopped themselves down at one long picnic table near the entrance, weary but satisfied as the festive glow wrapped around them. Wendy slid into a spot between Ruth and Luke. Ruth's shawl had slipped from her shoulder, so Wendy reached over to adjust it.

"For goodness sakes, Wendy, I'm not an invalid," Ruth chastised with gentle affection, pulling her shawl tighter.

Wendy smiled. "I know. But I also know you'll chill faster now that the sun's going down."

Ruth gave her a look, but then turned a mischievous eye toward Luke. "Speaking of going down, you all right, Luke? I'm impressed. You're still standing after all the work you put in today?"

"Oh, he's standing alright," Amy chimed in. "Even after Wendy put him through our version of festival training."

Luke chuckled. "I made it out alive thanks to my excellent guide."

"C'mon, Luke! You can't act like you haven't done hard work before. You write novels, after all. Those fingers gotta be used to heavy lifting," Leah teased.

Luke grinned, his gaze flickering toward Wendy, who tried to hide her amusement in a sip of cider. "You're right," he responded, deadpan. "It's tough filling that coffee cup just to sit and think about all the words I need to write."

"It's a good thing you've got us now. Plenty of work to keep you humble." Amy said.

"You're doing an impressive job of it, too," Luke responded. "Honestly, this is nice. We don't have community gatherings like this where I'm from—not like this."

His statement hung in the air for a beat longer than anyone expected. Wendy caught the change in his tone and turned to glance at him.

Martha, ever the one to fill silences, jumped on his comment, albeit with her typical blend of humor and candor. "Well, you better get used to it. There's always something like this going on here in Laurel Ridge. You dip your toes in, you might find yourself knee-deep before you know what happened." She cast a knowing glance at Ruth, who nodded in agreement.

"Small towns have a way of folding you in," Ruth said, adding to the sentiment. Then she snapped back to her sly self. "Especially during festivals—suddenly, everyone's your family."

A playful grin pulled at Wendy's lips. "Pretty sure they'll force-feed you until you sign adoption papers, Luke."

"Yeah, we can start on those papers right now if you'd like," Amy said. "You're practically a blood relative now."

Luke only smiled at the teasing but didn't say a word; his gaze was fixed again on Wendy. She tried to ignore how her pulse raced whenever his eyes locked on her.

"All this talk about adoption papers..." Martha muttered. "I expect a handwritten affidavit from Luke and his editor—that's how we will really know if he's got roots sprouting."

Leah perked up, her eyes narrowed as she turned her focus to Luke. "Speaking of which... let's hear it, Luke. How's that book of yours coming along, up in your cozy little cabin?"

Luke looked about as pleased as a kid called on to recite homework he was proud of. "It's... coming along well. I think I've finally got my first draft finished."

There was collective, exaggerated surprise from around the table.

"First draft? That's big news," Amy said, eyebrows raised. "But... you're being all mysterious about it," she exaggerated the word.

Luke chuckled, but held his position. "I guess I am."

Leah wasn't about to let it drop, though. "C'mon, don't leave us hanging—what's it about?"

Wendy could see the hesitation in Luke's eyes as they flicked around the table, like he was wading through an internal battlefield.

He kept things light. "Let's just say... it's different from other things I've written. Something new. Something that hits down deep. I still may add a few more things. A story is never really finished."

Martha narrowed her eyes. "What is it with writers? I swear, y'all love dancing around direct questions."

Luke laughed. "It's part of the job description."

Ruth wasn't fooled; she reached out, patted Luke on the arm with her weathered hand, and murmured, "Just make sure whatever you're writing... comes from your heart, son. The rest will follow."

"So, what do we think should be on Luke's agenda for tomorrow?" Amy asked, changing the subject.

"You know what?" Leah jumped in, laughing. "Maybe we could start something new and put Luke in his own authors-only booth. We could sell tickets to his first public novel reading of his work in progress."

Luke groaned but smirked anyway. "You do remember I'm trying to stay under the radar here, right?"

"Not on our watch, mister. The whole town's talking about you," Leah teased.

Martha's plate clattered against the table as she leaned back, crossing her arms over her stomach. "Alright, y'all. Let's give Mr. Author a break. No time to harass people who've still got ink wet on the pages."

Wendy stretched. Exhaustion had settled into her bones after the adrenaline of the day had worn off. As her eyes flicked around the scene—Martha still bantering, Ruth smiling, Amy and Leah throwing more jabs—it hit her how full her life in Laurel Ridge truly was. She knew she was extremely blessed to be surrounded by such great family, good friends, and a phenomenal community.

Glancing over at Luke, Wendy caught the weight of his gaze again, a soft expression lingering there, as if he, too, had been struck by the subtle magic of small moments like these.

"I think," he murmured, voice low enough for only her to hear, "I could get used to this."

Chapter 30

Wendy bolted upright in bed, her heart hammering in her chest. She fumbled for her cell phone, ringing nearby on her nightstand.

"Amy?" Wendy's voice came out in a panicked croak, still thick with sleep. "What's wrong, and why are you calling me when you're just down the hall? Or aren't you? What's going on?"

"I'm sicker than a dog," Amy groaned on the other end. "I caught that stomach bug going around. You know, the one Natalie Waters had last week? It's hit me hard. I'm completely out of commission. I've been up all night sick."

Wendy closed her eyes, inhaling. Her stomach twisted, a faint dizziness threatening to pull her back down onto the bed. Amy had been her right hand, her go-to for all festival crises and last-minute emergencies.

But now... she was on her own.

"No, no," Wendy whispered. This couldn't happen now. She pressed her fingers to her forehead, attempting to rub the tension away. It didn't work.

"I'm so sorry, Wendy," Amy said, her voice pained with guilt. "I know how important today is. I've already texted Leah, though. She's coming in early to help. Don't open my door. I don't want you to get sick, too."

"Don't worry about it. You just rest up. I'll figure it out." A glance at the clock on the phone sent further panic darting through her. The festival's main events started in just a few hours. "Drink lots of water and try not to worry."

"Yeah, I'll try," Amy murmured weakly.

"I'll stop in during the day to check on you, okay? Get some rest."

Clicking the call off, Wendy flopped back against the pillows, exhaling. She stared at the ceiling, anxiety churning up in her chest like an old habit.

"Lord, I need your help today," she whispered, letting her prayer scatter into the quiet morning.

***

The scent of caramel apples, popcorn, and cider wafted through the air. It was both beautiful and overwhelming in equal measure.

Wendy barely had time to appreciate it. Her mind was racing with a mental to-do list longer than the tractor ride circuit she'd mapped out earlier that week.

Leah's cheerful voice pulled her from her thoughts as she hurried over, clipboard in hand, her vivid auburn hair catching in the sunlight. "I've got the bakery vendors set up, and the game booths are all set. Visitors have started arriving. Jeb is down in the lower field handling the parking area. The store is open and ready to go. I hope you don't mind, but I need extra hands in the store today so I can help out here, since Amy is out of commission. Loretta and Mitch from the Book Nook are en route now to help us out."

Wendy forced a smile. Leah was always on top of it all when things came to push and shove? Wendy's anxiety spiked as she glanced around the bustling grounds. Families were spilling in, laughing, greeting one another. This festival was the heartbeat of their entire year, and now with Amy down for the count...

She swallowed hard.

"Leah, I—I need to reassign some of Amy's tasks," Wendy said in a rush. "Can you—"

"Wendy!"

Wendy turned at the sound of Luke's voice, her heart stuttering in a strange beat when she saw him. He was walking toward her, his posture a little stiff from yesterday's work. Still, his relaxed grin said he was more than willing to jump back into the fray.

"You look like you need a caffeine IV," he quipped, though his eyes were warm with concern as they scanned her face.

She chuckled, trying to tamp down her frazzled nerves. "I'll settle for a gallon of coffee this morning."

"What's going on?"

Wendy closed her eyes for a moment, pressing a hand to her forehead. "Amy's sick. Really sick."

Luke's smile slipped. "Ouch."

She nodded, biting her lip before opening her eyes again. "I'm not sure what I'm going to do without her. There's so much to take care of. We had everything planned out so perfectly, and now..."

Leah stepped in before Wendy spiraled. "We've got this. Don't worry. If anyone can pull this off, we can."

Luke's gaze lingered on Wendy and then shifted to Leah before settling back on Wendy. "What can I do?"

Wendy blinked at him, at a loss for words. "Wait, what?"

Luke shrugged, casual as ever. "I'm not much more than a glorified typewriter back in my cabin. I have all day to help. I'm all yours. What do you need, Wendy?"

"You really want to help?" she asked.

He nodded, his hazel-green eyes steady on hers. "Absolutely."

Wendy let out a long breath she hadn't realized she'd been holding. "There's pumpkin painting in the kids' area. I could really use an extra set of hands over there—the carving tables, too. It may be a little chaotic."

Luke grinned. "Pumpkin painting with a bunch of kids? Sounds right up my alley."

Luke nodded and walked to the children's area.

Leah gave Wendy a significant look, her lips quirking up into a knowing smile. "Looks like Luke's willing to jump right in again and help with whatever."

"Thank God for small favors for sure," Wendy said and headed toward the kids' pumpkin painting area as well. Maybe, just maybe, this day wouldn't unravel.

***

The children's area of the festival was alive with the excited hums of laughter and chatter. Kids sat, paintbrushes in hand, their faces focused with deep intensity as they worked on their creations. Small jars of paint ranged in hues from vibrant reds and yellows to delicate pastels. The kids' creativity was endless.

A little boy holding a paintbrush looked up at Luke and asked, wide-eyed, "Are you here to help us paint pumpkins?"

Wendy smiled at the child, though her heart squeezed at the anticipation in his small voice. "Yes, Mr. Carter here is an expert pumpkin painter," she said.

Luke squatted at the boy's eye level, arms resting casually on his knees. "Yes, I am. Now, let's think here for a minute. What can we do to this pumpkin to make it look really cool?"

The boy giggled. "You've got a neat voice."

Wendy laughed, catching Luke's amused glance.

"What do you think? What would make this pumpkin look spectacular?" Luke played along. "Got any ideas?"

The boy furrowed his brow in serious concentration. "You gotta start with giant eyes. Big, scary ones."

"That sounds like a plan," Luke said with a mock salute.

For the next two hours, the children's area became a hotbed of creativity—and a little chaos. Luke bent low over tables, helping kids paint or carve gory teeth, spooky faces, and one enthusiastic girl created an entire princess pumpkin, complete with a tiara painted in bright pink streaks.

"Having fun?" Wendy asked, bumping her shoulder against Luke's as she joined him at a table.

Luke straightened, wiping residual paint from his hands with a grin. "I think these kids might be more demanding than my editor. Don't tell her I said that."

Wendy giggled, watching as a small boy attempted to paint his pumpkin under Luke's patient instruction. The child wasn't much of a listener—he ended up painting a huge black streak across the top of the pumpkin.

Seeing the boy's lip tremble, Luke was quick to crouch beside him. "Hey, don't worry about it. It's not ruined. See? You just made a pumpkin that looks like it's wearing a hat!"

The boy blinked, awe dawning over his face. "I did?"

"Absolutely," Luke said. "Your pumpkin will be the first one today wearing a hat!"

"You're smiling," Luke pointed out, tilting his head as he caught Wendy's grin.

"Am I?" She arched a brow in deflection, folding her arms over her chest. "Maybe I just think the kids are doing a fantastic job."

"Or perhaps it's because everything hasn't fallen apart quite like you thought it would," Luke said, leaning closer in.

The kids' voices swirled around them, a chorus of giggles and excited chatter. But at that moment, Wendy felt like she and Luke were standing in a bubble of their own.

"Well, look at you two, setting quite the example." Martha's voice rang out, warm and full of mirth.

Wendy jumped back an inch, her face flushing as Martha approached, hands on her hips. The older woman cocked her head and gave a wily grin, her blue eyes sparkling beneath the sunhat perched askew on her head.

"I've always said nothing brings people together like good old-fashioned pumpkin decorating," Martha teased. Then, with a significant look towards Wendy, "Watch out, dear. He's falling for more than just the festival."

Wendy's jaw almost dropped while Luke coughed, scratching at the back of his neck.

"Martha!" Wendy sputtered, though she couldn't hide the smile tugging at her lips.

Martha waved a hand in dismissal. "Don't 'Martha' me. I'm just calling it like I see it."

Wendy's shoulders shook with restrained laughter. Trust Martha to turn a moment of mild flirtation into something way more obvious than it ever needed to be.

"You're lucky I like you," Wendy said with a shake of her head, trying to regain her composure.

"Oh, honey," Martha said, patting Wendy's arm before walking toward the next booth. "You love me!"

***

As the day wore on, the festival swelled with more and more people. Families flocked to the various booths, children ran through the towering hay bale maze, and the band in the barn began tuning up and practicing, the twang of the first guitar chords filling the crisp early evening air.

Wendy and Luke eventually wandered from the children's area. Volunteers had arrived to give Luke and Wendy a much-needed break. Walking side by side as they passed vendor stands and bustling crowds. Luke's easy banter had lulled Wendy into a relaxed state she hadn't thought possible earlier that morning.

"So, this is your life during an apple festival? It's pretty spectacular." Luke asked.

Wendy paused, taking in the sight of it all—vendors selling everything from cotton candy to popcorn and deep-fried cookies, craftspeople selling their hand-crafted wares, children with sticky fingers cradling warm cider doughnuts.

"It's chaotic. But it's mine. And I wouldn't trade it for anything."

Luke's smile was warm, and his hand found its way to Wendy's. The contact sent a soft thrill through her, steady and grounding. As they reached the doorway of the barn, Wendy paused, her gaze sweeping the interior. The band was on onstage, their fiddles and guitars blending into the ambient hum of the space. Only a few townsfolk were scattered along the sides of the barn, seated at picnic tables, sipping beverages, but it would soon fill with many more people.

"Shall we?" Luke asked.

Wendy, a smile tugging at her lips despite the uncertainty swirling in her chest. "Let's." she replied.

Luke led her to the makeshift dance floor beneath the twinkling string lights, the worn wooden planks of the barn floor creaking beneath their slow, deliberate steps. The soft melody of a fiddle drifted through the air, filling the space with an easy rhythm. Wendy's heart raced, though she tried to remain composed, her palm resting in Luke's as they moved in tandem, the space between them shrinking with every graceful turn.

It wasn't a dance of grand gestures or sweeping motions, but rather a soft, unspoken intimacy. Two people, locked in their own moment, oblivious to the world spinning around them. Luke's eyes never wavered from hers, and in their depth, Wendy saw a quiet vulnerability.

The flickering lights above cast soft light over Luke's face, and Wendy found herself smiling, not out of habit, but because being with him in this precise moment felt right.

She wasn't worried about the festival, the farm, or anything else.

"I could get used to this," Luke said, his voice a soft rumble that vibrated through her fingertips where they lingered in his.

Wendy tilted her head upwards, meeting his gaze. "Me too."

Luke's lips curled into a smile. Slowly others began joining them on the dance floor as the band picked up another tune, but for Wendy, the background sounds faded to nothingness, like a distant dream.

She could feel the warmth radiating from Luke's hand on the small of her back, guiding her gently with each step.

Her heart beat in time with the gentle sway of their slow dance. With each step, every soft turn, Wendy rediscovered something she hadn't realized she'd been missing all along—a feeling of belonging. Not just to her work or her town, but to someone else.

"This feels... right," Wendy admitted quietly, her words tentative, as if testing their weight. "I didn't think I'd be ready for something like this again—letting someone in."

Luke's gaze softened, the intensity in his hazel eyes giving way to something gentler, more vulnerable. He searched her face as though he were looking for the answer to a question he hadn't yet asked.

"I understand," he murmured, his voice low and steady. "I didn't think I could feel this... not again. But being here with you..." He trailed off, the rest of the sentence left hanging in the unspoken space between them.

In that brief, unguarded moment, something passed between them—fragile and real, like a fierce spark of connection.

The night stretched ahead, the autumn air cool as more couples joined the dance floor. But for Wendy and Luke, nothing else mattered at that moment–just the quiet understanding of two hearts, finding solace in each other.

As the song came to its slow, lingering end, Wendy glanced up at him, her voice barely more than a whisper, "What happens now, Luke?"

Luke paused, allowing the weight of her question to settle between them before offering her the most honest answer he could manage. "Everything…"

"Luke," a voice called out.

"Luke Carter!"

Luke froze as he turned toward the voice belonging to none other than Priscilla, his agent. Her appearance was startling—Priscilla Martelle, in the flesh, standing just inside the doorway. Dressed in her usual sharp, no-nonsense business attire, complete with a black trench coat, three-inch heels, and a disapproving frown, she stood out like a city-slicker dropped into the pages of a rustic storybook. Her steel-gray eyes locked with Luke's from across the dance floor.

Wendy felt the warm bubble they'd just been floating in pop instantly.

Chapter 31

"Priscilla..." Luke said, his voice tight, as the spell of the evening shattered into pieces.

The agent's presence was an abrupt, jarring reminder of the world Luke was trying to leave behind—his looming deadlines, his career, and everything that had kept him distant and emotionally attached to a life far from Laurel Ridge.

"Sorry to interrupt," Priscilla called, striding purposefully toward them. "But it's urgent."

Wendy's heart constricted. She stepped back from Luke, putting space between them, as if creating physical distance might somehow protect her from the reality crashing down on her.

Priscilla's gaze flickered between Luke and Wendy with thinly veiled disapproval.

"We need to talk, Luke," Priscilla continued, ignoring Wendy's presence. "London wants an answer about the tour dates. They're insistent and I—"

"Wait," Luke interrupted, holding up a hand.

Now he didn't look so relaxed—his posture stiffened, eyes hardening as they shifted from Priscilla back to Wendy.

"Can this wait?" Luke asked, his tone sharper than Wendy had ever heard it.

Priscilla raised an eyebrow, unimpressed. "No, Luke. It can't. I have spent the better part of my day driving all the way down here to this... this... quaint tiny mountain town to track you down because you've been ignoring my calls and emails." She crossed her arms, staring him down. "So no, this can't wait."

Luke clenched his jaw, turning back to Wendy with a flash of anger in his eyes. He motioned to Priscilla. "I'm... I'm sorry, Wendy. I need to deal with this."

Wendy swallowed hard, fighting the rising sense of dread in her chest. "It's okay," she said, though it didn't feel okay.

He squeezed her arm briefly—too briefly—and then followed Priscilla out the barn doors.

Wendy stood there, watching the two of them walk away, her heart sinking deeper with every step they took.

This was it—the reality check she'd feared. Luke was a part of a world she didn't belong to, and no matter how much she tried to convince herself otherwise, it was all coming back to pull him away.

She watched from a distance as Priscilla launched into her rapid-fire conversation. Luke looked back once, his eyes finding Wendy's, but his expression was unreadable.

And just like that, the magic faded, leaving Wendy standing alone amidst the twinkle of string lights.

***

Priscilla's heels clicked sharply against the gravel, her every step unsteady yet punctuated by impatience. Luke caught up to her, his jaw clenched, keeping pace as they moved further from the barn. The laughter and music of the festival faded into the background, replaced by the underlying tension between them.

"So, is this our new relationship? You ignoring my calls and emails?" Priscilla snapped, waving a stack of papers she produced from her large purse in front of him like a weapon. "And while you're busy playing farmer-boy, your entire career is sitting on the line. Do you even know what kind of opportunity this is? London will not wait, Luke."

Luke stopped, forcing Priscilla to turn and face him. His face was stern, like stone. "I've been thinking about this, Priscilla, and... I'm not sure if it's the right move. Not right now."

Priscilla's eyes widened in disbelief. "What are you talking about? This is precisely the right move. It's an international tour, Luke. Do you realize how hard I had to push just to get your publisher to focus on you for all this marketing?"

Luke ran a hand through his hair, the words Wendy had said earlier tugging at the edges of his mind. The quiet moments with her, the simplicity of the orchard and farm, felt so far from the high-pressure world he used to be immersed in. Yet, he was being yanked back into it with the force of a tide he didn't want.

"I'm not sure if that's what I want, Priscilla," he said, his voice quieter but firm. "I don't want to go back to chasing deadlines and touring just to keep up with the industry. I need something more... meaningful."

Priscilla stared at him. Her expression tightened, and when she spoke, her voice was clipped, sharp as a blade. "Meaningful? You didn't use to be someone who talked about meaningful things. You used to care about your readers. About your books. The important things that should be placed first in your career."

Luke's gaze didn't waver. "I still do. But my career needs to be on my terms now, not the industry's."

Priscilla's eyes flared in frustration. Years of partnership teetering on the edge of a cliff neither of them had anticipated standing on. "So, what's all this about? Some soul-searching journey because you're stuck in a backwoods town with..." She paused, glancing back toward the barn, her expression hardening. "Her?"

Luke's jaw clenched at the implication. "Her name is Wendy and no, it's not only about her."

"Oh?" Priscilla crossed her arms, her voice dripping with challenge. "Then why do I sense that she's undoubtedly what's derailing? She's not your future, Luke. This—" she waved the contract in front of him, "—this is."

Luke exhaled, trying to shake off the weight of her words. Luke was standing at a crossroads.

And the choices he needed to make were not just about his career anymore, but something much larger and more important.

Luke squared his shoulders, his voice no longer filled with tension, but resolve. "Maybe you're right. I wasn't expecting this—Laurel Ridge, Wendy, any of it. But that doesn't mean it's not what I need. For the first time since Sarah died... I'm finally starting to feel something real again. I'm reconnecting with myself, and honestly? That's more important right now than any book tour."

Priscilla's icy demeanor cracked, surprise seeping into her features. She stared at him, her mouth opening as if to argue.

"You mean to tell me you're willing to throw away everything we built for... for what? Some temporary fling with—"

"Careful, Priscilla," Luke cut her off, his tone like steel. "Wendy is more than a temporary fling, and I knew that the moment I met her. I need to stop this treadmill. I'm burnt out. If I keep going this way, I'll lose myself completely. I almost did."

There was a long pause as Priscilla looked at him, studied him. All the fight seemed to drain out of her, replaced by something almost resembling concern.

Her voice was softer when she spoke. "Luke... I get it. Really, I do. But think about your readers... about Sarah. About everything you've been working for. Is this really what you want?"

Luke swallowed hard at the mention of Sarah's name. She'd always been his anchor, his compass when he felt like he was drifting. But since her passing, he'd been moving without direction, driven by deadlines, expectations, and the emptiness of success without fulfillment.

As he stared down at the contracts in Priscilla's hand, Luke saw more than just pages of ink. He saw a life that had felt suffocating, one where he was constantly on the run from something—his grief, his fears, and now maybe even the possibility of something new.

He met Priscilla's gaze and spoke with clarity. "I will not do an international year-long tour. Something smaller stateside may be a possibility to finish my contract out."

Priscilla looked toward the barn, her coat fluttering in the breeze. "Luke, I just want you to be happy. And for your readers to be happy too. But take some time to think about everything. It shouldn't be difficult to sort it all out. The answers are right here in front of you."

With that, she shoved the papers into her bag. "I'm staying at the Laurel Ridge Inn. Meet me there tomorrow, 10 AM sharp, and we will discuss this further." And she turned and hurried back toward her car.

Luke stood there for several seconds, watching as Priscilla climbed in and sped off down the gravel road, leaving behind a cloud of dust.

"Luke?" Ruth called out from the darkened porch of the farmhouse beside Luke. He hadn't realized she had been sitting there and had witnessed the whole drama with Priscilla.

"Come sit, dear. Don't let that whirlwind girl steal all your peace," Ruth said.

Luke let out a long sigh and joined her, sinking into a rocking chair next to her, his mind still replaying everything that had just happened.

"You're at a crossroads, aren't you?" Ruth asked.

Luke's gaze stayed fixed on the horizon, where darkness stretched over the quiet hills of Laurel Ridge. "Yes, Ma'am, I truly am," he admitted.

"That girl—" Ruth began, motioning with her hand to where Priscilla had driven off, "—she's like a rushing river, full of force. But sometimes, Luke, it's the slow rivers that take you where you need to go. Steadier waters won't drag you under." She turned her gaze toward him, eyes filled with the kind of wisdom that comes only after a lifetime of living. "I think you know where the steady waters are. Just don't let fear keep you from them."

Luke knew this wasn't just about his career, or Priscilla's demands, or even the looming deadlines—it was about something more significant. Something deeper and more meaningful.

His eyes drifted back to the barn, where inside, Wendy was probably still dealing with the whirlwind of the festival and not even realizing how crucial of a role she played in shifting the direction of his life.

For a few minutes, Luke and Ruth sat without speaking. The sounds of the festival still buzzing, a reminder of the vibrant life happening just beyond the quiet refuge of the porch.

Ruth leaned back in her rocking chair, the rhythm of wood against the floor the only movement in the stillness. "You know, Luke," she said, "each person has their season. Sometimes we're meant to grow, sometimes we're meant to rest. The trick is knowing what season you're in—and trusting that God will guide you to where you need to be."

Chapter 32

Luke's gaze drifted toward the barn's wide doors again, just in time to catch Wendy disappearing into the dusky evening, her figure a blur. His heart sank. He sat motionless on Ruth's porch, Priscilla's words still grinding through his mind like a rusted gear. But even the noise in his head couldn't dull the sharper sting as Wendy slipped off—quietly and intentionally.

Luke's stomach tightened. This was his fault, no matter how he twisted it. He'd let the past intrude on what could've been a perfect evening between them, and now she was walking away, slipping from his grasp like sand through his fingers.

Ruth's voice cut through the stillness. "Steady waters, remember that. You won't find your way rushing to the rapids—or letting them carry you farther from what matters."

Luke clenched his jaw, his gaze locked onto the space where Wendy had stood just moments ago. "I don't even know where to start," he admitted, his voice raw, frustration heavy in the small exhalation that followed.

Ruth's slow sigh held more wisdom than comfort. "Start by not letting fear do the talking."

With one last glance at the older woman, he stood and descended the porch steps in a few long strides, heart thudding. Wendy was already disappearing beneath the canopy of orchard trees, and the farther she walked away, the heavier the distance settled between them.

His steps quickened as he moved along the path, weaving between the rows of apple trees now blanketed in twilight. "Wendy!" His voice cut through the orchard, but only the wind answered back.

She didn't stop.

Luke's pulse roared in his ears. Panic threatened to take root in his chest, but he pushed it back, lengthening his stride, determined to catch up with her. "Wendy, wait! Please!" The plea spilled out in a breathless rush, sounding far more vulnerable than he intended.

She paused, her figure still and tense, though she didn't turn to face him.

The hairs on the back of Luke's neck stood up with a mixture of nervous energy and urgency. The space between them crackled with unfinished words and unspoken fears. Wendy's rigid silhouette against the dark horizon made Luke's throat burn with the need to say something—anything—that would stop her from crossing an invisible line he would rather not face.

He slowed to a stop a few feet behind her, his heart pounding. "Wendy, can we talk?"

Her shoulders rose just slightly, and when she spoke, her voice was as cold and distant as the night creeping in around them. "What's there to talk about, Luke?"

The breath he'd been holding escaped in a slow, controlled exhalation. He took a cautious step closer, measuring every word as if each one held the power to either mend or break them. "Everything. We need to talk about everything."

Wendy still had her back to him, like a wall he couldn't scale. When she spoke, it was with a heavy edge, more resigned than accusatory. "I saw how she looked at you. You didn't even blink. She snapped her fingers, and you followed. You just... followed her as if she had some kind of control over you."

Her voice wavered in the last part, but she held steady. Strong. A fortress.

That fortress, though, was what unnerved Luke—the vast distance between her guarded front and the vulnerability he knew lay just beneath. He swallowed against the knot in his throat, taking another tentative step toward her, his hand lifting before falling back to his side, helpless.

"Wendy, it's not like that."

Wendy turned to face him, the look in her bright green eyes knocking the breath out of him. There was hurt there, sharp and raw, but beneath it was something even more painful. The unmistakable glint of resignation, a retreat into the safety of distance.

"Isn't it?" Her voice was quiet, but the question cut through the cool night air, thick with doubt.

Luke's chest tightened. The once solid ground between them felt like it was crumbling. The space they'd shared just moments earlier, filled with warmth and possibility, had been swallowed by an overwhelming sense of impending heartbreak. And now, staring into the eyes of the one person who had unexpectedly become essential to him, he knew he had no choice but to lay everything bare.

"I didn't ask her to come here," he said, taking a careful step forward, though it did nothing to soften the guarded look in her eyes. "She just showed up. And yeah, maybe I should've been better about responding to her calls and emails, but Wendy... that world doesn't hold the same weight for me anymore. Not like it used to."

"Used to." Wendy repeated, her lips twisting into a bitter, fleeting smile before it vanished. "You're a famous author, Luke. That's your life, your world. And me? I'm a farm girl. This place, this farm, it's everything to me. It's all I've ever known. All I've ever wanted. But you... you live a life somewhere else, in a world I don't belong to, nor do I want to. The moment Priscilla showed up, you went right back to it. Like...like you'd never even been here. So don't tell me it doesn't matter. Because one day... you'll leave. You'll go back. And when you do..."

Luke stepped closer, his hands raised in front of him, open, pleading. "You've got it wrong. What I see is you pushing me away, Wendy. It's easier for you to retreat. Easier to keep yourself safe than to believe me when I say... I choose you. I want this life. I want you. I want us."

Wendy let out a shaky breath, her voice trembling. "Safe?" She swallowed, the words almost choking her. "I am safe, Luke. You... you're not safe. You don't belong here."

Luke took another step forward, his voice steady but gentle. "I'm telling you, I want safe. I want real. I want something steady. Something I can build with you.

Her eyes sparked with frustration, blending with simmering fear beneath the surface. "And what happens when Priscilla calls again? What about when you're behind on your next book, with deadlines breathing down your neck and your readers demanding more? Will you just... run again? Is that what it's going to be like?"

Luke swallowed hard. The moment the question left her lips, he felt the weight of it. But he pressed on, his voice firmer now. "I can figure it out. We can figure it out. I'll find a way to balance it all, Wendy. I know I can."

Wendy's expression hardened, her words laced with an edge of finality. "But will you really want to? Will you really be willing to walk away when your world needs you? Trading it all for apple harvests and festivals? For..." Her voice faltered, her eyes searching his for answers she was too afraid to ask. Luke saw the vulnerability she tried to hide, her quiet fear woven into the silence between them. "For me?"

The question hovered in the air like a fierce wound. Waiting. Fragile. And real.

Luke watched her, sensing the deeper undertones beneath her words. It struck him like a punch to the gut—this wasn't only about his career. This was about trust. About love. About the unspoken fear of being abandoned yet again, just as she had been when her parents died, just as she had been with David.

"I don't want the life I had, Wendy." His words came out quiet, raw. "Not anymore."

She shook her head, her hair catching in the evening breeze. "I don't know if I can believe that. What happens if...when...you change your mind?"

Luke's heart twisted at the sadness in her voice, but before he could say anything, Wendy turned and started walking again, her movements mechanical. Like she was forcing herself to leave before she caved.

"You do what you need to do," Wendy said, her voice cool with finality.

Luke stood frozen, heart sinking as he watched her walk away, disappearing between the rows of apple trees that stretched ahead like endless roads.

He wanted to follow her. He wanted to run after her and try to get her to listen to him.

But he knew that wouldn't work.

This wasn't about convincing her with a quick fix or promises.

Luke stood there in the cool dusk, the orchard silent save for the occasional whisper of wind through the trees. His heart felt pulled in a thousand directions—from the expectations Priscilla had laid on him, to the depth of feeling that Wendy had stirred in him. Feelings he hadn't thought possible again.

Closing his eyes, Luke dropped to his knees beside one of the apple trees. His hand touched the rough bark.

"God…" Luke's voice was a whisper, but the words flowed out like a floodgate had opened. "I thought I could just write my way through life, push everything else aside, and focus on the work. I thought coming here would help me figure things out, help me find myself again."

His hands pressed against the rough bark of the tree, grounding him as he struggled to continue.

"But now I see… I see You've been guiding me all along. I see her, Wendy, right here in front of me, like you placed her in my life for a reason. But now…"

His voice cracked, emotion thick in his throat.

"Now, I'm not sure what to do. I don't know what You want from me. I don't know if I'm good enough—for someone as good as she is. She's so sure of who she is, so rooted in this place, and I'm…" He faltered, searching for words. "I'm lost."

Luke drew in a deep breath, trying to steady himself. The orchard swirled with the sound of rustling leaves, as if nature could sense the turmoil in his heart.

"If Wendy's meant to be part of my life… show me, Lord," he pleaded.

He leaned his head against the trunk of the tree, feeling the solid weight of it, and the stillness choked him. There was no immediate answer. No flash of inspiration to give him clarity, no voice from the heavens guiding his next move. It was just him, alone beneath the twilight sky, listening to the sounds of an orchard that wasn't concerned about book tours, deadlines, or publishers.

Chapter 33

Luke stood in front of the Laurel Ridge Inn, his mind swirling with a thousand thoughts. His meeting with Priscilla was just minutes away, and yet all he could think about was Wendy. How she'd looked last night. How her voice had trembled.

You do what you need to do, Luke.

Luke hadn't slept. After leaving the orchard the night before and returning to the cabin, something shifted inside him, and it wasn't subtle. A spark had ignited deep in his chest, spreading into a fire that consumed him entirely.

The cabin, once so quiet, had come alive. The sound of keys clacking beneath his fingers filled the air as he sat hunched over his laptop, furiously typing. Words poured out of him, each sentence sharper, more raw, than anything he'd written before. Entire chapters fell to the wayside as he hit the delete button without hesitation, making space for something new. Something better. Something truer.

In the glow of his laptop screen, long into the early hours of the morning, he reshaped his manuscript. The plot lines came alive with meaning. Characters breathed, their voices no longer stilted but rich with the depth they had always deserved. And the ending, the one he'd struggled with, seemed to write itself, natural, inevitable, like it had been waiting for him to find it all along.

This wasn't just another book.

This was THE book. The one that meant something beyond deadlines or sales.

He wasn't sure what he was walking into with this meeting with Priscilla, but he knew one thing for sure. Whatever came next, he wasn't afraid.

Inside the inn, the lobby was quiet. Soft classical music filled the space, and sunlight filtered through the tall windows, casting warm patches of light across the polished floor.

Priscilla sat in a large armchair by the fireplace, her back straight as she tapped on her phone. She looked exactly like she didn't belong. Sharp, polished, and made of steel, as she waited for Luke.

She glanced up, her eyes narrowing as they landed on him. "Right on time," she said with a pointed smile, tapping off her phone and sliding it into her leather bag.

"Did you give it some thought?" she asked, her tone professional, direct, almost like she was talking about a business proposition rather than someone's entire life.

Luke sank into the armchair across from her, leaning forward with his hands clasped between his knees. He had thought about it. More than she would ever know.

"I did," he said, observing her. He held his breath for a moment, considered his next words. Then he let out a slow breath, his heart steady. "And my answer's no."

Priscilla's brows shot up, the reaction immediate. She leaned back in her chair ever, trying to mask her surprise. "No? No to what, exactly? We haven't even—"

"No, to the tour. No, to the deadlines hanging over my head. No, to whatever it is that's pulling me away from what I want."

Priscilla raised one eyebrow in disbelief. "Luke, are you saying no to everything you've worked for? Your career, your readers? They're all going to feel the impact of whatever decision you make here."

Luke held her gaze and didn't flinch. He didn't feel the old fear of disappointing his readers, his editors, or even Priscilla tugging at him. None of that mattered anymore. It wasn't worth hanging on to if it cost him his future.

"I'm not giving up writing, Priscilla," he said, his voice calm. "The book is finished. It will fulfill my contract. It's the strongest and most meaningful novel I have ever written in my career. Things will be on my terms from here on out. Heck, I'm pretty sure I'll be self-publishing the next time around."

Priscilla's expression shifted, surprise giving way to skepticism. "Self-publishing? Seriously? After everything I've built for you, everything..."

"Yes." Luke cut her off, standing up from his chair with resolve in his heart. "I know this isn't what you wanted to hear, and I get that. But I'm not going back to the kind of life I had. And something else, you alone built nothing for me. Without me, there would have been nothing to build in the first place, and I think you've forgotten that along the way."

Priscilla stared at him for a long moment, then sighed and shook her head, letting out a short laugh.

"I sent my editor my final draft this morning. I will see this book through completion and fulfill my contract. From there, I will decide what happens next." Luke said.

Priscilla stood, adjusting the strap of her leather bag over her shoulder, her face a mixture of frustration and resignation. "Well, Luke, I don't think I've ever been turned away quite so... poetically." She attempted a smile, but it didn't reach her eyes. "I just hope you know what you're doing because you're walking a tightrope without a net from here on out."

He gave her a small nod. "I know. But it's my tightrope to walk."

She turned and headed for the door. As she reached the exit, she paused, her back toward him. "Luke... Just remember, every choice has consequences, and sometimes, they hit harder than you expect."

Chapter 34

Luke stood on the steps of the Laurel Ridge Community Church, the manuscript gripped between his hands. The weight of not just the paper, but every unspoken word, every unvoiced feeling, sent a shiver down his spine, making his breath quicken and his palms clammy.

He wasn't just holding his latest book. He was holding his heart.

The familiar voices of the congregation singing the opening hymn floated out on the breeze, the sound comforting but also ripe with tension for him. Inside, he knew Wendy was there.

Luke just stood, eyes closed, his lips moving in silent prayer.

God, give me the courage to do this. To put everything in Your hands. I don't know what's going to happen, but I need You to show me the way. Please—help me let go of my old life and make room for the life You've put in front of me.

Before doubt could creep in, his hand wrapped around the door handle, and he pushed it open, slipping inside quietly.

Immediately, his eyes landed on Wendy.

She was standing in one of the pews near the front, her head bowed as she looked down at the hymnal in her hands, her lips moving to the familiar tune of Amazing Grace. Her brown hair framed her face—soft wisps catching the sunlight streaming through the windows.

Luke's heart thudded in his chest, his pulse loud in his ears.

The hymn swelled around him—the familiar melody pierced him deep.

"Amazing grace, how sweet the sound... that saved a wretch like me..."

The words rippled, reminding him of the grace he'd found in the quiet hours last night, when the words for his book—his life—poured from him.

He had realized then that he wasn't running away anymore—from his life, nor from his grief.

He was running to something...something far better.

Swallowing hard, he slid into a row farther back from Wendy, setting the manuscript on the pew, and picked up a hymnal. His hands tensed, his fingers tracing the worn cover. He felt people glancing at him, some with curiosity, some with knowing warmth.

The song began to wind down, its final chords wrapping the sanctuary in a peaceful stillness. It was only in that brief pause between notes that Wendy glanced around, her green eyes finding him.

Shock crossed her face. A quiet, unreadable blink of surprise and her lips parted as though she meant to speak, but the words wouldn't come. She turned her attention back to the front of the church, gripping the hymnal tighter than before, her shoulders a tad straighter, like she was guarding herself.

***

The closing hymn, this one more upbeat, carried with it a sense of finality. Luke's gaze remained locked on Wendy, his heart pounding so hard it hurt. He would rather not overwhelm her, but if this went wrong...

He focused his gaze on the manuscript again, praying that it could speak any words his voice might stumble over.

Pastor Eli closed in prayer. The congregation stirred, rising from their pews, the creak of wood and the shuffle of feet filling his ears as folks began to file out.

Luke watched Wendy stand and exit her pew, cradling her Bible against her chest.

Luke also stood, rounding the corner of his pew as the congregation moved to exit the church. The sound of shuffling feet and quiet voices filled the room, but his eyes were locked on Wendy as she exited.

She blended into the drifting crowd of people, who broke into small groups in the open yard outside, chatting among themselves as they always did after church. Some gathered around the church steps, others closer to their parked cars, but Wendy moved purposefully, her pace quickening, her destination clear.

"Wendy!" he called, his voice breaking through the pleasant hum of post-service conversations.

She paused and turned to face Luke.

Luke hurried, weaving between clusters of people, offering rushed nods of apology to anyone he passed too quickly, his eyes never leaving her.

Luke reached her, breathless but resolute, standing just a few feet away with his heart wide open.

"Luke..." she said, her voice hushed, guarded.

She didn't meet his eyes. She didn't need to.

"I want you to have this." He held the manuscript out in front of her, hands trembling. The pages felt heavier than they had before—maybe because it wasn't just a book. It wasn't just some words he'd thrown together.

It was an offering. His heart laid bare.

Her eyes flicked to his, then to the manuscript. Slowly and hesitantly, she reached out, her fingers brushing against his for the briefest of seconds as she took it from his hands. The movement was tentative, like she wasn't sure whether to accept it or push it back into his chest.

"What... what is it?" she asked, her voice a mixture of curiosity and wariness. She turned the manuscript over in her hands, her brow furrowing.

"It's everything..." Luke hesitated, rubbing a hand against the back of his neck, struggling to find the right words. "It's everything I've been carrying this whole time. My work, my past...my heart. Everything I haven't been able to say to you."

She lifted a brow, her lips pressing together as she looked down at the stack of paper in her hands. Tension crackled in the air between them, thick and wavering, both of them unsure whether to step forward or retreat.

Wendy stared down at the pages.

"Please read it," Luke continued.

Her eyes darted back up to his.

"I'm not asking you to do anything else, but read it," Luke said, his shoulders dropping with the gravity of the moment. "I know you think I'm going to leave. But if you'll give me this chance... if you'll just read it."

"I don't expect your trust right now," Luke continued, lifting one hand as if to give her space to breathe. "I know I've given you reason to doubt me. I won't rush you. I don't expect anything in return. I just need you to see me, Wendy. See all of me...at my best and my worst. Then, if there's no room in your life for me... well, at least I'll know I tried with everything I had."

Tears welled up in Wendy's eyes, holding the manuscript closer to her chest now.

Then, without another word, she turned and walked away. The manuscript clutched in her arms like a lifeline.

Luke stood there, rooted to the spot, watching her go. The ache in his chest deepened... but so did the quiet faith he was clinging to.

"Well, now..." a familiar voice drawled behind him. "That was something."

Luke blinked, turning to find Martha standing with Leah and Ruth, all three of them watching him with amused expressions on their faces.

Ruth tilted her head. "You sure know how to make a girl stop in her tracks, don't ya, Luke?"

Leah grinned, tossing her long hair over one shoulder. "It sure looks like he knows how to write a love letter, too, from the size of that stack of paper."

Luke chuckled under his breath, shaking his head. "I... I don't know if it will work. I guess we'll see."

Martha rocked back on her heels, arms crossed. "Well, if it doesn't work, son... I don't know where you go from here because...what I just witnessed... Mercy, my heart is a thumpin'!"

Chapter 35

Wendy couldn't shake the knot of tension coiled in her chest. It had clung to her ever since she'd left Luke standing in the church parking lot. The manuscript sat beside her in the truck.

The drive back to the farm was uneventful, but the silence in her truck felt louder than it should've been.

Her thoughts churned, racing between anxieties.

As soon as she parked the truck beside the farmhouse, she let out a deep breath.

Wendy got out, grabbed her Bible from the passenger seat, and slipped the manuscript under her arm.

She slipped inside the farmhouse and headed upstairs with purpose. Stopping outside her sister's room, she knocked on the door.

"Ames? You up?" she called, leaning against the door frame, listening for the telltale rustling from within.

"Barely," Amy croaked, her voice thick with congestion. "I feel like a pumpkin that's been left out long after October... all mushy and gross."

Wendy smiled despite herself, shaking her head. "You need any-thing?"

"Just a new immune system," came the muffled reply.

Wendy suppressed a soft laugh.

"All right," Wendy said. "I'll let you rest. But call my cell if you need Tylenol or... lemongrass tea or whatever."

Amy muttered something unintelligible.

Wendy stepped away from the door and walked to her room, quickly changing out of her dress and into a pair of leggings and an old T-shirt.

She paused before leaving her room and glanced through the back window to the gazebo that rested down by the creek, a small, peaceful place on the edge of the orchards. It had been her sanctuary in the chaos of farm life for as long as she could remember, an anchor of stillness in what sometimes felt like a restless world.

***

The chirping of birds and the bubbling sound of the creek were a calm to Wendy's anxious heart as she neared the gazebo.

Her fingertips grazing the weathered wood as she ducked under the climbing ivy that wrapped lazily around the posts and the outer edges of the gazebo. Ruth had once told Wendy that she remembered playing nearby when she was a little girl as her daddy built it, brick by brick, for the foundation and board by board for the frame. It was a labor of love to give his family a peaceful gathering place.

Wendy had always found peace here.

She lowered herself onto a bench, setting Luke's manuscript on the table in the center of the gazebo, and looked out at the gently flowing creek. Twisting her fingers together, she closed her eyes and tried to let the tension roll off her shoulders.

God, I don't know what to do here. I'm scared. I don't know if I'm strong enough... but You are. Please show me the way.

Her heart fluttered with nerves as her gaze drifted back toward the stack of papers waiting in front of her.

***

Luke paced the creaking porch of the cabin, running a hand through his hair for what felt like the millionth time that day.

He couldn't stop thinking about it. About her. There wasn't much chance she'd read it already, was there?

Of course not. That would be insane.

It hadn't even been but a little over an hour since he'd handed it over...

This could go either way. Wendy could either accept his vulnerability, the spill of words and confessions within those pages, or... she could close the manuscript, and close the door on him as well.

Why was waiting always the hardest part?

His phone buzzed in his back pocket, and he sighed with mild relief the moment Bill's name appeared on the screen.

Luke pressed it to his ear. "Hey, Bill."

"Well, well, Luke. I got your message. Now, what's this about you throwing your manuscript directly at the feet of a woman you're in love with? I thought you were going to be Mr. Emotionally Cautious?"

Luke chuckled despite himself, shaking his head as he leaned against the porch railing. "If by emotionally cautious you mean tongue-tied and mildly terrified, then yes, I'm exactly that. But throwing the manuscript at her feet? That might be an exaggeration."

"That so?" Bill laughed. "Well, you've got to admit, it's a pretty Shakespearean move you pulled there. The 'manuscript of my heart' approach. Who knew Hemingway could get so romantic?"

"Don't exaggerate," Luke groaned, though his lips twitched into a faint smile. "I don't think Hemingway left his heart anywhere but on the battlefield."

"True. But he could've used some practice in the love department. You, on the other hand, seem to have cleared that bar."

Luke hesitated, his smile fading as his gaze drifted toward the cluster of apple trees that led to Wendy's farm, his pulse quickening again with that tight ball of nerves lodged deep in his chest. "I guess you could say I'm trying... but it doesn't feel like I've cleared anything just yet."

"Oh, c'mon," Bill said. "Give yourself some credit, Luke. You poured everything into this new book—sounds like it's more than just a story. You're not just fulfilling a contract now, you're asking Wendy to trust you with more than that. That's no small thing."

"Yeah, I know," Luke murmured, rubbing his temples. He paced the edge of the porch, aching for any sign, any sign at all, to tell him things would turn out the way he desperately wanted them to. "Do you think I've lost my mind, walking away from the life I built? From everything that got me where I am today?"

There was a distinct pause on the other end, then a soft sigh. "Luke, we've been friends for a long time, and I've watched you gain and lose a lot. And in all that time, I've never seen you, as you've been these past few weeks. I think what you're doing...it's not walking away. Not really. You're moving toward something. Something a lot better from the sounds of it. That can't be wrong, can it?"

"Feels like waiting for a train you're not sure is coming."

Bill's laughter rang across the line, dry and knowing. "Buddy, all the best things in life feel like that. But I've seen enough in life to know when something's worth the risk... and from everything you've told me? Wendy? This life you're chasing there? It's worth it."

Luke closed his eyes, thankful for having a friend who understood. Someone who wasn't blinded by the demands of fame or success, someone who knew there were more important things in life because Luke had nearly forgotten it himself.

"You're right," Luke mumbled. "I just need to hold on a little longer."

"And if it helps," Bill said with a smile in his voice, "You're not the first guy in history to be pacing, waiting for a miracle."

Luke chuckled. "Thanks for that."

"No problem, Romeo," Bill shot back. "Now quit stalling and go live that story you wrote. I want to hear how it all pans out."

Luke smiled, his nerves loosening just a little. "I'll keep you posted. Thanks, Bill."

He slipped his phone back into his pocket, glancing toward the farm again. The wind rustled the leaves in a soft, comforting sound, echoing through the quiet afternoon air.

Just as he settled into a chair on the porch, attempting to pull his thoughts together, the familiar hum of a golf cart reached his ears. He'd come to recognize that sound well over the past few weeks.

Ruth Kincaid.

She had a knack for showing up just when she was needed. Ruth had visited often during his stay, always leaving small tokens of care, homemade bread, cider, or a thermos of hot coffee, quietly placed on the porch without disrupting his writing. Ruth never knocked or disturbed whatever flow of creativity he might have been in. Instead, her visits were gentle reminders he wasn't alone—that someone was thinking about him even in his solitude.

Occasionally, though, she would insist he take a break, coaxing him to sit beside her for a few precious moments. They'd share quiet conversations on the porch, and those simple pleasures, though brief, had meant something to Luke. Ruth's soft nudges and her warm smile reminded him that sometimes, life wasn't just about the words on a page, but the people who stepped into your story along the way.

"Well, now, if it isn't the man of the hour," Ruth called out, her voice cutting through the afternoon air as the cart came to a stop with a gentle squeak of the brakes. She tipped her straw hat back, her sharp eyes glinting with a knowing mischief. "Thought I might check on you and chat a bit. Care to go for a ride?"

Luke couldn't help but smile. Ruth had that way about her, always swooping in with impeccable timing, her presence somehow soothing even the most tangled nerves. There was no denying, if Ruth had something to say, it was probably best to listen.

He crossed the porch and sat in the passenger seat beside her, folding his long legs into the small cart. "I could use a little ride," he said with a soft chuckle. "And if I had to guess, you have some wisdom to deliver."

Ruth grinned, her smile warm and grandmotherly, but her eyes were sharp.

With a satisfied hum, she shifted the cart into motion, steering them down toward the winding path that led through the orchard. The breeze whipped through the trees, carrying the scent of ripened fruit.

For a few moments, they rode in comfortable silence, the rolling hills and quiet, steady rhythm of the engine filling the spaces between them. Then Ruth spoke, her voice strong and steady. "Wendy's been awfully quiet since last night," she said, more a statement than any genuine inquiry.

Luke nodded, the knot tightening in his chest again. "I'm hoping my manuscript will change that." He swallowed, his voice hoarse. "I just hope it's not too much."

Ruth kept her eyes on the path ahead, her hands firm on the wheel. "Wendy's not a woman who scares easy, Luke," she said. "But she's had her trust broken before. Loss of trust does some funny things to a person."

Luke stared out over the rows of trees. "And you think... you think maybe I'm asking her for more than she can give?"

Ruth slowed the cart, turning it off the main path and stopping under the long shadows of a nearby apple tree. She angled her body to look at him, her expression kind but serious. "Luke, I've lived long enough to know that love—genuine love—it asks you for all you've got. And that's a scary thing. But the thing about Wendy is, she knows that better than most."

"She's spent almost her whole life holding this farm together. She's strong. Not in a flashy way, but in a quiet way that sneaks up on you." Ruth leaned back in her seat. "If you're asking her to trust you with her heart, you better believe she'll think long and hard about whether you're steady enough to hold it."

Luke inhaled, his chest tight with doubt. "But... what if I'm not?" his voice was low, scared. "What if I'm not enough?"

Ruth chuckled, her eyes crinkling at the corners. "You're asking the wrong question, son."

He frowned, confusion filling his thoughts. "What do you mean?"

"Don't wonder if you're enough," Ruth said, her voice soft but firm. "Wonder if you're willing. Love isn't about being perfect. It's about being present. Can you stand beside Wendy through the good and the bad, not just in some grand gesture, but in the everyday moments that pile up?"

Luke swallowed hard, his throat thick with emotion. Ruth's words pierced straight through the countless fears swirling inside of him. He stared down at his hands, calloused and trembling.

Standing beside Wendy wasn't just about the big, romantic moments. Could he run a farm with her? Could he handle the slow rhythm of life in a small town when the world he'd come from was so different?

"When you handed her that manuscript," Ruth continued, "did you hand over a part of yourself that's ready to stay, Luke? Or was it a piece of you still looking for an exit? 'Cause trust me when I say this, Wendy will know the difference."

Luke blinked, the weight of Ruth's insight hitting him like a stone. He thought back to the moment he'd handed over the manuscript, the vulnerability that had coursed through him. The promise he'd made to himself.

"I'm not planning to leave," he said, his voice strong with the strength of that truth. "But I guess... I need to show her that."

Ruth's smile softened, and she nodded. "That's all you can do, son. Take it one day at a time and let Wendy do the same. Trust is built brick by brick, especially when it's been knocked down before."

Luke nodded.

Ruth revved the golf cart back to life and guided it down the orchard path once more, her voice bright and steady. "Now, let's head to the house. We've got apple butter to make! No use in frettin' over what isn't done yet. And you young man... you are going to learn the fine art of making magic happen with a few apples today."

Chapter 36

Luke stood in the middle of Ruth's kitchen, shifting awkwardly in place as the oversized apron hung from his neck like a kind of surrender flag. Cinnamon, sugar, apples—everything said home cooking in that room, but none of it came naturally to him. Ruth's comfortable kitchen felt like another world. A world where everything slowed down, and nothing pressed with the weight of deadlines or expectations. But that didn't mean the learning curve was any less steep.

"How's that stir, young man?" Ruth asked, her sharp yet kind eyes glancing over at him as they stood in front of the large industrial-size stove. She was standing guard over her own enormous pot, the aroma of apples bubbling into the air.

Luke lifted the spoon he was wielding, looking like a soldier, not entirely sure which end of his weapon to hold. He gave the pot a stir and then froze, realizing it was too fast.

"More like a whirlpool than a calm creek," he muttered.

Ruth chuckled, setting down her wooden spoon. "Luke, you're stirring it like you're trying to outrun a train. Slow it down. Apple butter's not something you race through. It's all about patience. Like life, if you want to avoid burning it, slow it down."

Behind him, Martha snorted as she leaned against the counter, arms crossed, a smile hidden behind her eyes. "Yeah, city boy, you've got to settle into the rhythm of it. You know, pass the apple butter test before anyone around here considers you a true local."

Luke groaned, eyeing both women. "First apple picking, then festival bootcamp, now an apple butter rites-of-passage? What's next? Do I have to plant an apple tree from seed?"

Ruth exchanged amused glances with her sister-in-law. "Don't give us any ideas," she said, winking. "Though, I reckon, if you planted some seeds, folks around here wouldn't mind. Planting's a good metaphor for life, don't you think?"

Luke held back a smile. What was it about these women who always made him feel like they saw more in him than he could see in himself?

He gripped the spoon again and followed Ruth's instructions, slower this time. Much slower.

"Good, good," Ruth said, peeking into his pot. "Look at that. Already smoothing out."

Martha leaned over his shoulder, teasing. "Well, you might pass out from lack of air moving that slow, but at least the butter'll be fine."

As the afternoon drifted into that pleasant rhythm of shared tasks, Luke couldn't help but marvel at these two women. Ruth with her steady, grounded presence, and Martha with her lively and spirited teasing. Between the soft clinks of measuring spoons and the bubbling of hot apples, the three of them fell into simple conversation.

"So," Martha started between bites of an apple slice, "how're you likin' small-town life so far, Luke? I always say, you can tell how well someone's settling in by how good their first batch of apple butter turns out, ya know?"

Luke smirked. "I hope this turns out, then. If not, I'll be labeled the city boy writer who couldn't stir for his life."

Martha cackled, waving her hand in front of her as if to dismiss the title. "Oh, we've had worse stirrers. Earl Smith burnt a whole batch some years ago. The stove wasn't the only thing smoldering that day!"

Ruth shook her head, her expression one of fond exasperation. "You're never gonna let Earl live that down, are you?"

"Not if I can help it!" Martha winked.

Luke glanced around Ruth's kitchen, light pouring in through the windows, glinting off old copper kettles and worn cutting boards. The room exuded warmth, the kind that reminded him of those homes in picture books he had used as settings for his characters. It hit him then. This wasn't just a kitchen or a place people cooked together. It was sacred ground, where stories steeped, slow and deep, as rich and comforting as the foods they made together.

Martha, unaware of his moment of reflection, turned to grab something from the pantry. "You know, Luke," she said. "If you keep up with this stirring, we might make a spot for you in next year's apple butter competition. We could probably convince Wendy to be a competitor, too."

Luke's stirring faltered. He cleared his throat, trying to recover from the unexpected twist of her comment. "I thought we weren't going to bring up Wendy for the rest of the day..."

Ruth gave her a warning look. "Martha, the boy's already nervous enough. No need to stir the pot anymore...if you catch my meaning."

Martha shot a cheeky grin. "Oh, I'm just sayin'. You know, Wendy's got the best stirring technique in town. Could give Luke here a run for his money, or maybe teach him a few things."

Luke managed a weak laugh, but he could feel the tension curling deep in his gut. Wendy.

"Who's to say that I'm not learning from the best right now?" he said, hoping to shift the conversation elsewhere. He didn't trust himself to talk about Wendy right now, when even her name made him feel like he needed to sprint through the nearest orchard to burn off his nerves.

Ruth, mercifully, changed the topic, steering them back toward the apple butter and more lighthearted banter.

"Do me a favor, Luke," Ruth said as she handed him a smaller spoon. "Try mixing it with this." Her voice softened. "Sometimes, you don't need the biggest tool to get the best result."

Luke chuckled but nodded, understanding the life lesson Ruth had tucked beneath her words.

By the time they reached the part of seasoning the butter, Luke had spilled spices, over-scooped sugar, and nearly sent the pot flying when he misjudged a ladle size.

"Who designed this thing?" Luke questioned, staring down at the ladle in his hands, half-covered in spilled cinnamon and sugar. Ruth laughed so hard she had to lean against the stove and regain her composure.

"Good heavens, Luke! It's just apple butter, not rocket fuel. Stir it slower...like you've got all the time in the world," she chastised affectionately, patting his shoulder. "Apple butter, like most things worth doing, benefits from a little care and patience. It isn't a race."

"Care...patience," he muttered under his breath. "Got it."

"That's the spirit." Martha patted his back, throwing in a smirk. "And don't think I didn't see that look on your face when I mentioned Wendy earlier. You, uh, want to share?"

"Nope," he blurted. Then, with a sheepish grin, "I'm focusing on my stirring technique."

With the late afternoon sun trickling through the lace curtains and the pot of apple butter ready for the whatever was next, Luke stepped back, taking in the surrounding scene. The jars lined up neatly on the counter, their glossy tops catching the light. Ruth and Martha had slipped into a gentle rhythm of jar-sealing and clean-up. Their conversation had the comfortable cadence of people who knew each other well.

Luke leaned against the counter, watching them.

There was something so simple about today, yet so profound. Here he was, a bestselling author, engrossed in nothing more than apple butter and small talk. Yet, it was more meaningful than awards dinners or book signings.

He glanced out the window. The trees outside swayed with the wind...constant, unfailing, certain.

"You're quiet, Luke," Ruth said, wiping her hands on her apron. "Got somethin' on your mind?"

He hesitated, then smiled back. "Just... thinking about how good it feels to be here. A part of this."

Ruth nodded, as if she had known it all along. "Well, that's what life is, isn't it? Being present in the simple things. One day, you'll look back and see that it wasn't the biggest moments of your life that made you who you are. It was the steady beats of days like this."

***

Ruth placed a jar of the sealed apple butter onto the counter with more care than was necessary, then stood beside Luke.

"You know," she began, "I learned something from making apple butter a long time ago. Sometimes, the slow and steady things...those end up being the best, 'cause they have time to flavor just right. Nothing rushed is worth a lick."

He nodded, appreciative and humbled by Ruth's words.

"I'm willing, Ruth," he said, his voice steady. "I want to show her I'm here for the long haul."

Ruth rested a hand on his arm and patted it tenderly. "I know you do, son."

As the ladies finished sealing the last of the jars and stood back to admire their day's work, Martha chimed in, a mischievous twinkle flickering in her eyes, "Well, now that you've survived the apple butter initiation, Luke, next up is the town's Fall Festival. Maybe you could give Wendy a little run for her money and learn how to bake a pie and enter the best pie of Laurel Ridge competition."

Luke groaned, though he wore a soft smile. "I thought we said no more Wendy talk."

"Well, it's only a matter of time before she knocks on your cabin door to give her review of your...err...stirring technique." Martha winked, dodging the peppered look Ruth shot her way.

"Tell me more about this Fall Festival," Luke asked, his curiosity piqued despite himself.

Ruth's eyes lit up, and she glanced at Martha, who eagerly jumped in to explain.

"Oh, the Fall Festival," Martha said, her excitement bubbling over. "It's a town event, similar to our Apple Festival, but smaller. We have pie contests, hayrides, live music, and crafts—all the good small-town things that make Laurel Ridge the cozy place it is. It's all held downtown, streets are blocked off and people come from all over. We have a special church potluck dinner and let's not forget the pie contest. It's serious business here." She said. "If you want to win over Wendy, you might want to sharpen those baking skills, starting with the cranberry-apple combination she swears by."

Luke chuckled, shaking his head. "I'm not exactly pie competition material."

"Well, you didn't think you were apple butter material either," Ruth quipped, patting him on the back. "But look how well you did."

Luke glanced down at the rows of apple butter jars, sealed and glowing. A tiny smile tugged at his lips.

"Grandma." her voice called out from the back door, and everyone froze, looking at one another. Martha, Ruth, and Luke hadn't expected Wendy to come by.

"Wendy!" Ruth exclaimed, turning with a quick glance at Luke, who had gone stiff as a wooden spoon. "We were just finishing up some apple butter. Come on in, sweetheart."

Wendy hesitated at the threshold, her eyes snapping from Luke to the jars of fresh apple butter lined up on the counter. The scent of cinnamon and apples swirled in the air, but there was an undeniable tension sparking through the room, one that didn't have anything to do with apple butter.

Luke's heart thudded in his chest.

"Smells good in here." Wendy's voice was careful, guarded, as she stepped into the kitchen. She avoided Luke's eyes, focusing on Ruth and Martha. "I hope you didn't wear him out too much with this."

"Not at all," Ruth said with a knowing smile. "He took to it like a natural...gave me and Martha a good laugh here and there, but we got it done, didn't we, Luke?"

Luke could only manage a half-hearted smile. But Wendy's face remained neutral as she reached for one of the sealed jars, scrutinizing it.

"Looks like you did all right," she noted, her tone light but lacking the playfulness he'd grown used to with her. She still wasn't looking at him. "I'll have to see if it tastes as good as it looks."

Luke swallowed hard. Was she still upset? Did she need more time with the manuscript, or had it driven a wedge between them? It was impossible to tell.

Martha, always eager to nudge things along, couldn't help herself. "Oh, trust me, Wendy. He's stirring up more than just apple butter today."

Ruth shot Martha a warning look. Wendy's cheeks flushed, her eyes grazing over Luke's form for the briefest of moments before darting away again.

Luke's throat tightened.

He took a breath, steadying himself. "Wendy..." His voice wavered, but he pressed on. "Did you have time to read the manuscript?"

The room fell quiet. Martha busied herself with the dishes, although her ears were perked. Ruth, ever perceptive, shifted focus to wiping down the counter.

Wendy remained silent, her expression unreadable as she held the jar of apple butter in her hand. Then she nodded.

"I read some of it," she said, lifting her eyes to meet his. There was a mix of hesitation and something deeper in her gaze. Something that made Luke's chest tighten. "But I'm not finished yet."

Luke exhaled, feeling a brief flicker of relief, even though the tension in him remained. "Thanks for taking the time to start reading it. That means a lot." He wanted to say more, to ask how she felt, if her heart had softened at all...but he held back. He reminded himself of Ruth's earlier advice...patience.

The silence between them was thick, tinged with uncertainty. Wendy's gaze stayed on him, guarded, but with a trace of something still open.

Then she spoke again. Her voice was stronger this time. "Here's the thing, Luke. I'm not going to read any more of your manuscript."

Luke blinked, caught off guard. Before he could react, Wendy held up her hand, stifling any protest.

"Don't get me wrong. What I've read so far... it's good," she continued. "Really good. So good that the afternoon just slipped by while I was reading. I got all the way through the parts about the man, lost, stuck in a rut. And the woman he meets, who, by the way, sounds wonderful. Strong, grounded. I like her grit."

Luke stood still, daring to breathe as Wendy went on, so focused on her words he hadn't noticed that Martha and Ruth had paused what they were doing, their attention on the exchange now.

"The parts about the man falling for the woman? Oh, I was hooked," Wendy said. "I could practically feel my heart swooning right along with hers."

Luke stood there, apron still dusted with sugar and cinnamon, feeling the energy in the room shift. He dared not move, waiting for her to finish.

"I really loved the moment when he starts to realize he's falling for her, and they both begin opening up to each other. You know how to craft a good love story, Luke," she said, her tone deepening with sincerity.

If a pin had dropped at that moment, it would've been as loud as thunder in the stillness of Ruth's kitchen.

"I read up through the part where the man begins to feel like he's losing her," Wendy continued, taking a measured step closer to him. "That moment when he hasn't fully decided yet...whether he's going to stay or go. The part where he can feel her slipping further and further away, and it terrifies him because he doesn't know what to do next."

Luke stood there, his heart a thunderstorm in his chest, uncertainty hanging heavy in the air. His life, his future, all of it seemed to rest in Wendy's next words.

She took another step, closing the distance between them, eyes locking with his. "Here's the thing, Luke. I don't want to keep reading to see how that story ends," she said, her voice steady and firm.

Luke swallowed, anxiety building as he wondered where she was headed with this.

"Why?" he asked, his voice barely more than a whisper.

Wendy's green eyes locked onto his with an intensity that sent tremors through his chest. "Because," she said, her voice warm yet full of determination, "I want you to show me. Show me how our story continues."

Silence swept through the room like a gust of wind.

Martha's voice cut through the stillness, flustered. "Well, heavens to Betsy. I need some fresh air." Without missing a beat, she grabbed Ruth's hand and whisked her out the door, leaving Luke and Wendy standing alone in the kitchen.

Chapter 37

The kitchen remained still, the air thick with unspoken words. Luke blinked, still processing Wendy's last statement. Her words had landed heavily between them, carrying the weight of a challenge, a nudge forward...not toward an ending, but towards a future. The silence lingered, defined by the ticking of the old clock hung above the pantry door, each second stretching into eternity.

Wendy stood before him, her green eyes expectant, strong in a way he hadn't seen before. Not the guarded woman who had walked into this kitchen moments ago, nor the ever-capable owner of Nature's Gifts. No, Wendy was determined. Strong and in charge, bravely staring down whatever future they might navigate together.

"Show you?" he said, taking an instinctive half step closer, as if the gravity between them was pulling tighter. "I want that. More than you could know."

Wendy's lips lifted, the barest hint of a smile. Her gaze didn't waver. She folded her arms across her chest, but it wasn't a defensive posture.

It felt more like she was holding herself steady, standing as still as she could in the vulnerable space they now shared.

"You've given me pieces of your heart through that story about us, Luke," Wendy said, her voice quiet but firm. "But a story on paper's not enough. I need to see it...for real. I need to live it. Can you show me who you are, beyond the pages of a manuscript? Can you live the words you wrote?"

Luke didn't respond right away. He didn't know if he could find the perfect words to match this perfect moment.

He reached for her hand. His calloused fingers brushed against hers, tentatively at first, but then firmly wrapping around them. He felt her pulse quicken under his touch.

Luke exhaled, the air escaping like it had been held in for years, and finally let go. "I'll show you," he said, his voice no longer trembling. "Brick by brick, moment by moment, Wendy. I'll be here. In the thick of it. Whether we're making apple butter, picking pumpkins, or weathering any storm life throws at us—I'm not going anywhere."

Wendy's eyes softened then, her lips parting ever so slightly as a flicker of emotion passed across her face.

Wendy stepped forward and closed the final gap between them, her hand tightening in his. She wasn't standing apart from him anymore. There was no distance, no space to keep them separated from all that could be.

"They warned me about you," she said with a soft laugh. "Said you had a way with stories."

Luke smiled, feeling the warmth of her presence wrap around him. "This is one I never want to stop writing."

They lingered there for a moment, letting the promise settle between them. Then, without fanfare or expectation, Wendy leaned in and kissed him.

As he wrapped his arms around her, Luke knew this wasn't the end of their story. It wasn't the final page or the resolution.

It was the beginning of a never-ending chapter.

***

Two women sat outside beneath the open kitchen window during that special moment between Luke and Wendy, soaking in every word exchanged. They held hands, not uttering a single word. When all was quiet and no words floated through the kitchen window anymore, Ruth and Martha gazed at each other, tears slipping down their weathered cheeks as they shared a knowing wink.

They had known this moment was coming, of course. Both women had watched the gradual dance between Wendy and Luke...the tentative steps, the hesitant pauses, the way their lives had seemed to orbit each other without ever fully colliding.

Martha dabbed at the corner of her eye with her apron, her voice a whisper as she broke the silence between them. "Well, I'd say he passed the apple butter test, wouldn't you?"

Ruth, still clutching Martha's hand, gave a small, knowing smile. "Oh, I reckon he's done more than that," she murmured, her heart too full to say much more.

The hum of crickets filled the evening air as the last rays of sunlight drifted lazily behind the mountains. Inside the kitchen, nothing stirred—only the gentle rhythm of two hearts, finally finding their sync.

Martha and Ruth sat outside a little while longer, listening not just to the rustling of the trees but to the quiet sound of hope adding its own flavor to the breeze. And though they didn't speak another word, they both knew tonight was the start of something neither Luke nor Wendy could ever write or plan.

Some stories, after all, are better lived than penned.

Leave A Review

If you enjoyed this book, please consider leaving an honest review on Amazon or Goodreads.

Visit Our Website:

www.tarabaisden.com

Visit Our Amazon Author Page HERE

Find Us On Social Media:

Facebook

Instagram

TikTok

Pinterest

GoodReads